D1423071

FALCON'S CLAW

When her father dies, lovely young Gida Falcon is alone and afraid in a world filled with violence and intrigue. Her innocence does not last long when she enters the service of a legendary lord and his ravishing wife. In the arms of a lover forbidden by every law of God and man, Gida learns both how dazzling and dangerous is her beauty, how strong is the pull of her passions, as she moves towards her inexorable fate as a Falcon . . .

Books by Catherine Darby
Published by The House of Ulverscroft:

CATHERINE DARBY

◆

FALCON'S CLAW

Complete and Unabridged

ULVERSCROFT
Leicester

First published in Great Britain in 1981 by
Robert Hale Limited
London

First Large Print Edition
published 1999
by arrangement with
Robert Hale Limited
London

British Library CIP Data

Darby, Catherine, *1935* –
   Falcon's claw.—Large print ed.—
   Ulverscroft large print series: romance
   1. Love stories
   2. Large type books
   I. Title
   823.9'14 [F]

   ISBN 0–7089–4131–1

Published by
F. A. Thorpe (Publishing) Ltd.
Anstey, Leicestershire
Set by Words & Graphics Ltd.
Anstey, Leicestershire
Printed and bound in Great Britain by
T. J. International Ltd., Padstow, Cornwall

This book is printed on acid-free paper

1

1399

Old people tell tales to their grandchildren of how the world was when they were young and green. I, Gida Falcon, am only in my middle years, but my winter is come upon me swiftly these past months and no grandchild will question me about my life. And if some child did ever listen my tale would not be believed. It is too strange, too soaring, too far removed from what ordinary folk call reality. Yet I feel the need to set it down for my own benefit, and then, perhaps, as I write some things that now are clouded will blaze into clarity in my own mind.

There was a mystery at the beginning. I know only that it centred around my father, Pierre de Faucon. He was a French knight captured in the Scottish war and brought south to Kent.

There were many Frenchmen awaiting the arrival of their ransoms in the castles and manors of England. Some served out their time and went home again. Others stayed here and settled and took English wives.

This my father did, marrying a woman called Alfreda. And of that marriage there were twin children, myself and my brother, Godwin, and we were born at Marie Regina in Kent.

When I was very tiny I thought that Marie Regina was the whole world and the people I knew the only ones in it. My mother was the best loved, for I never knew her angry or unjust, and I believed she was beautiful. She had hair that was the colour of the copper beech when the sun gilds it in autumn and brown eyes that slanted at the corners, and she was as slim as a twig with brown hands and face. She never raised her voice or slapped us as Dorothy did, and yet in many ways Dorothy was closer to us. She was the widow of an archer and had been housekeeper at the castle for years. She was fatter than my lady mother with a more comfortable lap, and bright blue eyes like little beads set in her plump face.

My mother brewed herbs and sewed exquisite tapestries, but it was Dorothy who made us gingerbread men, and played Blindman's Hood and Kiss-in-the-ring, and scolded me when I asked too many questions.

'How is it that my father never comes to see us?'

I remember that I asked that question

one day when she was making quince pies. We were in the kitchen behind the great hall, next to the women's quarters. I can remember too that it was a hot afternoon, that the other maids had gone to pick berries, and that Godwin had the toothache and was in the Solar having his sore gum dressed with cloves.

'Your father has duties elsewhere,' Dorothy said.

'But he never comes,' I said.

'Because he has better things to do,' she said vaguely.

'Better than looking after his castle?' I persisted.

'His castle! Why, it doesn't belong to him!' Dorothy exclaimed. 'All this land belongs to the Abbot but he leases it to the Lady Joan, and your father is Constable of it.'

'Isn't the castle ours then?' I asked in astonishment.

'No indeed. Lady Joan's father leased it as a hunting lodge. The Lady Joan used to come here often, but since she wed Sir Thomas Holland we scarcely see her.'

'And who is the Lady Joan?'

'Why, she is cousin to the king and a very great lady,' Dorothy said.

'Greater than my lady mother?'

'She has more money,' Dorothy said, with

3

an air of ending the conversation.

I was not to be silenced so easily however. 'If my father is Constable of this castle, ought he not to stay here to guard it?'

'We have men at arms to do that. Your father is a knight and knights have many duties.'

'Is he really dead?' I asked.

'As far as I know he's very much alive, just busy,'Dorothy said curtly.

'The Abbot must be a very rich man to own all this land.'

'Well, it's church property. He doesn't own it personally, though it amounts to the same thing.'

'Then why — ?'

'I haven't the time to answer any more questions,' Dorothy said firmly. 'Get out from under my feet now and go into the fresh air.'

I went reluctantly because there were dozens of things I wanted to know. It was of no use to ask my mother for if I did she would look at me in her gentle, remote fashion and say nothing. Yet she did occasionally speak of my father, and then her eyes would glow and her voice would be soft.

'He is a fine man. Tall and straight with blue eyes and fair hair. He came here first as a prisoner but he loved the land so well that he stayed. Oh, he is sometimes in France, fighting as knights must fight, but England is his home now. He is very often at Court with the king and the great nobles.'

No, I could not ask my mother why my father never came. I did think sometimes of asking the Abbot, but whenever I was actually face to face with him I dwindled into littleness and couldn't think how to frame the question.

The monastery was three miles distant and stood on a high tor at the other side of the river. It was not a very large monastery, but it was cool and spacious, with herbs and flowers planted around it and the path winding like a snake down to the wooden bridge.

On our side of the river the trees grew thickly down to the bank and among the trees was a wattle hut. My mother told us once that she had lived in the hut before she married, and I knew that sometimes she went back there by herself. She took me there with her once and I picked some of the wild iris and lilies that grew close to the water and made a wreath for myself, and she sat in the open doorway of the little hut, her thin brown fingers clasped, her eyes raised to the sky as if she saw pictures there.

I was still too small to sit comfortably at table when she began to teach me how to grow and recognise herbs and make some remedies out of them. There was a room behind the kitchen where she pounded and infused the leaves and petals with which she treated ailments and injuries.

'Daffodil roots mixed to a paste with honey soothe the angriest burn, and wallflower leaves mixed with salt are excellent for the ague, but for gout then you must make an ointment of mallows, daisy leaves and butter.'

Her long fingers tapped the neatly labelled jars. Coltsfoot for coughs, wood sorrell for weak stomachs, willow bark for corns, snapdragon to avert the evil eye, linden for ulcers in the mouth, valerian against plague, rosemary for bad breath — I learned all their names and qualities, and how to pound and boil.

'And as you put them into the jars you must say 'To the glory of God and in honour of the holy Raphael I dedicate this remedy'.'

Raphael was the Archangel of Healing, and my mother prayed to him often. I used to imagine him as a shining being hung about with leaves and roots and grasses.

There were other jars too with red labels

pasted upon them and in those jars were foxglove, poppy seeds, wolfsbane, aconite, monkshood, nightshade, and yew.

'Dangerous poisons,' my mother said. 'Yet sometimes a few grains of one may counteract the effects of another. Remember that in Nature everything has its use.'

I asked her how she knew so much, and she laughed saying the Abbot had taught her when she was young. I thought then that the Abbot must surely be the cleverest man in the world.

We saw him every week at Mass, of course, when we went to the chapel with its gilded altar and jewelled statues and painted windows with scenes from the life of Our Lord on them in colours that flashed fire when the sun shone.

My Lord Abbot was very tall and his nose jutted out of an old face, seamed and creased like oft used leather, with black eyes and a thin mouth. His voice was deep and rich, like the honey that Dorothy trickled over her plum puddings, and there was a beautiful ring on his hand, a sapphire cut square and engraved with a cross.

I liked the services though Godwin fidgeted, but I loved the sound of the Latin words rolling out onto the incense filled air, and the clear, cold chanting of the

Brothers who stood, cowled and sandalled, their hands folded within their wide sleeves. One of them, Brother Agnus, was a particular favourite of mine. He was even older than the Abbot, and as gnarled as a tree that ought have been cut down but still goes on giving shade.

He spent nearly all his time in a room just off the cloisters, where he copied manuscripts all day long at a sloping table. This room had big windows filled with diamond panes of glass, and on a bench along the wall were hundreds of tiny jars filled with coloured inks, and tiny brushes. When Brother Agnus had finished copying a page he would choose a selection of paints from the bench and draw elaborate and beautiful pictures spiralling out of the initial capital letter down the margin. Red, blue, emerald, purple and gold twined together leaves and flowers, with minute birds and butterflies and even animals peeping from the brilliant foliage.

I would stand for ages, while my lady mother talked to the Abbot in the parlour, and watch Brother Agnus as he filled in the colours, using first one brush, then another, every stroke sure and delicate. And once, glancing smilingly over his shoulder at me, he swiftly drew in a face, a child's face with tiny dots of blue for the eyes and golden hair. Tiny as it was it still looked like me.

'Now you will be here for ever,' he said. 'People will read this book in the centuries to come, and your face will still be there.'

That was a strange thought. I remember it now as I write and wonder if he spoke truly, and if anybody will ever wonder who the child is who peeps out from behind the leaves.

My mother came in one day with the Abbot while I was watching Brother Agnus, and after a moment or two, the Abbot said, 'So you like books, little Gida?'

I hung my head, being shy, but he put his ringed finger under my chin and said, 'Come, there is no shame in liking books. Is it the pretty colours that draw your eyes?'

'And the shapes of the letters,' I said. 'And each shape has a sound of its own.'

'And when you see the shape you hear the sound? Alfreda, this little maid is ready for the lessons. Bring her and Godwin to me in a day or two, and we'll make a start.'

After that we went nearly every day to the monastery and the Abbot sat us on stools and began to give us lessons. He was a patient teacher and I was an apt pupil, but Godwin hated having to sit still for so long. He was restless and over active even then, wanting to be off with the men-at-arms or riding his pony in mock attacks against the Saracens, and he thought reading and writing and ciphering were a great waste of time.

'A knight must use a lance and sword, and ride like the wind, and rescue people,' he declared.

'If you learn to read and then commit a crime,' the Abbot said, 'then you will be able to claim benefit of clergy.'

It was an odd thing to say to a little boy, for an instant the Abbot's eyes were clouded as if he looked into a sad future. And then he rapped Godwin sharply over the knuckles and told him to get on with it.

When we were not doing lessons with the Abbot, Godwin and I went our separate ways. Oh, we had affection for each other, but my brother was at the age when he considered girls to be a nuisance. He had a great admiration for the men-at-arms, and hung about them copying the way they held their weapons and wore their hats and swaggered. Once or twice he copied the way they talked too, but Dorothy grabbed him by the ear and washed out his mouth with soap.

I preferred to help my lady mother when she mixed her brews. She would sometimes let me pound leaves with pestle and mortar, or add something drop by drop to an ointment. I went with her to gather the plants too, for there were certain phases of the moon when a particular plant could best be found and plucked, and other times when they could be planted.

I went to watch Brother Agnus too, and once he let me paint in a tiny gold leaf in the margin of the page he was on. He made it clear that was a very great honour for me, and not one he would have accorded to anybody else, but I know he considered me neat and careful, and unlike most females I didn't talk a lot. I heard him say as much to one of the other brethren.

And then my father came home. My lady mother had gone on a journey, the first one I ever remembered her taking, and the Abbot and two of the monks went with her. I asked Dorothy where she had gone, but she snapped that little girls ought to mind their own business. My mother was a grown woman who could go where she pleased without having to explain herself. I thought that perhaps she had gone to find my father, but I decided later that I must have been mistaken, because while she was away, my father came home.

I guessed it was my father as soon as he rode into the yard. He was not as tall as the Abbot but I still had to tilt back my head to look at him, and he had features such as Godwin would have when he grew into a man. His eyes were as blue as mine, his hair yellower than mine and not so curly, and his voice was deep with a strange accent.

'Who the devil are you?'

'Gida, sir.' I dipped into a curtsey as my mother had taught me. 'I am Gida Falcon.'

'Are you indeed? Then you must be — '

'Your daughter, sir,' I put in. 'Godwin is in the stables, tending to his pony.'

'I heard she'd had twins.' He had dismounted and now stood, looking down at me as if he were not certain whether to be glad or sorry I was there. Evidently he decided to be glad because he took my hand and said, 'So you are Gida? Where is Alfreda? Where is your lady mother?'

'She has gone on a journey with my Lord Abbot,' I said. 'We did not have word of your coming, else I'm certain she would have stayed at home.'

I looked at him rather anxiously, fearing he would be displeased at her absence, but he didn't seem to mind if she was there or not, because he merely smiled and said. 'Then we must make shift till she returns. Go and tell Dorothy I'm home and that I've gone to the stables to seek my son.'

Dorothy came in a fluster, declaring there

was nothing fit to eat in the place which was untrue, and that Sir Pierre ought to have sent warning, which was true. Then my father came in from the stables with Godwin jumping up and down at his side, and boasting about how skilfully he could hit the butts.

With the arrival of my father a new vitality came into our lives. He was a vigorous, handsome man with a way of talking that made you want to listen though what he actually said was not always very interesting to me. He talked a lot about battles and campaigns, and Godwin never stopped asking him what it was like to be a knight.

'Often very dangerous and uncomfortable,' he said. 'When it rains and your armour rusts to your joints, or the sun blazes and then you feel as if you are being roasted alive, then you wish yourself anywhere but in the field. Yet even then it is better to be in the open than forced to endure the tedium of Court life. The hours I have spent listening to trivial gossip and long political speeches!'

I wondered if that were true, why he hadn't come home before. Then I decided that the king must have needed him and valued his services so highly that he had been unable to come.

My mother returned shortly afterwards,

riding with the Abbot down the northern road. We were both out with my father, hunting for squirrels or hares. Godwin was skilled at setting traps for all that he was so young. I thought them cruel and hated to see the poor creatures being tormented, and I was glad that we hadn't found any. Then we saw my mother and as she came nearer I saw her whole face light up. She looked beautiful then, but my father didn't seem to notice. His own face never changed though he went forward and kissed her with a smile on his mouth.

With my father and mother at home, life subtly changed, though not in a manner I could understand. They shared the big bed now up in the tower room and Godwin, on my father's orders, left the women's quarters and was put to sleep with the men. But it was more than that. My mother looked younger and put bright ribbons in her hair, and I knew she was happy because my father was in Marie Regina again. Yet I sensed that he was not so glad to be here. He never said anything, and he was always kind, and perhaps that was why I knew. I never heard him shout, or lose his temper. He behaved as if he were a visitor, staying with us for a time, and would soon be going away again.

We still went to the Abbot for lessons and

I spent a lot of time still helping my mother with the herbs. I had expected her to spend more time with my father and to have less to spare for me, but they never seemed to want to be alone. So we still gathered the plants and she taught me the phases of the moon and the names of the earth spirits who blew life into the seeds and made them swell into plump fertility.

Then everything changed again, quite suddenly, between one day and the next. My mother came back from a ride over to the monastery, and went up to the tower room where she and my father were closeted for a long time. The next thing I knew was that we were being bundled into our warmest clothes and put up on our ponies, and then my parents mounted their own horses and we rode away.

I cannot remember the actual journey, only the start of it and the end when we came into cobbled streets with high buildings at each side and so many people passing up and down that I was bewildered.

'This is London,' my mother said. 'I was never here before, so keep close behind us.' We came at last to a bustling street with tall houses and a rail outside where horses could be tethered. There were goods on display in many of the windows, more than I had ever seen on the pedlar's cart.

Looking back I realize that, although we may think we remember the past, in truth we remember it only in flashes. We never retain every waking second, only those incidents stand out clearly because, in a way, they are linked with what is to come.

We had come to stay with the Astons. Ralph Aston had been my father's squire but he had saved his money and was now a wool merchant, having been apprenticed to that craft when he was a lad. His wife, Enid, had been a needlewoman and after we came to their house she often made pretty dresses for me in the latest London fashion with hanging sleeves lined with contrasting colours and tiny crystals sewn into the bodice to catch the light.

There was a garden at the back of the house, and while I can't remember the furniture or the rooms within the house I do remember there was a big pear tree in the garden whose branches overhung a stone bench. I remember my mother sitting there with an expression on her face that I couldn't understand, and my father turning away from her and striding towards me as I came out of the back door. And he swung me up in his arms and said, 'Come and bid me farewell because I am to go about my duties again.'

'At the Court?'

'No, in France. The treaty is broken and the king intends to invade. You must be a good child and stay here.'

I wondered why we couldn't go back to the castle, but he had already set me down, and was calling Godwin who was playing about in the storeroom.

I knew, with a child's instinct, that something had happened. Sometimes, after Godwin and I had been put to bed, I heard the Astons and my mother talking together far into the night, but I could never distinguish any words.

The next thing I remember is a snatch of conversation that I did hear. I came into the parlour one afternoon, and my mother was sitting by the fire, not doing anything, just sitting there looking into the flames. Mistress Aston was with her, and as I paused at the door she said,

'Now that the king is home again he will surely come.'

'Unless the Lady Joan has need of him,' my mother said. 'You know he will drop everything and run when she beckons.'

That was all because they noticed me standing there then and began to talk about something else very quickly.

Everybody said there had been a magnificent

victory. The king and the Black Prince had ridden with the younger princes through the streets of London, and there had been tournaments and balls and a marvellous pageant with free wine flowing from the conduits.

Godwin had gone to see the procession with the Astons. My mother asked me if I would like to go too but something in her face made me say that I didn't want to go. It was very nearly true, because I did get nervous in crowds. I liked people in ones and twos, not bunched up together and shouting. So we stayed in the garden and later, after the candles had been lit, the Astons brought Godwin home.

He was chattering his head off about everything he had seen.

'The king had a purple cloak and a golden crown on his head. I saw him clearly through the gap in the crowd, and the Black Prince too. He really does wear a suit of black armour, and he rode a white stallion. And the other princes rode behind. Lionel of Clarence is bigger than any man I ever saw, and John of Gaunt and Prince Edmund were at each side of him.'

I wondered if my father had been in the procession, and then I saw my mother give an enquiring look at Mistress Aston. She shook her head and my mother turned away, her shoulders drooping.

Sometime after that, I don't know how long, our lives changed and we rode back to Marie Regina again. This time the Astons came with us, closing up the shop and bringing three packhorses loaded with goods. Mistress Aston had just had a baby, a little boy they called Ralph after his father. He was a nice baby and I liked to help Mistress Aston to take care of him.

I was pleased to be going home again, the city was too noisy, too crowded, and the people moved too fast and talked too quickly.

It was Godwin who asked why we were going back to Marie Regina. I thought my mother hesitated for a moment and then she said. 'There's a plague in the city. It's better to be away.'

What she said must have been true because the road out of the city was jammed with horses and wagons. People had wound scarves about the lower parts of their faces and many of them carried bunches of herbs to ward off infection. But from the look on her face I guessed there was another reason for our leaving the city and it had something to do with the fact that my father hadn't come back. I hoped it would be different again now that we were going to Marie Regina.

It was different, but not in the way that made us any happier. It was, instead, as if during our absence, some black cloud had spread itself over that part of the land I loved the best.

Dorothy was unchanged. She never did change, and from then on she represented security in a dangerous world.

The Astons had lived in the castle before, when Ralph Aston was my father's squire, and they settled in quickly with the baby. Nobody mentioned my father and I wondered again if he had been killed in the wars, but when I hinted as much to my mother, she shook her head and said, 'He will come home to us when his duties permit.'

We had been at home only for a day or two when I rode over to the monastery. I was not really supposed to go so far afield by myself, but I was nearly nine years old and felt it was time that everybody stopped treating me as if I were a baby. Anyway I wanted to see the Abbot and ask him when we could begin lessons again, and I suspected that if I told anyone they would make me stay near the castle for fear of the plague.

As soon as I reached the top of the winding path I dismounted and ran through the herb gardens to where the cloisters arched against the sky. The door to Brother Agnus's room was open, and I went in quietly as I had been taught.

The cowled monk who turned round at my step was young with a freckled face and gingery hair sticking in tufts from under his hood. After a moment he smiled and said, 'Why, 'tis a little maid! Were you looking for someone?'

'For Brother Agnus,' I said.

'Brother Agnus?' He wrinkled his forehead. 'I don't think there is anybody of that name here. Do you mean Brother Andrew?'

'No. Brother Agnus,' I said. 'He illumines and copies all the manuscripts. He lets me watch him.'

'Is anything wrong, Brother Sixtus?'

Another strange young monk had entered and was staring at us both.

'This little girl is seeking a Brother Agnus,' the ginger-haired one said. 'We don't have a lay-brother of that name here, do we?'

'No. There is a Brother Andrew,' the other said. 'Perhaps you got muddled.'

'Brother Agnus,' I said firmly, wondering why people always imagined that children got muddled. 'If he is not here, or has died, then I will see my Lord Abbot.'

'The Abbot is far too busy to be bothered

21

with little girls,' the monk said, not unkindly. 'I am Brother Laurence. Perhaps I can help you.'

'But the Abbot always sees me,' I said in bewilderment. 'I do my lessons with him every day, or I used to do them before I went to stay in London.'

'Do you have a name?' Brother Laurence asked. 'I am Gida Falcon,' I said. 'My brother, Godwin, and I live at the castle and come to the Abbot for our lessons. But we went to London and now are home again.'

'It must be one of the Constable's children,' Brother Sixtus said. 'I heard there were twins, a boy and a girl.'

'And now we are come home again,' I said patiently, 'so may I see the Abbot now?'

'Child, let us go into the cloister,' Brother Laurence said, 'and leave Brother Sixtus to get on with his work.'

I went with him more puzzled than ever, but also afraid. Something was wrong. There was a different feeling about the monastery as if something had been taken from it.

'The Abbot who gave you your lessons is — no longer here,' Brother Laurence said at last.

'Has the Abbot died?' I asked.

The monk looked down at me and nodded

gravely. 'And Brother Agnus? Has he died too?'

'Yes. Yes, Brother Agnus too.'

'Then who is to give me my lessons?' was my first selfish reaction. 'Will Brother Junius do so? He is very quick at ciphering.'

'Brother Junius is no longer here.'

'Has he died too? Have they all died?'

'The Abbot and Brother Agnus died,' said Brother Laurence. 'The other Brethren left about a year ago.'

'All of them?' I stared at him. 'Did they all leave then?'

'All of them,' he said. 'We are new Brethren here — all new to this monastery, I mean.'

'But why did they leave?'

'That's a matter for adults,' he reproached, 'not for children.'

'Was it a plague? There is plague in London now.'

'Something like that,' he said vaguely. 'Now, Gida, you must ride home again. Your parents will be anxious.'

'My father has duties at Court,' I said importantly. 'My mother is at the castle.'

'I will visit her to pay the respects of the community,' he said.

'But my lessons?' I persisted.

'I will discuss the matter with your lady

mother when I come,' he said.

I lingered a moment to say, 'I play sometimes in the garden here, and I go into the room where the books are copied, and into the infirmary to watch all the potions being mixed.'

'We will see about that too later,' he promised. 'You will be at Mass on Sunday?'

'Yes, Brother Laurence.' I curtsied and mounted my pony, aware that he was gazing after me with an anxious expression on his face.

I must have seemed a hard, insensitive little girl, not to weep to express grief for the Abbot or Brother Agnus. The truth is that I was afraid, because I knew that something very bad must have happened and nobody would tell me the whole truth because I was only a child. And I felt, in a strange way it was all bound up with our sudden departure for London the previous year. As I rode down the hill I decided that I would make one more effort to talk to my lady mother and find out what went on in that strange adult world from which I was excluded.

But as I went into the great hall my mother ran down the stairs, one hand outstretched to ward me away.

'Enid has the sickness,' she said, and she was paler than I have ever seen her. 'It is the plague. I thought we fled the city in time but we must have carried the infection with us. She is very sick, very sick indeed. No! You are not to come near me. You must go to Dorothy and stay with her. She will take care of you and Godwin and the babe, and Ralph and I will have the nursing of Enid between us. And send one of the lads over to the monastery to say we will have need of the prayers of the community.'

'The Abbot is dead,' I said, 'and Brother Agnus too.'

I had not meant to blurt it out like that, but she merely nodded her head and said, 'I knew that. I have known it for a long time.'

'And my father? Is he coming home again or is he at Court?'

'Your father is in the service of the Lady Joan,' my mother said, and she gave a laugh that was like the taste of bitter aloes. 'He is her liege knight.'

'But doesn't he want to come home?' Something drove me to say the words. 'Doesn't he love us at all?'

'Child, of course he does! You must never believe otherwise of him!' my mother exclaimed. 'He loves us very much, and he will come home as soon as he can. But you must understand that the Lady Joan has need of his services, and she is a very great lady.'

'Then she is a wicked one too!' I said passionately. 'She keeps him away from us.'

'She is a sweet and gracious lady,' my mother said. 'You must always believe that, Gida. The Lady Joan is very dear to me, as well as to Pierre. Go to Dorothy now, and remember that you are only little and don't understand.'

But I was not too little to understand that my mother, for all her brave words, lied, and I knew that she lied. If my father had truly loved us not all the great ladies in the world could have prevented him from coming home.

2

Enid died the next day and then Ralph fell sick. My mother thought at first that he would recover for he only had the disease lightly, but I think he had lost heart after he buried Enid. Brother Laurence rode over from the monastery, and he and my mother worked together using every remedy they could devise, but none of them were of any use.

Godwin and I were sent to play out of doors though it was damp and cold, and the rest of the time we were kept with Dorothy who was crosser than usual because the baby was teething. The other servants, except for Jem, all left us, though I doubt if there was any real escape from the plague. It had even attacked the monastery, so Brother Laurence said, and prayers were being redoubled.

I don't remember how we were told that my lady mother had died. I suppose it was Brother Laurence, but I cannot remember the words he used or how I felt about it at the time. I suppose I cried but I don't remember that either.

I do remember that it rained all the time,

and that Ralph fretted with his teeth, and that Brother Laurence came over often to do what he could. He was Master of Novices, it seems, and so had more freedom than the other monks. I grew quite fond of him, but there was not the same power in him there had been in the Abbot, and the Abbot was a tight-lipped, squat-shouldered man with a high, nasal voice that sounded silly when he was on the altar.

My father came home too. It seemed that he had left the service of the Lady Joan, or at least left his Court duties because he was still Constable. He was changed too, but by something other than my mother's death. The spring had gone out of his step and his face was older, harder. He was still very kind to me, but he took more interest in Godwin. That was only natural, I suppose, but with Dorothy always fussing over the baby it did mean that I was left alone a great deal. I never minded that because I had never craved the company of other children, but it made me too old for my years.

We started lessons again at the monastery, but with Brother Laurence. He was a well educated man and, once he had got over the surprise at a female who was quick at her books, he devoted much energy to me. Under his guidance I learned to read and write fluently in Latin and French, and to add up columns of figures. He taught me to read English too which was being spoken more and more widely, not just by the peasants but by well born people too. Parliament had even began to frame laws in English, so that at least people would know which ones they were breaking.

After a while I begun to watch Brother Sixtus copying the manuscripts as I had once watched Brother Agnus, and I helped Brother Andrew in the infirmary. He was surprised at my knowledge and told me that if I were not a woman I could have become an apothecary. Privately I didn't think being a woman had anything to do with it. I still feel that way although Maudlyn tells me that I'm wrong, but the young always think they know best. I was the same myself.

We lived so retired at Marie Regina that we heard little of what went on in the outside world. But we did learn from a pedlar who came by in the autumn that the Lady Joan, whose husband had died the previous year, had married Edward, the Black Prince.

'By special dispensation because she is his father's cousin,' the pedlar said. 'Three weeks after the ceremony she miscarried of a dead boy. It's said that both king and queen dislike the match and wished for a foreign bride, but the prince had loved Lady Joan for years and would have none other for all that she is two years older than he is.'

Everybody seemed to be in love with the Lady Joan. Even Dorothy, when I asked what she was like, said she was the loveliest lady in the world. Perversely I made up my mind to dislike the Lady Joan exceedingly.

But I was interested in news of the Court, perhaps because my father never spoke of his time there save to grumble about various inconveniences he had suffered. I thought of the king and queen and the royal family as always wearing golden crowns and sitting on high platforms above other people's heads. Apart from the Black Prince, the king had four sons. Lionel of Clarence was a giant, over seven feet tall and very amiable, which was a blessing for other folk. He and his wife, Elizabeth, and their little daughter had gone to govern Ireland.

'Though the Irish are no better than painted savages!' the pedlar snorted.

I imagined the painted savages all bowing down before the gigantic prince.

John of Gaunt was married too and had great tracts of land, as did Edmund of Langley.

'And when Prince Thomas is grown there won't be much land left for him,' the pedlar grinned. 'He was an afterthought you might say.'

The king's daughter, Isabella, was married also, to a Frenchman who had been taken prisoner in the wars. I pricked up my ears at that because it sounded like my own parents, but the pedlar said that Princess Isabella was a very dull woman, and not nearly as pretty as her sister who had died of the plague some weeks past.

So royalty was not immortal, but subject to the same ailments as everybody else. Even the king, said the pedlar, was not the man he'd been before he went away to war.

'Though Alice Perrers doesn't seem to mind,' the pedlar said.

'Who is Alice Perrers?' I asked with interest. Dorothy glared at me and said crossly that it was no business of mine. The list of matters that were not my business seemed to grow longer every day, I thought, glaring back and slipping from the stool where I had been perched.

It was a fine spring day and I just passed my tenth birthday. In the year since my mother's death I had grown taller and the mirror in the tower room told me that I was very pretty with my father's blue eyes, pale golden hair that curled without tongs, and a clear skin. Even Dorothy, who never paid idle compliments, had said I was 'passably beautiful', and Brother Laurence considered it his duty to warn me against vanity.

It was too sunny to remain indoors, so, though there were no lessons that day I saddled my pony and rode over to the monastery. I came and went there more or less as I pleased, the monks never taking any notice of me. Indeed I think it gave some of them an innocent pleasure to see a pretty young girl in the grim cloisters. I thought of them now as grim, and when Brother Andrew asked me once if I had any leanings towards the religious life I had shaken my head in horror.

Yet I was still drawn there, over and over as I had always been. It was as if the monastery was as much my home as the castle, even though the Abbot had died and the other monks had gone.

There were one or two lay-brothers planting in the fields below the tor. From the top of the winding path they looked like small brown ants scurrying about in ordered confusion.

The monastery itself was as silent as ever. The Brethren would probably be in the refectory at this hour having their midday meal. They ate twice a day in summer, three times a day in winter, except on fast days. I looked in at the open door of Brother Sixtus's room but it was empty. Beyond the cloisters a square entrance hall with long stone passages leading off it gave onto the Abbot's parlour. I had been there often in the old days, but this new Abbot had no time for children. I think he only tolerated my comings and goings because Brother Laurence had told him I was an apt pupil.

On impulse I pushed open the door of the parlour and went in. Formerly there had always been a carafe of wine and a dish of sugared almonds or marchpane on the table, and even in summer the Abbot had enjoyed a fire. Now the hearth was empty, the surfaces swept bare, the only ornament a carved silver paperweight.

There had been two paperweights, I remembered, of ivory and gold, and a beautiful statue of Our Lady carved out of ebony and gilded. These were gone now, as were the rich carpet that had hung against the wall and the embroidered silk screen. I wondered where they were, and if the new Abbot disliked beauty. Everything looked so grim and grey, and the spring sunlight merely emphasised the bleak aspect. I moved round to the big, flat-topped table where I had so often seen the Abbot sit, wine at his elbow, the square cut sapphire on his long hand. There had been a power in the old man that had flowed out into the room. It came to me then that he had been either a very saintly man or a very wicked one, or perhaps both at the same time.

'What are you doing?' The voice was sharply querulous and belonged to Brother Simon, who was always in a sour humour.

'Nothing,' I said truthfully. 'Nothing leads to mischief,' he said, 'and the devil — '

'Finds work for idle hands to do,' I said promptly and pertly.

'You have no business to be in here without permission,' he said, fussily severe.

'I often came here when the Abbot was alive,' I argued. 'He used to give me sweetmeats and tell me of when he was a young man, fighting against the Saracens in the Crusades.'

'Hush! you are not to mention such things, or talk about the late Abbot.' To my surprise he made the sign against the evil eye.

'The Abbot died, didn't he?' I asked. 'Why is it wrong to talk of him?'

'Brother Laurence said you were too young to know,' he mumbled.

'Too young to know what?'

'That he was burned,' Brother Simon said

unwarily, and promptly scowled at his own indiscretion.

'*Burned*?' I stared at him in horror. 'Why who would do such a thing?'

'The Abbot was a very evil man and he was burned. There is no need for you to know any more.'

'Then I will have to ask Brother Laurence,' I said sadly.

'You are not to mention it,' the old monk said sharply. 'You would get me into serious trouble for my indiscretion.'

'Then why was he burned?,' I asked.

'Because he worshipped the devil.' Brother Simon looked furtively around, then dropped his voice. 'He worshipped the Evil One, and led his community into the worship of the Evil One too. Someone found out and informed on him, and he was burned for his heresy. Burned and his community dispersed.'

'And Brother Agnus? Did they burn him too?' 'No, no, he was old and died. The Abbot was burned though, and has gone to hell. He died unrepentant, you see.'

'And Brother Laurence didn't wish me to know.' 'He and my Lord Abbot agreed you were too young. Only they and I and a few of the others know the truth, but we keep it to ourselves. Even the memory of evil should be stamped underfoot.'

'But he had great power,' I said.

'So has the Evil One, and we must be ever on our guard.'

I remembered how we had ridden through the night to London, and was suddenly afraid.

'You must say nothing,' Brother Simon was insisting.

'My lady mother was very friendly with the Abbot,' I said blankly.

'I believe there was some talk at the time of her being questioned, but naught came of it.'

Because we rode to London and so avoided questioning, I thought.

Aloud, I said, 'The Abbot gave lessons to my brother and me.'

'And that troubles you?' He looked at me more kindly. 'You need have no fears on that score. None, I assure you. He did not corrupt you with any of his ideas. Brother Laurence has assured us of that. You have been very fortunate, my dear, for he had been practising all manner of abominations for years.'

'May I go into the chapel?' I asked abruptly. 'It is of no use to pray for the Abbot,' Brother Simon told me. 'His soul is in hell now. But you may pray for Brother

Agnus, and the rest of the community for they repented.'

I nodded silently and he stood aside, saying as I passed, 'You'll not say anything to Brother Laurence about our little talk?'

'I'll not tell,' I said, and went out into the hall and through the cloisters to the chapel.

It was empty save for a young laybrother spreadeagled in penance at the foot of the altar. I knelt down where I always knelt at Sunday Mass, folding my hands primly, resting my chin on the tips of my fingers.

The Abbot had chanted the Mass so beautifully, the rich cadences of his voice matching his slow and stately gestures. I could not understand how he could have been a follower of the Devil. And if my lady mother had been involved, then it was all the more mysterious, for I never knew anyone further separated from evil than she had been. Yet we had gone to London and when we came home again everything had changed.

Someone must have laid information against the Abbot, and so they had burned him and scattered his community. I wondered who could have done such a thing and if they had been rewarded. And I remembered the golden paperweights and the ebony statue.

The laybrother, having finished his penance,

rose, dusted himself down with his large, red hands, and bowed. As he turned to go out I saw his sentimental glance at me. I must have made a touching picture, my eyes fixed on the gilded altar, my small hands clasped. I imagined him telling the others that I looked like a little angel, that it was possible I had a true vocation. And all the time the only thought in my head had been to wonder who had informed on the Abbot and where his treasures had gone.

I rode away slowly, waving to the laybrothers still planting the slopes below. They were simple countrymen, able to read and write a little, but not clever or learned. Yet there was a kindliness in their weatherbeaten faces and a gentleness in their hands that reminded me of my mother when she touched the leaves of first one herb and then another, telling me their names and the virtues of each.

Suddenly I wanted my mother very badly, not because she might have answered my questions for she never had, but because she had been an unchanging part of an ever shifting world. I crossed the wooden bridge and led my pony among the trees towards the wattle hut. I hadn't been near since the plague, but as I crossed the weed starred grass I saw that it was still in good repair, though the heavy rains of the previous autumn had broken through the roof in a couple of places.

A horse was cropping the grass a few yards away, and within the hut, through the open door, I could see a figure sitting on the three legged stool which was all the furniture the hut contained.

I paused, just beyond the threshold, staring at the cloaked lady. The hood of the cloak was pushed back to reveal curled golden hair in which tiny brilliants glinted. In the gloom of the hut her face was a pale oval.

'Don't be afeared.' Her voice was warm and clear, with a ripple of laughter threading its way beneath the surface. 'You are not a fairy child, are you?'

'No, mistress. I am Gida Falcon,' I said.

'Alfreda's daughter.' She spoke the words on a long intake of breath.

'She is dead, mistress.' I came further into the hut, blinking as I tried to accustom my eyes to the dim light.

'So I heard, and wept to hear of it. She was a gracious soul.'

'Did you know her?'

'As well as I know the fingers of my own hand. And so you are Gida.' She put her head on one side studying me.

'And Godwin is my brother,' I volunteered.

'And you are ten years old now? Is that right?'

'Last month,' I said.

'Tell me about your brother,' she invited. I would have preferred to talk about myself, but I said obediently. 'He is fair like me, but bigger and stronger. He is very pleasant most of the time, but he doesn't like sitting still. And he doesn't enjoy doing his lessons.'

'Do you?'

'Yes, very much.' Enthusiasm warmed my tone. 'I love reading and writing and finding out about things.'

'Who teaches you now?'

'Brother Laurence does. The Abbot used to, but he was — '

'Burned for heresy. Yes, I know.' She bowed her head briefly.

'My lady mother taught me about plants,' I volunteered. 'I can mingle potions and pound ointment, and I know the phases of the moon.'

'Your lady mother was wise as a child is wise, but she was not bred for happiness. The Abbot was wise too.'

'They say he was wicked.'

'As to that you must make up your own mind,' she said. 'If you are what I believe you to be then you will never take anything

40

for granted. You will always try to find out things for yourself.'

'Yes, mistress.' But I was disappointed because I had hoped for a real answer.

She seemed to know what I was thinking because she gave a throaty little laugh and said,

'You will understand my meaning when you are older. There is wisdom in you already that is not like other children. You can keep a secret.'

It was not a question but a statement, and the eyes looking at me were suddenly piercing.

'Yes, mistress.'

'One day you will want to know the truth about the Abbot. Use this key and you will open the door that guards the truth, but its meaning will lie in your own heart.'

I stared at the big iron key she was holding out to me.

'The door is at the head of the snake just within the wall,' she said. 'When you find the door you will know it is time for you to use the key.'

I took it feeling the cold weight of it on my narrow palm.

'It is a secret then between us?' she questioned. 'Yes, mistress,' I said bewildered but obedient.

41

The lady for all her friendly manner, was evidently accustomed to command.

'I have a gift for you,' she said now, and reached again within her dark cloak. 'Keep it safe because it is very old.'

'Thank you, mistress.' I stared at the ring, its circle formed of twisted silver with tiny rubies set in each link.

'The ring came from Jerusalem many years ago before you or I were born,' she said. 'It came from the holiest place on earth and once belonged to a Saracen princess. It was given to me when I was a child, and now I give it to you.'

I knew, without having to ask, that it was the Abbot who had given her the ring. It throbbed a little as I held it.

'Keep it safe,' the lady said. 'And keep your own counsel. We who follow the Old ways know that.'

'The Old ways?' I stared at her.

'They are still there for the wise to tread,' she said. 'Go home now, and remember what I've said.'

'Yes, mistress.' I stared at her a moment longer, then ventured to ask. 'How did you know I would be here? Was it magic?'

'I hoped you might be,' she said, 'but I'd no way of being certain. So I sat and willed you to come. It is possible to will almost anything to come to pass.'

I was silent, while there passed through my mind a bewildering series of images. My mother living in this hut close to the river and waiting for someone to love her. My father riding away to his Court duties and leaving her under the pear tree in the Aston garden. The Abbot bound to a stake and writhing in bright fire.

'I enquired your whereabouts,' she said, laughing as if she took pity on me. 'One of the men working in the field told me that you had gone up to the monastery. So I came here, and willed you to come. Now you must go home again.'

She leaned forwards and tapped me lightly on the cheek, and I curtsied and went out into the clearing where my pony grazed. Before I mounted I hid the key and the ring under my cloak, and took another look back towards the hut where the lady still sat, gleaming in her dark coverings, within the dimness.

My father was at home when I reached the castle. I had barely run to secrete my gifts in a box where I kept my few treasures hidden when I heard him calling me.

'I'm here.' I ran into the great hall where, still in high boots and short cloak, for he had been hunting, he stood in the window alcove near to the raised table where we all sat for meals. There was a queer, excited look on his face as if something inside him had been stirred to life again.

'You've been away all morning, child. Dorothy was fretting,' he began, but his voice was more absent than scolding, as if he were only saying what he believed a father should say.

'I rode to the monastery,' I said, but he had already rushed on without waiting for my excuse.

'I am going away again,' he said. 'Not to war this time, though if there is a campaign I will join as is my duty.'

'Where will you go?' I asked.

'To Gascony. Prince Edward is to establish his Court there and has asked me to make one of his household.'

I frowned a little because as Constable in Marie Regina my father was absolute master, but in Gascony he would be one of many knights serving their Black Prince. Then I remembered the Black Prince had married the Lady Joan, and remembering that, I felt suddenly cold.

'Have you had a message from the Lady Joan?' I asked.

'Not more than an hour since. She passed through with her escort but had no time even to take refreshment. She said she had other business in the district.'

Down at the wattle hut, I thought, and felt sickness rise up in me because I had felt such a strong pull of affection between me and the woman I had vowed to hate. I had even accepted gifts from her and listened to her words.

'Gida, I know it must be hard for you,' he said, 'to have to stay here while we go away.'

'We?'

'I am taking Godwin with me. He is ten years old now and must begin his knightly training. He is not a studious child as you are, but he will take to shield and lance as easily as the sons of the noblest men in the kingdom.'

'Godwin will be pleased,' I said, swallowing my disappointment.

'He will have much to learn, but he needs the company of other boys,' my father said.

'And I am to stay here?'

'For a time. Brother Laurence tells me that you are an apt pupil, clever beyond your sex and years. He wishes to continue in charge of your education for a year or two. When you are a little older you will be taken into a noble household and reared in the graces that make a fine lady.'

45

'Like the Lady Joan?' I asked.

'I wish she had had leisure to stay,' he said, and there was a note of boyish admiration in his voice that made me acutely uncomfortable. 'Long years ago, when I was taken prisoner at Neville's Cross, she bought my ransom and I gave her my fealty. She has had it all through the years.'

'And my mother?' I had to ask the question. 'Your mother was brought up here and knew the Lady Joan long before I came. In many ways they were like sisters.'

I wanted to ask why, if that were true, the Lady Joan had lived in a castle and my mother in the wattle hut down by the river. And I wanted to know what the Abbot had had to do with them, and who had given information against him. All the questions were whirling round in my head, but overriding them all was my own childish disgust at having been tricked into feeling affection for the Lady Joan.

Because of her my father had gone away for years, and never truly loved my mother. I knew that though I was not certain how I knew it, and it seemed to me that by accepting her gifts I too had betrayed something.

'You're very silent, my little Gida,' my

46

father said. 'In fact you're like your mother. She said less than most women, but what she said was nearly always wise.'

'When I do leave Marie Regina where shall I go?' I asked in a small voice.

'To some noble household where you will be treated as befits a gentlewoman,' he said. 'But I will come back and we will discuss it fully before you leave. For the time being you will stay here with Dorothy, and continue to study with Brother Laurence. He has hopes of you for the cloister, but I confess I would prefer to see you married. It is my belief that most women are happier when they are married.'

I was silent, wondering if my mother had been happy. I supposed that she must have been, because she loved my father and he had married her. I was still too young then to understand that loving someone does not automatically bring happiness.

'I will wait here,' I said. 'I will wait here until you come back, as my mother did.'

I think he heard the new sharpness in my voice because his colour rose and an odd, guilty look stole into his eyes. He might have explained something of it all to me then, but Godwin ran in from the stables, with his news bubbling on his lips.

'I am to go to Gascony with the Black

Prince! What do you think of that, Gida. I am trained in valour and chivalry as a knight must be trained. I will learn to ride the fiercest horse I can mount, and joust against the greatest champions in Europe.'

'You must begin by learning not to interrupt conversations,' my father said firmly. 'Remember the most important virtue a knight can have is good manners, and you are never too young to practise that.'

But he smiled as he spoke because he could never be severe with either of us for long. It was why I went on loving him, though I knew there was a weakness in him and that weakness had to do with his feeling for the Lady Joan.

They left within a few days and there were only Dorothy and me and a couple of retainers to occupy the castle. It was fortunate that in England life was becoming a little more peaceful, else it would have been most dangerous for two females to live alone with so little protection, but as it was, we were left unmolested and I rode my pony about the neighbourhood without ever coming to harm.

Those were the sunlit days. When I look back now I see every one as a summer day, and this perhaps is the mark of happiness, that winters be forgotten. Only sometimes, when I was by myself in the tower room which I had now taken as my own, did I remember that strange meeting down by the river and the gifts the Lady Joan had given me before I knew who she really was.

I was fourteen in the spring of thirteen hundred and sixty-six, and past childhood, my breasts swelling out my bodices, my courses having begun the previous year. And with the dawning of womanhood there rose in me new feelings that were uncomfortable and exciting. There were long hours when I wanted to do nothing but sit dreaming at the window, and other times when I was so full of energy that I could not tire my pony out swiftly enough. Sometimes the smallest incident would send me into helpless giggling, and at another moment the sight of fish leaping in the river would make me weep. And I had longings too, for something I had never known and could not fully understand.

I remember a dream that came to me at this period, not once, but many times. In the dream I stood in a courtyard, holding a stirrup cup out to a man on a chestnut stallion. I never saw the man's face, but his gloved hand reaching for the cup bore about the wrist, a bracelet of emeralds, and I knew in that moment that I loved the man, and

I woke in tears because I would never love anybody else.

I had dreamed that dream the night before I rode to the monastery as usual for my lessons. Brother Laurence was waiting for me at the door, which was unusual in itself, but one glance at his expression brought fear into my throat.

'You have ill tidings,' I said, and he nodded gravely, motioning me into the parlour where the Abbot sat at the table.

'We have received word from Gascony,' the Abbot said.

'About my father?' I said 'about' and not 'from', because I had already sensed what the news would be.

'Your father died of the fever two months since,' the Abbot said, and crossed himself. 'We must be thankful that he was shriven and so died in the mercy of God.'

I said nothing, because my throat had closed up over a lump and my eyes were blurred. At that moment I forgot how I had never seen my father for more than two or three out of my fourteen years. I forgot how he had left my mother to serve the Lady Joan, and returned without warning. I remembered only that he had been kind to me and that now I had no parents at all.

'Your father made provision for you,'

the Abbot said. 'Sit down and listen to me now.'

I took my place on the stool and looked at him attentively, trying to set aside my grief.

'Your father had some land in France inherited from his father. It has been neglected in recent years, but he sold it for as good price as he could obtain. That money has been set aside as a dowry for you. Your brother, Godwin, is to remain in the household of the Black Prince. He will complete his knightly training there. And you — ' He hesitated, looking at me from under lowered eyebrows.

'My Lord Abbot wonders, as I do,' said Brother Laurence, 'if you had any thought of taking the veil. You have great intelligence, more than any pupil I have had. Within a convent you could practise the arts of herbalism in which Brother Andrew tells me you are most proficient. You could quickly become Abbess.'

'I have no wish to enter a convent,' I said hastily.

'Your father thought that the choice should be yours,' the Abbot said. 'One may, it is true, serve God in the holy estate of matrimony. If that is your will then your dowry will be saved for that purpose. I did urge your father before he left to contract you to a boy of good family, but he believed you were too young. And, of course, he had no way of knowing that he would not live to arrange the matter himself. He was only forty-two years of age, scarcely in middle life.'

'Then where am I to go?,' I asked.

'In the event of his death,' the Abbot told me, 'he left instructions that you were to be taken into the household of the Duchess Blanche. She is the wife of Prince John and is noted for her gentleness and beauty.'

I was silent, thinking that very soon I would see for myself the royal family of whom I'd heard bits and pieces all my life. And I was afraid, wanting to stay in Marie Regina.

'Dorothy?' I began chokingly.

'She receives a pension and will return to the Aston's house in Cheapside with Ralph.'

I had forgotten Ralph who was six years old and must soon be breeched. He was a pleasant child who stayed close by Dorothy, and was destined to be a merchant as his father had wished.

'Yes, of course.' It was selfish of me to want to keep Dorothy by my side, just as it was foolish of me to want to stay where I no longer had a home.

'You will be leaving for Windsor in a few days,' the Abbot said. 'Two of the lay brothers will escort you.'

'I would like to go into the chapel for a while,' I said, because I felt the suggestion was expected of me.

The Abbot gave me an approving look.

'Masses will be offered for the soul of your father,' he said. 'His grave is in Gascony, but I am assured that everything was done as he would have wished.'

I thought, a little bitterly, that that was probably more true than he realised. Even in death my father would not have wished to rest for long at my mother's side.

Brother Laurence went with me to the chapel door and there left me tactfully alone. But my desire to weep had left me as it always did at the most solemn moments, and when I knelt before the gilded altar it was not of my parents that I thought but of the Abbot who had been burned as a devil worshipper. I thought of the flames leaping up around him, and of our riding to Cheapside, and the shadow that had fallen over the monstery when we returned, and I thought of the key that opened the door in the wall nearest to the head of the snake. There was very little time left in which to find that door.

3

Dorothy's reaction to my father's death was typical of her. She had a hearty fit of crying, then dried her eyes, embraced me fervently, and bustled off to see to the condition of my clothes.

'For we cannot have you arriving at Court like a beggar maid,' she said. 'It is just like a man to give us so little time in which to prepare ourselves. They don't understand the importance of making a good first impression. And you have grown out of nearly all your bodices these past months! I will have to see what can be done in the letting out of seams. And your shoes need mending. Someone will have to ride into Maidstone for new ribbons. I always think that a bit of ribbon livens up an outfit.'

She went off, apparently not having thought about the fact that she too would soon be leaving. I wonder now if her bustling and fussing were not her way of avoiding her uneasiness at the prospect of leaving Marie Regina for a new life in the city.

A few of the men were to remain to guard the castle. There were no more than half a dozen of them left, three past active service age, two of them younglings. But the place would no longer be my home. When I returned, if I ever returned, it would be as a visitor. I had been born in the castle, lived there for all but a year of my life, and I had never really looked at it. Now I saw it with a new clarity. The tower that reared up above the great hall with the kitchens behind, the cobbled yard with the stables and the loft where the lads slept, the garden where my mother had cultivated her plants, the long room where all the jars and the bottles were stored — all these were the background to my growing up. The tapestries were shabby; the plate chipped; the hearth smoked when the wind blew from the east, but it was my home, and I had not known until now that it was part of me, as were the woods and fields and the bridge across the river. Even the monastery was part of me, or had been when I was little and the old Abbot had been alive. And that reminded me again of the key the Lady Joan had given to me. That was four years since and in anger I had put it out of my mind, but now it teased my thoughts. The key would open the door within the wall at the head of the snake. The only thing that remotely resembled a snake was the path winding up the tor. The door must be one of the doors in the monastery. There were wine cellars and store rooms, and punishment cells under the main buildings, I knew, and many doors that I had never seen opened. The key must fit one of the doors in the outer wall.

I took it from its hiding place in the box, mounted my pony, and rode over to the monastery. I had timed my arrival carefully so that the Brethren would be at their devotions. I feared that one or two of them might be working in the garden, or pacing the cloisters, but when I reached the top of the path there was nobody in sight. I dismounted, tethered my pony to the iron ring jutting from the wall, and went beneath the arch into the first enclosure.

The door was easy to find. I must have passed it a thousand times without giving it a second glance, for it was set deeply into the wall and had been painted over to resemble the stone. For a moment I feared that they had painted over the keyhole too, but a moment's search relieved my mind. I stood for a moment, the path snaking behind me, and drew a long breath. Then I fitted the key into the lock and after a little struggle managed to turn it. The door swung inwards slowly and creakingly and a long, stone passage twisted down into the darkness.

On a narrow shelf within was a tallow lamp with flint and tinder box at its side. I kindled the light and lifted down the lamp, blowing on it gently until the flame was clear and bright. Then I went into the passage. It sounds so simple when I tell it, but it was not like that. Inside I was shivering and the lamp in my hand shook, sending its flame shadows tilting over walls and roof. The passage widened into a small chamber with two high backed chairs and a low table there. Behind the table hung a curtain that had once been black but was now grey with dust and cobwebs.

I stood looking at that curtain and, young as I was, I knew that once I lifted it I would never be the same again. Everything that had gone before would take on a new meaning, and everything that was to come would be subtly changed by what I had been led to understand.

Then I lifted the curtain and passed through into a great stone chamber with iron sconces around the walls and a floor squared in black and white. In the centre of the apartment was an altar of shining black stone and at the four quarters were high backed chairs carved from the same stone. I suppose they had been left because they were too heavy to move. Whatever else had been there had been destroyed or stolen.

What impressed itself upon me was the sad loneliness of the place. I imagined it glowing with light and colour, with robed figures moving about it, and I wondered what their ceremonies had been like.

Behind each throne was a figure painted on the wall. It was a wonder they had not been defaced but perhaps those who sacked this great chamber had not been anxious to stay very long.

I moved closer, lifting the lamp, steeling myself to meet horned devil, and gazed into the eyes of the archangel I had imagined all my life to be hung with herbs and remedies.

Raphael wore a yellow robe and his wings were folded in much the same fashion as a physician rolls up his sleeves before he begins work. On his golden head was a neat straw hat and there were sandals on his feet and bunches of leaves at his waist. In one hand he held a pair of scales and in the other a long staff up which twin snakes twined. He looked as familiar and friendly as if he had just stepped out of my own mind, and I found myself smiling at him as if we had met after a long absence.

The terror had drained away and I felt as if I were at home in this echoing place. Slowly

I walked round, lifting my lamp to each archangel. Michael was a knight in shining armour with scarlet wings blown backwards like the folds of a cloak and a great, shining sword. Gabriel had wings of silver shot with lavender and a blue and silver cup in his hands. The russet garbed angel in the north with his great sheaf of wheat puzzled me for a moment until I remembered some words of my mother.

'Uriel is the least known of the Shining Ones but he guards the north, the cradle of darkness out of which all life emerges.'

I came round to Raphael again and stood gazing up at him.

One thing was clear. The Abbot, whatever else he had done, had not worshipped the devil in this place, for against the might of the Shining Ones the devil cannot stand.

There was another door at the far side of the altar. I went through it into a much smaller chamber, completely empty, beyond which a short passage ended in a cobwebbed door which yielded to neither my hand nor the key. The air in here was as fresh as it had been in the large apartment and I guessed there were slits nearer the roof for there were no windows.

My lamp cast its glow on the walls with their smooth slabs of stone and picked out marks on them, scratched deeply as if with a knife. A five pointed star, a looped cross, a triangle within a circle. The symbols meant nothing to me but they must have meant something to somebody once, for they had been most carefully incised.

I ran my fingers along them and then looked closer noting that the edges of the inscribed stones were not flush with the others. I inserted my fingers in the crevice and pulled. My father had kept coins in a wall cavity at home and this looked as if it worked on the same principle. It resisted for an instant then swung out on its pivot. In the small cavity revealed was a small, thick volume. I drew it out, opening it as well as I could with one hand, but the words were written too small, so I tucked it beneath my cloak and went back into the great chamber.

The present Abbot had spoken to me about the snares of the devil, of how even the saints had been tempted by the beauty of the demons sent to lead them astray. But I could not possibly believe that the figures of the archangels had gazed at devil rites.

I had spent too long here. One of the Brethren might have passed and seen the open door. I started back along the passage and saw that what I had taken to be a cleft in the rock a few yards within the door led in fact, into a lower cavern, not of polished stone but in its natural state with plants and grasses twining over the rocks and water trickling into a shallow pool. I looked within, holding my lamp high, and the fear of unknown things rose up in me again because this place had no ordered dignity but a wild and primitive quality that roused something equally primitive in myself.

Shivering, I withdrew and hurried back to the daylight, locking the door firmly behind me.

The scene had not changed. My pony still grazed peacefully on the short grass, and from the chapel I heard the bell ringing the angelus. Three times a day it sounded across the fields and woods, and on the slopes beneath the tor the laybrothers paused in their work and bowed their knees.

I watched them now, little brown ants bending to the earth they had tamed, and thought of the undisciplined cave and the echoing chamber where the archangels gazed down, and I wondered if it would ever be possible to reconcile the two. Perhaps the old Abbot had tried and that was why they had burned him.

I rode down the path and across the bridge into the woods. Not until I had dismounted near the hut did I take out the book and begin to read. On its leather cover stamped in gold were the words, 'Grimire of Baphomet.' Within, inked in black and gold and scarlet were figures and signs and what looked like prayers and recipes all jumbled together.

One page began, 'To the glory of God the Father, God the Mother, and God the Son,' and I stared at that for a long time. I had never thought of the Creator as being female before, and the idea pleased me, the present Abbot said that women were weak and evil to be controlled by men. But if all men were made in the image of God then surely women were made in His image too, and so in the Creator male and female combined.

I turned the page and read on, how to conjure the spirits of air, water, fire and earth to visible appearance and bind them within the triangle of art, how to brew a potion that would make a man fall in love, how to make oneself invisible — I wondered if anybody had ever tried that and if it had worked.

I read on in the spring sunshine with the river rippling nearby and my mouth dropping open with astonishment. And so I came to the last page and saw there, inked in a different hand, the name Eadgytha, and beneath that the name Alfreda, and beneath that the name Gida. My own name writ in a book of spells, with space beneath for more names, more children. Girl names, for my brother's was not there. Perhaps, I thought, the real power lay in women and the Abbot had known this and so they had burned him.

I no longer hated the Lady Joan, though the remembrance of her puzzled me. She must have known of the book and hoped that I would find it when the time was ripe, and that meant that she had trusted me not to betray her. Yet, at the last, someone had betrayed the Abbot and all his valuables were gone.

At last I rose, hiding the book away carefully, took a long look at the wattle hut where my mother had once lived and where the Lady Joan had willed me to her, and rode slowly back to the castle.

That evening for the first time I questioned Dorothy. My boxes were all packed and I was to leave very early on the next day. We sat in the tower room she and I, with a jug of wine between us. I had encouraged her to drink a little more than she usually did, and by degrees her tongue became looser. She began to talk of the old days before I had been born, when her husband had been alive and she had been a laundress at the castle.

'The Lady Joan came here often then for the hunting season. She was wed to the Earl of Salisbury then, but it was never a happy union, and so it ended in divorce which caused a great scandal and then she wed Sir Thomas Holland. I think she was more content in that marriage, but she came less often to Marie Regina after that.'

'Did you like the Lady Joan?' I asked.

'Like her? Of course I liked her! Nobody could help liking her. She is said to be one of the loveliest women in England. Golden hair and blue eyes and skin white as milk. Oh, it was a treat to look at her and hear her laughing. The men couldn't drag their eyes away and my own man was no better than the rest of them, but looking never did any harm.'

I wondered if in my father's case he had stopped at looking, or if my mother had had true cause to be unhappy.

'Did the Abbot like the Lady Joan?' I asked. 'I mean the old Abbot who was here when I was little?'

'She was friend to everyone,' Dorothy said. 'The Abbot had a great admiration for her.'

'Did you know the Abbot?'

'Well, not to say *know*,' Dorothy said. 'He

was a very distinguished man, very important, with little time to spare for ordinary folk.'

'My mother was very friendly with him.'

'Your mother was never ordinary,' Dorothy said.

'Why not?'

'As to that I couldn't say,' Dorothy said vaguely. 'She was not like the rest of us.'

'They burned the Abbot, didn't they?'

Dorothy's hand jerked and a little of the wine spilled on the table.

'You were not to be told of that,' she said.

'I've known for years. Why did they burn him? Was he a devil worshipper?'

'So it was said. Nobody asked my opinion, and I never enquired. It's wiser to keep out of such things.'

I poured more wine for her. 'Did you never guess?' I coaxed. 'In all the years you've lived here did you never guess?'

'Oh, we all knew something was going on,' Dorothy said tapping the side of her nose. 'At the great festivals — the old country feasts, why we kept within doors and nobody asked questions when others crossed the bridge. But I knew little of such matters myself.'

'Didn't you ask my mother?'

'Alfreda kept her own counsel, as did the Lady Joan. I never asked them and they never told me.'

'And after they burned the Abbot? Was it here they burned him?' I looked at her in horror as the thought occurred to me.

'They took him away,' she said. 'We heard afterwards what had happened to him. Then other monks came to the monastery and a new Abbot. There were rumours of a Temple — a heathen one, but I never listened much.'

'We were in London then.'

'And I am to take young Ralph there soon.' She looked at me, moist-eyed. 'Me to Cheapside and you to Court. Well, I've no family of my own and living in town will be a change.'

'You must be very old,' I said.

'Close on fifty. I never feel it though, except when the rains come and my joints ache.'

'You must have been here when my grandmother was alive.'

'What do you know about her?' she asked.

'Only that her name was Eadgytha and she is buried in the monastery garden.'

'Ah, well I was only a young wench when Eadgytha died. She seldom came to the castle, but lived down by the river.'

'And my grandfather? Who was my grandfather?'

'It was never told,' Dorothy said. 'Eadgytha never wed.'

I stared at her, struck by a new idea. When I spoke my voice was low and excited.

'Was the Abbot my grandfather? Was he, Dorothy?'

'Lord bless us!' she exclaimed. 'The Abbot was a celibate! Whatever put that notion into your head? No, your grandfather was — ' She stopped, her fingers flying to her lips.

'A man of no account,' I said carelessly, 'since nobody ever mentions him.'

'Of no account?' Her plump cheeks flushed. 'Would you call the king of no account?'

'King?'

'King Edward himself,' she nodded. 'Didn't he come here for the hunting one summer? The Abbot hadn't been here long at that time. He'd come back from the East, from the Crusades. And the king came to hunt. He was a young man then, of course, not long wed, not settled in his ways. And Eadgytha was very pretty. Oh, nobody said much, but everybody knew. I was working in the kitchen then, but I kept my eyes open.'

'What happened?' I was leaning forward, the wine forgotten.

'The king went back to the queen,' Dorothy said, 'and Alfreda was born. Her mother died and the Abbot took her under his protection.'

'So the king is my grandfather.' I tried to accustom myself to the idea.

'Not that His Grace ever acknowledged the fact,' Dorothy said wryly. 'They do say he has more bastards than he can count. But don't you go imagining your grandsire was of no account. He was a king and you may hold your head as high as any when you go to Court.'

I wanted to ask more but she was growing sleepy, and after a while she began to talk about her husband whose active service had been ended by an arrow deep in the thigh.

The next morning I was awake before dawn, and swallowed some breakfast with difficulty because the pain of leaving was suddenly mitigated by the excitement of going to Court. I would see for myself the royal beings about whom I'd imagined such pomp and glory, and though they might not know or acknowledge it a little of their blood flowed in my veins.

I wished I had a beautiful Court dress in which to dazzle everybody, but although Dorothy had done her best my wardrobe was modest. For the long ride I wore a green shift under an open sided gown of brown wool. My brown cloak was lined with yellow, and my hair was drawn back under a cap of frilled white lace.

Dorothy evidently had a headache, or perhaps she was truly sad to part with me, for her eyelids were red and her lips drawn in. Ralph jumped about me, chattering, 'Will you come to London to see us, Gida? Will you come to Cheapside?'

'If my duties at Court allow,' I said, and thought that I sounded like an echo of my father.

When I came into the courtyard where my pony waited, with my luggage strapped to the pack horse behind, I was pleased to see Brother Laurence there.

'I came to wish you Godspeed,' he said. 'My Lord Abbot wishes me to convey his good wishes and his blessing. And this is for you.'

He gave me a narrow box in which lay a carved wooden rosary set in silver. Looking at it I thought, 'Now I have a book of spells, a Saracen ring, and a Christian rosary. I wonder how I can reconcile the three.'

'You are not a child now,' Brother Laurence was saying. 'At court you will meet many subtle temptations. Faith and courage will help you to resist them. Brother John and Brother Martin will ride with you and return tomorrow. I hope you will find time to write to us occasionally. I would not like to see your learning go to waste.'

I promised that I would write, and hugged Dorothy who said gruffly I'd likely grow into a fine lady and forget all about her, and I mounted my pony and took a last look up at the high tower, and then we clattered through the gate into the fields, with the two monks, cudgels in their hands, riding close at each side.

I suspect they hoped for a little excitement on the way, but there was none. Our way lay across the downs and the fine weather made the riding easy. As we went the two monks lost their shyness and began to talk more freely. They were not local men, but had come from Lancashire and their thick accents made their speech difficult to follow.

Neither of them had ever thought of being anything but monks. It was a good outdoor life, they said, with regular meals and a place in Heaven assured for them if they kept their vows. They could both make shift to read and write, and had enough Latin to follow the Mass, but they liked best to be out in the open, planting and reaping. The Abbot was a strict man but fair, and Brother Laurence was very learned.

I asked if either of them had known the old Abbot, but they shook their heads, saying they understood that he had died. I think they assumed that he had perished in the Death.

They said that my father's death must have been great grief to me, but that it was a wonderful chance for me to be able to go to Court. Their ideas about the king were as childlike as my own. He was a very powerful man, said Brother John, who could still hold his own in a tournament though he was in his mid-fifties, and his queen was a most Christian lady. They had never seen the Lady Joan of Kent, but she was said to be most beautiful. Years before she had dropped her garter at a ball and King Edward had founded the Order of the Garter in honour of the incident. She had four children by her second husband, but her marriage to the Black Prince had brought no living child, and as she was close on forty her time was getting short.

It was all innocent, pleasant gossip as the miles fell away behind us. At Kingston we stopped to water the horses and eat at the inn. I had a purse of gold coins that the Abbot had given to me, but the laybrothers had been entrusted with a little money to defray the expenses of the journey and insisted on paying for the meal.

'It is not often,' said Brother Martin, 'that we have the pleasure of taking out a young lady. This journey is a real treat for us.'

'And with you,' I said, 'I feel I can travel safely.'

'Our habits save us from molestation,' Brother John said, 'not to mention our cudgels.'

They would certainly have made sturdy opponents, I guessed, with their brawny arms and broad country faces. But after the meal we rode on again without incident. We were in the woods by the time the sun was setting and, long before we reached the castle, its walls glimmered golden above the trees as the sky changed from blue to the scarlet of evening.

King Edward had, I knew, many palaces but Windsor was said to be his favourite one. He spent as much of his time there as possible, hunting in the forests, arranging jousts and tournaments, continually embellishing the great halls and chambers. He went to London only when the business of state demanded his presence at Westminster.

The crowded streets of London had impressed me when I was a child, but this many towered structure of stone was grander than anything I had seen, and as we clattered beneath one of the arches I began to feel small and young again.

There were guards everywhere and a

bustle of lackeys, ostlers, esquires and pages hurrying up and down, each one seeming to know exactly where he was going.

I dismounted and stood in bewilderment, wondering what to do. Brother Martin however drew himself up to his full height, which was considerable, and called loudly to a passing stable boy to take the horses and to see that the luggage was delivered to the right place. I hoped, as I saw the pack horse being led away, that the boy knew where the right place was and that my modest wardrobe would turn up again. Brother Martin, however, was already striding across the courtyard, waving his letter of introduction and informing anyone who cared to listen that Mistress Gida Falcon had come to Court.

Either his voice was more penetrating than people could bear, or we were unusually fortunate, because a plump young man stopped, bowing politely, and enquiring if we would care to follow him. We did follow him, up and down stone steps, down long corridors and round corners. He went at breakneck speed, puffing a little as he sped along, and brought himself up short in an antechamber where he held out his hand for the letter, motioned us to a bench, and vanished through a doorway.

He was out again in a few moments, smiling and talking in an unexpectedly deep and pleasant voice.

'Mistress Gida, I am Geoffrey Chaucer and I had the honour of knowing your father slightly when I was a boy. I am sorry to hear of his death, but pleased to hear you are to join the Duke of Lancaster's household. The Duchess Blanche is greatly beloved. Philippa will show you to the maiden's quarters.'

'The queen?' I was rather shocked to hear her referred to by her Christian name.

'Heavens, no! Philippa de Roet is one of Her Grace's attendants and my own betrothed. She will help you to change your dress and escort you to supper. If you will wait here she will be with you directly.'

He was looking questioningly at the laybrothers, and I said hastily, 'Brother John and Brother Martin brought me here. Can their needs be supplied until they leave tomorrow morning?'

'Our needs are very simple,' Brother John assured him, 'but we would take it as a great favour if we could see the king and queen. Just a glimpse of their Graces, to be able to go back to our community and say that we have seen them.'

Geoffrey Chaucer's face warmed into a beam, and he reached up to clap Brother

John on the shoulder.

'Nothing easier! I'll have a word with one of the chaplains and see that you get a place at table where you can see everything.'

'Then we're very much obliged to you, sir.' Brother John turned to me, holding out his hand. 'We leave very early, so we'll make our farewells. Our prayers will be with you.'

We clasped hands firmly, and when they had gone I felt as if two friends had deserted me. Then another door swung open and a thin girl with a hooked nose and curly brown hair came towards me.

'Gida Falcon? I am Philippa de Roet. Come with me and I'll help you to make ready. The Duchess Blanche is at Kenilworth with the two children, and the duke is in Gascony, but we expect him back in a week or two, and then you may travel in his train. He is very amiable, as she is, and you find her duties very light. I have not been to Kenilworth myself, but my sister is governess there, and says it is a vastly more comfortable place than Windsor, and Windsor has more draughts than any place I've ever known! Mind the step! It goes down steeply here and 'tis easy to lose your balance or twist your ankle.'

I had followed her chattering voice and rustling skirts up and down passages and round more corners than I could count, and now we landed in a long, high-ceilinged room with rows of curtained beds down one side, and massive chests and wardrobes ranged down the other. An immense fire burned at one end of the apartment and dozens of candles strengthened the fading light slanting from narrow windows high in the walls.

'Your things have been put here.' She swished back a curtain and disclosed my trunks. 'What will you wear? We ought to be down there already, but I have leave to wait for you. Normally we would be fined. Oh, but this is a very pretty gown! You must wear this.'

She had already unbuckled the straps and flung back the lid, and was holding up a dress I had only worn once because it was too good for every day. The undergown was of yellow silk, the high-waisted houppeland of coral with a collar and wide cuffs of dark green. There was a coif of coral silk with tiny yellow beads stitched over it, and I remembered that when I'd put it on Dorothy had said I looked far from plain.

'You are Geoffrey Chaucer's betrothed,' I said shyly, taking off my cloak.

She rippled with laughter. 'So he tells everybody, but it is not official yet. I swear

I will not wed him until he is promoted body squire to His Grace. And he swears he will carry me off by force, to which I reply that he had best lose a little weight before he tries to pick up anything heavier than a spoon!'

'You don't love him then?'

'Love him? Of course, I love him madly, but I'll not tell him so. Have you a comb, for your hair is sadly tangled.'

I fished out my comb and sat on the edge of the bed while she teased my hair into little quiffs and coils, and all the time she talked as if we had known each other all our days.

'There are ten of us here now again. Ermina used to have your bed, but she fell in love and so into pregnancy, and had to be wed in a great hurry. She was only thirteen and the queen was very cross. The queen is a very moral lady and has no vice save that of extravagance. She says as much herself, so it is perfectly alright for me to repeat it. No, let that curl peep out of your temple. It softens the line. Are you in love with anyone?'

'I don't know anyone,' I said truthfully.

'Oh, we are all in love with somebody or other,' she said cheerfully. 'There is not very much else to do, and as few of us will be allowed to marry those whom we love, we take what we can while we can. Eleanor de Bohun now is deep in love with the

Captain of the Guard and writes poems about him. The other day he spoke to her in the courtyard and she declared her knees shook so much she couldn't make answer. All he said was that it looked like rain, but he said it with a meaning glance! Not that anything can ever come of it. She is to marry Prince Thomas who is a most unpleasant boy, and she has coaxed her father into letting her wait until she is fourteen but she is nearly twelve now and time rushes by. I am seventeen but I don't intend to take Geoffrey Chaucer until I am twenty, even if he were to be made body servant within the hour. There! You are ready now and we can go down.'

Incredibly I was, for she had never stopped talking!

As we went back through the confusion of corridors I let her chatter on, while I wondered if I would be able to find my way about the place as easily as everybody else seemed to do.

Philippa stopped talking suddenly and drew me back against the wall. A little group of ladies were approaching from an intersecting corridor, and as my companion sank into a curtsey, I realised it was the queen. I had an impression of glittering gold and silver, and then the queen paused.

'Are you Her Grace of Lancaster's new attendant?' I began to stammer some reply, but Philippa answered for me.

'Gida Falcon, Your Grace.'

'From Marie Regina.' The queen studied me, and in that moment I felt as if she knew all about my background, and who my grandfather had been, for she heaved a sigh as if she were remembering some past heartache, and said, 'I trust you will be happy with us and do your best.'

'Yes, Your Grace.' This time I did manage to speak coherently, and she smiled a little, a tired elderly smile quite unlike the glorious image of my imaginings and went past, her ladies following.

One of them, a slit-eyed young woman in a gown of dark red, hesitated and glanced back at me, a crooked smile tilting a corner of her thin mouth.

'The lady in red.' I caught at Philippa's sleeve, whispering, as we began to follow them.

'What of her?' She spoke sharply. 'I wondered who she was, that's all.'

'Alice Perrers,' Philippa said. 'She is the king's harlot, and a bitch into the bargain. I cannot understand how the queen tolerates her.'

I said nothing, but my brain was racing

as we came into the Great Hall. On the index finger of her left hand Alice Perrers had worn a square cut sapphire. I knew that cross-carved jewel, for I had seen it many times on the hand of the Abbot who had been burned for devil worship.

4

My first days at Windsor are jumbled now in my memory, as dreams are jumbled with flashes of clarity interspersed with grey, shadowed periods when one wanders in a kind of limbo. So I remember certain scenes, even conversations, very vividly, and other hours, whole days, are blurred in my mind as if I looked back at them through a veil.

Under the surface bustle and confusion, life at Court ran with surprising smoothness. The king was the hub of this great wheel of activity. His tall figure with waving grey hair and beard was continually here, there, and everywhere, followed by his chaplains and advisers, body squires, valets and pages. He spoke to me only once, pausing to look down at me as I sat in a window alcove. I would have risen, but he motioned me back, his eyes travelling from the crown of my head to the tips of my toes.

'You are Gida Falcon, from Marie Regina?' he said at last.

'Yes, Sire.'

'To be attached to the household of the Duchess Blanche?'

'Yes, Sire.'

He gave me another searching look, and then he said, 'I knew your grandmother,' and laid a small purse in my lap. There were coins in it judging by the weight, but I was too angry and humiliated to open it. If he hoped to buy an easy conscience by paying me off then I would not give him that satisfaction.

I heard my own voice, as sweet and cold as ice. 'I thank Your Grace, but my father made provision for me, and I have no need of anything more.'

I handed back the purse and, out of surprise I think, he took it and stared at it as if he had never seen it before. Then he gave it to one of his attendants, nodded in a manner that was not entirely displeased, and strode on, his robes billowing about him.

So my grandfather had known or guessed who I was, and cared very little. Tears of rage stung my eyes and my hands clenched in my skirt.

The queen spoke to me more than once in those first days. It was as if she sought to make up for her husband's lack of concern, and at the time I thought it could not have been easy for her to be reminded of his early indiscretion. Now I realise that she felt very little pain because the king had enjoyed many mistresses and sired many bastards, and yet none of them meant as much to him as she had done. She had never been beautiful, and in middle life she had put on so much weight that her features were blurred in fat, but she had pretty hands and a kind smile, and I could understand why she was popular.

She never said more than a few words to me, but each word was designed to make me feel at ease, for she told me that I must send letters whenever I wished to my brother in Gascony, and she would write to her son to ask him to take an interest in the boy.

When she spoke of the Black Prince her blue eyes glowed with pride. His feats as a warrior, his reputation for chivalry, were matters on which she loved to dwell. She said nothing about his marriage and once, when one of her ladies mentioned Joan of Kent, I glanced at the queen and saw that her lips had thinned and her heavy face was stiff with disapproval.

'It is rumoured that the king himself was once enamoured of the Lady Joan,' Philippa de Roet confided to me. 'She would have none of him, but Her Grace was jealous.'

It was strange that a wife should feel more jealousy about a woman who had not been her husband's mistress than the ones who had. I wondered if my mother had been in the same position, wishing that my father would sleep with the Lady Joan and so discover that she was only an ordinary mortal after all.

Philippa de Roet was a great gossip, and much of what she said was true. She was the daughter of Sir Payn de Roet and had only a small dowry, a fact that worried her not at all. Her younger sister was already wed but separated from her husband and much happier at Kenilworth where she looked after the Duchess Blanche's two little girls.

'Pippa is six and Bet is two. They are beautiful children, but then the Duchess Blanche is very beautiful. I think she is the most beautiful woman I ever saw, save for the Lady Joan. They are both fair but the duchess has paler hair and skin and is not so curved. There is a great discussion as to which is the most fascinating. Geoffrey Chaucer says I am more fascinating than either of them, but he is in love with me and so cannot be expected to judge sensibly.'

She had gossiped about the other members of the royal family.

'The Princess Isabella didn't wed until she was thirty. Her husband is a Frenchman, very rich, and very much in love with her for they waited many years before they were married. But she is very sour at times is

Madame Isabella, and her daughter Philippa is a horror.'

It was confusing that the three grand-daughters of the queen were all named after her. Lionel, the king's second son, had a daughter called Philippa too. The first time I saw Prince Lionel I must admit to feeling terrified. He was over seven feet tall with a mane of yellow hair, and a booming voice, and enormous hands that looked as if they could crush the life out of a person in a moment. His wife had perished during the Death and it was said he would never love another woman, though sooner or later he would be obliged to take another wife. Fearsome he might look, but one could not be more than five minutes in his company without realizing that he was one of the kindest and simplest of men. He adored children and was rather like a gigantic child himself.

'He and Prince John are the nicest of the king's sons,' Philippa de Roet said. 'Prince Edmund is very clever, they say, with his nose always stuck in a book, but he likes to spy on people and carry tales about them. And nobody has a good word for Prince Thomas. He cannot keep his temper for more than two minutes together. I don't believe even the queen has much affection for him, but she is his mother and so has to pretend.'

The younger princes took no notice of me at all. I doubt if they noticed my existence, for though I was pretty I was of small account compared to the bejewelled young girls who served in the royal household. They were daughters of the great nobles and barons of the land for the most part, brought from their father's estates to ornament the Court and carry out light duties until they were wed. Most of them were already betrothed, not for love, but for profit or the settling of an old quarrel. Those few who were not held out the inducement of comely faces and comelier dowries to the sons of noble families who, like themselves, had been sent to Court.

Our duties were very light. We rose early and were expected to attend Mass before we broke our fasts on bread and beef and ale. In the forenoon we took turns to accompany the queen wherever she wished to go, but as she disliked walking and had lost her taste for riding, most of the time was spent at our needlework, or in reading aloud to her, for like many women of middle age she adored romantic poetry. It was clear that she adored the king too. Her face lit up when he visited her apartments and a caressing note came into her voice whenever she spoke of him.

'We met in a garden,' she said one day when we sat in one of the rose arbours dotted about the grounds. Philippa de Roet was there and Eleanor de Bohun who, as the future wife of Prince Thomas, was often with the queen. 'His Grace was the Prince of Wales then for his father still lived, and I came into my father's garden and we both looked at each other and loved in the same moment. I was only fourteen and we were wed in a very few months.'

I could imagine her as a big boned, flaxen girl with a sweet smile and pretty hands.

'My affections have never wavered,' said the queen, and a brief shadow crossed her face. I wondered if she were remembering the many times he had been unfaithful to her, and then I saw that the king had come into the garden with Alice Perrers at his side.

There was nothing pretty about Alice. She was thin and tall with a sallow complexion and narrow eyes and lank hair, but she dressed like a peacock in scarlet, turquoise, emerald and orange, and always on her finger was the cross-carved sapphire ring. She didn't sleep in the dormitory with the rest of us, but had her own apartments.

'They say she is married but nobody knows where her husband is,' Philippa de Roet whispered to me. 'She has two little girls already, Jane and Joan, and it's an open secret who fathered them, but nobody knows who fathered Alice. Nobody is even sure how she came to Court in the first place. There are all kinds of tales, but I don't believe half of them myself.'

I said nothing, but I watched Alice whenever she was in the company. She moved gracefully, I conceded reluctantly, and she had a way of arching her long neck and smiling sleepily that a man might find attractive. I admitted that and went on disliking her.

It seemed that she was also watching me for I often saw those narrow eyes slide in my direction, and then she would look away again, her glance veiled by blackened lashes, for though she was not yet twenty she already painted heavily.

The Court dined at noon, though the queen often had a nuncheon in her own apartments and she never went far without a bag of sweetmeats into which she frequently dipped, licking her shapely fingers free of sugar. After we had eaten, those who had attended Her Grace in the morning were more or less free to do as they chose. There were many entertainments at Court — tournaments and hunting parties and games of chance. We had instructions in dancing, and in archery, and in the arranging of flowers, and the queen was always pleased when one of the girls requested permission to go into the great library to read one of the books there.

Before supper there was another service in the chapel, and at the meal itself we took turns to serve their Graces with the various dishes after they had been tasted by the food tasters. To be late for church or supper meant a fine, and to be absent meant a scolding and a day kneeling in penance in chapel. I had not been late or absent, however, when Alice Perrers sent for me. She did not, to be fair to her, phrase her summons like that, but it was a summons all the same. I might have refused but I was filled with curiosity. I had never been inside Alice's apartments, and I wondered too what she wanted of me.

The lad who had brought the message led me through the great palace, where I still found the directions confusing, to the stairs that spiralled up to the apartments that had been set aside for the king's mistress. There was a guard at the door as if she were a person of great consequence, but he stood aside as I went in.

The chamber was one of the most luxurious I had ever seen. The walls were hung with brilliant arras and, instead of rushes, on the floor were carpets woven in many shades. There was a fire burning though the evening was warm and all about the room were rich ornaments of silver and jade. As if by magic my eyes were drawn to the golden paperweights. I had always liked those paperweights when they stood on the Abbot's table at Marie Regina. And looking at them now I knew who had betrayed him.

Alice Perrers sat in a high backed chair by the fire. She wore a loose robe of a bright orange colour and there were diamonds in her ears and around her long throat. She watched me as I stood looking at the paperweights and there was a sly amusement in her face. Then she indicated a chair opposite to her, and I sat down and looked at her with my eyebrows raised. I was determined not to speak to her until she spoke to me.

When she did her voice was gentle and confiding.

'I have wanted to talk to you for a long time, Gida Falcon. You and I have much in common.'

That did surprise me. My head jerked up and I stared at her.

'You are the daughter of Sir Pierre de Faucon and the woman called Alfreda.'

'Yes.' I went on staring at her.

'Is the wattle hut still there, down by the river?' she asked softly. 'And the bridge that leads to the top of the tor?'

'You've been to Marie Regina.'

'I was taken there when I was very small,' she told me. 'Your father took me there. He and Ralph Aston found me in a village in Norfolk. I was born in that village and orphaned when I was — oh, too young to remember! A woman took care of me, a peasant woman, she lived in a miserable little hut with skins to sleep on. We were hungry, not just before meals but every day. The harvest was very bad that year, and it rained all the time. There was even talk of sacrificing a child, to give blood to the earth so that the crops would grow. The woman kept me in the hut for fear they might seize me and kill me. I was only little, but I knew I was in danger. And then Pierre came with Ralph Aston, and the woman sold me to them.'

'Sold you!' I stared at her in horror. 'She was a poor woman,' Alice said. 'And I wanted to be rich. I wanted to eat regularly and wear pretty gowns and shoes with leather soles. I knew it was best for me to go with them. So they took me to Marie Regina, and Dorothy took care of me at the castle.'

'She never told me,' I said blankly.

'She wouldn't,' Alice said. 'She never liked me very much, and she liked me even less after — '

'After you betrayed the Abbot?' my voice snapped out.

'The Abbot.' She looked down at the ring on her finger and smiled. 'The Abbot told me that I was a vain child and told me that I must pray for humility. He told me too that I must always be grateful to those who rescued me from a life of poverty. He sat there, the great ring on his finger, and lectured me as if I was nothing. And I kept watching that ring, that beautiful ring. I made up my mind then that one day I would own that ring. One day I would own all the lovely things the Abbot possessed.'

'So you betrayed him?' I didn't trouble to keep the scorn out of my voice.

'The king gave you a purse of gold,' Alice said, 'and you gave it back to him.'

'I didn't want charity,' I said stiffly.

'Then you're a fool,' Alice said calmly. 'Only a fool lets pride stand in the way of progress. Money is protection against hunger and cold and danger. I knew that even when I was little.'

'There's honour — ' I began, but her laugh cut me short. 'Only the rich can afford honour,' she said. 'Men can make their fortunes in war, but we women must use other means. We must be subtle and clever, and forget our pride.'

'How did you come to Court?' I asked.

'The Lady Joan came to Marie Regina and said she would bring me to Court. She was very kind to me. I learned later that she was kind to everybody in an unthinking way, because it was too much trouble to be cruel. But it was a fine opportunity and I set myself to learn. I learned that when others talk it is best to remain silent and listening, and when others are silent then is the moment to speak — to the right person and in private.'

'So you told lies about the Abbot.'

'They were not lies,' she said. 'I was too young to understand, but I did know that things went on at the monastery at certain times. Alfreda and Pierre went by night across the bridge and the Lady Joan went with them. I followed them once and they went into the great temple in the side of the tor.'

'And you betrayed them? You put them all in danger!'

'There was not much danger for the Lady Joan or your parents,' she said. 'His Grace was anxious to keep his cousin's name free from any scandal. But the Abbot had once been a Templar Knight and the Templars were suppressed long ago because thay had turned to devil worship.'

'But you couldn't be certain. You couldn't be certain,' I said.

'I wasn't,' Alice said. 'I let a word pass here and there. I asked a question or two. I had the ear of the king by then, for he thought me clever and amusing. And when I told him that I had never seen the Lady Joan go to the secret place — why, he was so grateful that he said I could have what I chose from the Abbot's possessions.'

'They burned him,' I said. 'Don't you understand? They burned him! They took him away and burned him, and scattered his community. And it was because of you.'

'If he had been entirely innocent they would have found him so, and my words would have made no difference,' Alice said.

'You must have hated the Abbot,' I said slowly.

'I'll not be spoken to as if I were nothing,' Alice said. 'I will be rich and safe, and my daughters will be safe too and make fine marriages.'

'Was that all you wanted to say to me?' I asked, rising.

'I wanted to talk to you,' she said. 'I am — lonely here at Court. They are polite because they dare not offend the king, but I know they despise me even while they envy me. I care nothing for that, nothing at all. But you are Pierre's daughter, and he was kind to me. I hoped you might understand.'

'I understand that because of you the Abbot died horribly,' I said. 'If my father had known how it would be he'd have left you in that village to be killed as a sacrifice. I wish he had left you there.'

I thought she flinched a little, and I was glad of it. I am sorry now. My only excuse is that I was very young and the young see everything in terms of black and white. Forgive me, Alice, wherever you are now, because I could not recognise in you that frightened child hiding from danger. I only saw the hard, mocking young woman who cared nothing for honour or decency.

I turned and went out, my heart burning with resentment. I was certain that Alice Perrers was an evil woman, and I made up my mind never to think kindly of her. I have altered my mind, but it is too late now.

At the time I was so angry that I picked up my skirts, and ran down the stairs, and along the corridors without noticing in which direction I went. I came into a small panelled room where I banged my fist down hard on a table and said aloud. 'I hate Alice Perrers! I hate her! I hate her!'

'Child, it is very wrong to hate,' said Queen Philippa.

I had thought myself alone and swung round in fright. Her Grace had evidently been at her private devotions, for a rosary was twined round her fingers and she carried a Missal. Her voice was chiding but my feelings at that moment were too intense to be contained, and I burst out, 'She is an evil woman, and an ugly woman, and keeps the king from your bed!'

I could have bitten out my tongue, not only because I must surely be sent away from Court in disgrace for speaking so, but because her kind face was full of pain. Then she motioned me to a carved bench against the wall and drew me down beside her.

'You speak aloud what many others keep in their private thoughts,' she said. 'I am aware of the glances and the whispers. But there are reasons for my keeping quiet, for my toleration of Alice Perrers. You have heard of Abishag?'

'No, Your Grace. Is she one of your ladies?' She smiled at that.

'When King David of the Jews grew old he took into his bed a young virgin, Abishag, to lift the melancholy of his old age and restore his failing powers. Alice is the king's Abishag.'

'But you — ' I stopped, looking at her.

'I have a lump in my breast,' the queen said. 'It causes me no pain as yet, but it grows larger and I know what it portends. The king will be lonely when I am gone. He will need Alice then.'

She rose, patting my arm as if I were the one to be consoled, and went away. She did not force silence upon me, but she was wise enough to know that I would say nothing.

I had been at Court for almost a month when we had word that John of Gaunt was returning, and that the duchess, weary of his absence, had travelled to the coast to meet him as he disembarked.

'They are much in love and cannot bear to be separated,' Philippa de Roet told me. 'They are to come to Windsor, and then I suppose you will travel up to Kenilworth with them. They are bringing the two little girls and my sister will be with them. It will be pleasant to see Katharine again. She and I were very close but then she was married to Hugh Swynford and I was brought to Court, and we seldom write. So there will be much to talk about.'

I could imagine that and I wondered with

some amusement if either would listen to the other.

'There will be a great banquet to celebrate their return,' Philippa said. 'Will you wear your coral dress? 'Tis the most becoming one you have. I think I will wear my yellow. Geoffrey prefers the blue, but the colour makes me look too sallow! Not that Geoffrey has any taste as far as women are concerned. Look at me! I am not pretty and my nose is too big, but he thinks I am completely lovely!'

'And you feel the same about him,' I interrupted.

'I certainly don't think that Geoffrey is lovely!' she exclaimed. 'He is too fat, and he treads on my feet when we dance, and he sits his horse like a bag of turnips. But I cannot imagine that I could ever be happy with anyone else, so that just shows how foolish I am.'

She laughed again and whisked off to talk about clothes with some of the other girls.

There was certainly an air of excitement running through the household. The queen could not talk sufficiently about the splendours of her magnificent son.

'He is so handsome that it is difficult to fault him. And I find it impossible to decide whether he or Ned is the better horseman.

Ned sits the straighter, but John has the more graceful bearing. I tell you, ladies, a mother with such fine sons is a happy woman!'

I was pleased by her good spirits, by the pleasure she took in her family. And I wondered if, in the midst of her gaiety, she ever thought of the king mounting the spiral stairs to the room where Alice Perrers waited, to play Abishag to his waning powers.

The Duke and Duchess arrived. By that simple statement I try to convey something of that great cavalcade which swept up the broad avenue to the main courtyard. Men at arms, pikesmen, archers, halberdiers, knights with their visors raised and plumes in their helmets, pages in satin tabards embroidered with lions and leopards, in rank after rank they came.

'The duke doesn't visit Court. He invades it,' Geoffrey Chaucer said in my ear.

I made no answer because I was dazzled by the brilliance and the rhythm of beating drums and the blaring of the trumpets. And in the midst of it all, mounted on chestnut stallions, were two glowing, golden figures. The duke was clad in silvery armour and his cloak was of bronze velvet, its high collar faced with ermine. The duchess wore a loose robe of silver over a gown of gold tissue, and her fair hair was braided and pinned with long combs of ivory. They were the most beautiful people I had ever seen, exactly as I had pictured royal personages to be before I came to Court and found out that they were only ordinary human beings.

The king, his face beaming, embraced his son as he dismounted while Queen Philippa enfolded her tall daughter-in-law with what was obviously genuine affection.

The babble grew louder as the rest of the party dismounted, spurs jangling, weapons clashing, greetings exchanged, gossip beginning between the ladies of the Duchess Blanche's train and the queen's attendants. I was swept along with the rest, bewildered by it all.

'A smooth crossing,' John of Gaunt had a pleasant but penetrating voice. 'And what do I find when I reach dry land but my disobedient wife who will not stay quietly at home but travels to meet me with all her household! I was never so surprised in my life.'

'Pleasantly, I hope?' The duchess had an unexpectedly deep voice.

'Can you doubt it, my love?' His hand reached out to clasp hers, and the brightness was all about them as if they stood in some enchanted circle of their own.

'We have a Thanksgiving Service in honour

of your safe return,' Queen Philippa said.

'And a tournament on the morrow,' the king said. 'Will you test your lance against Lionel?'

'And have my neck broken in the first fall? I'll take on Edmund,' the duke said.

'And me? Will you joust with me, John?' Prince Thomas was clamouring.

'If you promise not to toss me in the first round,' the duke said kindly.

'My dear Blanche, you must rest before the Service,' the king was saying. 'You will be worn out if you overtax your strength.'

'I am much stronger than I used to be. The air of Kenilworth agrees with me,' the duchess said.

'She wears herself out in the service of others,' her husband said. 'I wish you could impress upon her, my lady mother, that she is not responsible for every orphan in the land.'

' 'Tis a good fault,' the queen said indulgently. 'Have you news of Ned?

'Long letters from him and from Joan. Both are well and keep a fine Court, but my brother is restless for more conquest. He has a mind to go campaigning again.'

'And nobody can stand against the Black Prince!,' Lionel of Clarence boomed. 'I've a mind to join him, Sire, and earn enough to pay off my debts.'

'While you rush around Europe incurring more.' The king looked up at his huge son with exasperated affection. 'You would do better to marry again, to take some rich heiress.'

'Violante Visconti is rich, and very beautiful.'

'And her father is tyrant of Milan.'

'But a useful ally if you decide to carry your campaigning into Italy.'

'There is civil war in Spain between Don Pedro and his bastard brother. You would do better to give your support to Spain.'

'And bring in Bernado Visconti as an ally for Don Pedro.'

The conversation eddied back and forth, and I stood on the fringe of it, listening and watching. They were so vivid, so full of life, so vital and colourful. If I can close my eyes I can still see them as they were then, and see myself on the edge of that glittering group in my coral dress with my hair hidden under the beaded patterned coif.

The Service over, we trooped into the Great Hall where extra trestles had been covered with white cloths and long benches brought in to accommodate the Lancaster servants. There were musicians in the gallery, tumblers springing and somersaulting between tables, a troupe of acrobats forming a human cobweb up the west wall, a sloe eyed dancer in crimson doublet and hose to leap and twirl on pointed shoes. There was too much to watch, too much to eat and drink, and my head was spinning long before the fifteen courses were done.

'Gida, you are wanted at the high table.' Eleanor de Bohun had to shout the words into my ears until I could make out her meaning.

I rose from my place and threaded my way through the dancers and the serving women, until I had reached the dais where those members of the royal family who were present sat above the salt, the velvet canopy over their heads muting the din in the main body of the hall.

'This is Gida Falcon,' the queen said, indicating me to the duchess as I sank into a curtsey.

'The Lady Joan recommended you to us, Mistress Gida,' the duchess said, turning in her chair to look at me. 'My Lord Duke was acquainted with your father who was a most noble gentleman, and I understand that your brother is in the service of Prince Edward.'

'Godwin is a page at the Gascon Court. I have had no word of him for years,' I said.

'Men are not noted for their fondness of writing letters,' the duchess said. 'John, do you recall a Godwin Falcon when you were at Ned's Court?'

The duke pondered an instant, then shook his head. Like his parents he was fair, but his long hair was more red than gold.

'Ned has pages and squires all over the place,' he observed. 'They chatter like monkeys and eat like horses. I cannot tell one from t'other.'

'If you wish to write to your brother when we reach Kenilworth, I will see that the letter reaches Gascony,' the duchess promised.

'I'll carry it myself.' Her husband raised his goblet, nodding at me in friendly fashion. 'We can stay but a week, and then I must take my brood back into Warwickshire and settle them there before I return to France.'

'He is at home so seldom,' said Duchess Blanche sadly.

'My love, I am not yet eight and twenty. Would you have me don a nightcap and sink into old age?' he teased.

'I would have you home, my dear,' she answered, and there was sadness in her glance.

'You will require money for this new expedition,' the king remarked.

'That's why he is visiting us,' Prince Thomas said. There was a sly spite in his narrow, dark face.

'I can call a Parliament,' the king said, frowning at his youngest son. 'They may grant a loan.'

'May? Surely they cannot refuse?' the duke countered.

'The lords will agree but the Commons are growing more vociferous, and require account of our spending.'

'Knights of the shire to require account of royal spending! You jest!'

The duke's handsome, high coloured face flushed deeply.

'I wish that I did. But our subjects are not French or Gascon peasants,' the king said. 'They are proud of our conquests but complain they see none of the profits.'

'Let them turn mercenary then and earn their own profits,' John of Gaunt said sharply. 'Or let them lend money in hope of an increased return.'

'They have done so, and have seen no return,' Prince Edmund said. 'Your expenses outweigh your plunder.'

'Because I have my men to equip, or do these little shire knights imagine that an army marches on air. You ought to hang a few to teach them better manners!'

The queen, seeing that I still knelt there, said, with quick tact, 'Men with the kindest hearts often speak the most fiercely. You are excused, Mistress Gida.'

I rose and made my way down the steps into the noise and the music again. As I reached the lowest level Philippa de Roet tugged at my sleeve.

'Come and meet my sister,' she invited. 'Katharine has been seeing to the children and so was pardoned from supper, but she will join us later for the dancing.'

I went with her out of the Hall and across an inner court to the apartments that had been prepared for the Lancaster family. Two small girls, miniature editions of the Duchess Blanche, were tucked into a high bed under the window, and as we entered a tall girl, brown hair caught into a heavy knot at the back of her head, rose from a low seat by the fire.

'Katharine, this is Gida Falcon who is to join you in the Duchess Blanche's household,' Philippa said. 'She is new to Court and is as innocent as a babe, so you must be good friends with her.'

'That would be my pleasure,' the girl said, 'but I fear I will not be long in your company. My husband has sent word that he requires my presence, and he has the right in law. Duchess Blanche has promised to perform what service she can for me, but she cannot stand between husband and wife, even if the wife wishes it.'

I clasped her hands and murmured something polite, and then Philippa began chattering again and one of the children lifted her head from the pillow, demanding a story. Nothing told me that I had just met the woman who was unwittingly to be my ruin. No inner voice warned of the heartbreak to come. There were only the faint strains of music and laughter coming across the courtyard, and a lamp flickering in the draught from the open door.

5

At the end of the week we travelled north to Warwickshire. It was a week of gaiety, of balls and tournaments and hunting parties. The queen kept the Duchess Blanche close by her side, for it was evident that the two were deeply attached to each other and welcomed the opportunity to be together a little while. They often talked in private and once, I saw the Duchess coming from Her Grace's apartments with such a sad look on her face that I wondered if the queen had told her of the lump in her breast.

Alice Perrers rode out with the men, holding her head proudly, her eyes sliding between king and duke. I asked Philippa de Roet why the king's harlot should trouble to ingratiate herself with the king's son.

'Because John of Gaunt is one of the most powerful men in the kingdom, silly,' Philippa said. 'Oh, the Black Prince is heir, but he is in Gascony, and he disapproves of Alice. If anything happened to His Grace Alice would need a protector. Prince Lionel is good-hearted, but sails on the prevailing tide. The Duke of Lancaster would be a powerful friend.'

'She sits at the king's side,' I said. 'She dances with him while the queen looks on, smiling and saying nothing. She wears the most rich dresses and jewels and more costly perfume than any of us can afford.'

'And looks uglier than any of us,' Philippa giggled. Then she grew solemn again, her eyes filling with tears. 'My sister will be going back to her husband. He has sent for her, and as his legal wife she must go to him. She was so happy at Kenilworth that I hoped she might be allowed to stay there, but Hugh Swynford demands his rights.'

'Perhaps it is best to remain unwedded,' I said.

'Unless one has a stronger nature than one's husband. Katharine is gentle. She submits, but I am of different stuff.' Philippa wiped her eyes with a look that boded ill for Geoffrey Chaucer if ever he tried to assert his rights when she was not willing.

Katharine herself said nothing of the matter. She was a pale, silent girl with little fire in her glance. She seldom smiled and never laughed, but she seemed to find pleasure in the company of the two children. They were always at her side and she treated them as if they were her own. Soon, she would have babes if her husband kept her with him for long. It must be hard for a woman to submit to a despised embrace, I thought, but even as I thought it there moved in me the desire for an unknown experience.

On the day before we left the queen sent for me. She sat in her favourite room, a solar that overlooked the herb garden and was itself filled with jars of sweet smelling pot-pourri. It was a sunny room with bright cushions scattered over the stools and chairs.

'So you go to Kenilworth with the duchess? Sit down, my dear.' She patted the cushions by her side and I sat down, my eyes on her kind, plump face.

'I have received a letter from the Abbot of Marie Regina,' she continued. 'He thinks highly of your intelligence, so highly that he actually regrets that you were not born a man! According to him you might have made a name for yourself in the world had you been male.'

'I like to learn, Your Grace,' I said shyly.

'Books are very fine,' the queen said, 'but true wisdom comes from human nature. You are not always wise in that, but you are still very young. At Kenilworth you will find yourself in a very happy family. My son and his wife are a devoted couple, and from them you will learn much of what is beautiful and noble in human nature.'

'I look forward to it,' I said truthfully.

'But there will come a time when you will have to deal with people who are not generous or kindly,' she said gravely. 'You are apt to be impulsive, I fear. Cultivate patience and tolerance.'

I promised that I would, wondering what was coming for young I might be but I was not quite as foolish as she seemed to think.

'I have a gift for you to take into your new life,' she said, and laid a purse in my lap. From its pattern I recognised it as the purse I had given back to the king, and my first impulse was to fling it away. Then I looked up and saw that she was watching me, waiting to see what I would do.

'I will accept this from you, Your Grace,' I said at last, 'as payment for the duties I have carried out while I have been at Court.'

'You're proud and stubborn,' the queen observed, 'refusing to take anything you've not earned, even from the highest in the land. Keep your pride, child, and your strong will. There may come a time when they are all you have to sustain you.'

It was the last time I ever saw Queen Philippa, and I wonder now if she realised how prophetic her words would be. I wonder if, seeing her own death draw near, she was permitted to look a little further. Probably not, for if she had divined what was to be, she would not have been so tranquil.

Our riding away from Windsor was as noisily spectacular as had been the arrival of the duke and duchess. I contrasted it with my own demure ride to Windsor between Brother Martin and Brother John. I had never bothered to write to them, and a stab of conscience troubled me and then was lost in the general excitement of mounting, and waving goodbye to Philippa de Roet. The last person I saw as we turned away was Alice Perrers. She had come out to stand by the king, but he had moved away to give the duchess one last embrace, and for a few seconds Alice stood, alone and defiant, staring after us as if she too wished to penetrate the veil of the future.

We took four days to reach Kenilworth, not because the weather was bad or the going hard, but because the duke seemed to regard a journey as a public procession. At every stopping place we were surrounded by people, clamouring to present petitions, complaints, letters from lawyers setting out the evidence for their particular cases, earnest young men claiming benefit of clergy for some misdemeanour, friars with begging bowls, serfs declaring their lord would not accept their manumission money, widows crying that the heriot tax was too burdensome. I had not known there was so much misery in the land, and yet the duke remained cheerful, eating heartily of the fare provided when we pitched camp each night, always solicitous of the Duchess Blanche.

'You take the grumbles of these people too much to heart,' I heard him tell her once. 'It is their pleasure in life to make complaint against their betters.'

'Holy Mother Church bids us succour the needy,' she said.

'Then let Holy Mother Church make a start by unloading some of her own wealth,' he retorted. 'I tell you there is enough gold in our chantries to feed half the beggars of the kingdom.'

'Then you must give me leave to feed the other half,' she said.

He threw up his hands in mock despair and they laughed together.

As always there was a glowing circle around them, and I slipped quietly away, unwilling to intrude upon them. They were seldom alone, but they created their own world with a host of loving glances. I envied them those glances, not for myself, but because I had never seen such glances exchanged between my mother and father.

The tents had been pitched and the guards set. I walked slowly across the meadow towards the river that bordered its edge. It was wider than the river at Marie Regina, and there were only a few trees overhanging the water's edge. I sat down by one of them, shielded by its branches, and looked down into the water. It was shadowed and dark beneath the surface as if night crept on before its appointed hour.

'All alone?' One of the squires had approached me and stood, smiling at me, his arms folded. I recognised him as Cullen Beaumont, a young man training for the knighthood, who had been for a time in Prince Lionel's employment. I had spoken to him only once or twice, but it was pleasant to see a familiar face, and I smiled back at him.

'I was thinking of my home,' I said. 'There is a river there too, but the woods grow more thickly down to the bank.'

'You're from Kent, aren't you?' He came closer and squatted on his heels.

'From a place called Marie Regina,' I nodded.

'And your name is Gida Falcon?' I nodded again.

'We will be at Kenilworth by tomorrow,' he said. 'Do you look forward to it? I visited the castle once when I was a child. It's magnificent, but then anything that John of Gaunt does is magnificent! Don't you think he is a splendid man? And the duchess is an angel! She is so lovely, so exquisite. Don't you think so?'

'I can see that you think so,' I said, and felt amused as if I were older and wiser then he.

'I noticed you, Mistress Gida, because you looked a little like the duchess,' he went on. 'Has nobody told you that before?'

'No.'

'Then I am happy to be the first,' he said. 'I am nearly nineteen and have less than three years to wait before I am eligible for my spurs.'

'I'm sure you'll be successful,' I said. 'My own home is in Warwickshire,' he confided. 'My two older brothers are with the Black Prince in Gascony.'

'As is my brother,' I said. 'I've not seen him for years.'

'And Philippa de Roet told me that your father had died.'

'Father and mother, both,' I said.

'I am sorry for it.' He gave me a sympathetic look. 'My own house is no more than an hour's ride from Kenilworth. I will ask the duchess if she will give you leave to visit my mother. She is something of an invalid, but very interested in all that goes on at Court.'

'Thank you,' I said briefly. He was very kind, but his chatter was beginning to get on my nerves. At that moment I really wanted to be alone, under the tree by the darkening water.

'I feel sorry for wenches,' Cullen said, insensitive to my mood. 'They seldom have the opportunity to travel, or to make a name for themselves, but must go where they are told, and do as they are bidden. I have no sisters but I have often heard my mother complain. She wishes she had been born a man, but is condemned to lie in her day bed for much of her time. She will be happy to see me again and unhappy to see me go to Gascony.'

'Very natural,' I said.

'Do you truly mean that?' His face brightened. 'Dare I hope that you will also regret my going?'

'Why, you must choose what you wish,' I said in bewilderment.

'I must do what the duke orders me to do,' he corrected. 'He has had my wardship since my father died, but I am eager to make my name in the lists, so the spell of duty in Gascony will be most useful to my progress. You can appreciate that, Mistress Gida.'

'Yes, of course. Most useful.' I wished he would go away and leave me alone.

'Perhaps, when I go into Gascony, I could do some service? I could carry a letter to your brother for you if I choose.'

'Thank you, that would be very kind.' I wondered what I could find to say to Godwin. My twin and I had never been close and it was so long since I had seen him.

'If there is any other service I can render you?' he was stammering.

I wanted to tell him to vanish but that would have been unkind, so I smiled sweetly and asked him to fetch me a cloak because the evening was growing chill and I wished to sit longer by the river. He was off at once, long legs flashing beneath the short cotehardie he wore, and I forgot him directly and looked down again into the water.

A breeze had risen and ruffled the surface and my image was not so clear as it had been. I leaned closer and it was as if I were dissolving into spray, becoming one with the water, losing my own identity. If I closed my eyes I could imagine myself merging into another being that twined itself, lank haired and insubstantial as a dream, before me.

There was a roaring in my ears and the cold shock of water rushing into my nose and mouth. There was a sharp tugging pain at the roots of my hair, and I crawled, gasping and spluttering, up the bank.

'You ought to take off your gown before you take a bath,' the duke said dryly.

'I was not taking a bath!' I gulped, shaking water out of my eyes.

'And you could not drown in two feet of water unless you were truly tired of life.'

'I was not trying to drown myself either!' I snapped, struggling to my feet and trying to wring the water out of my skirts.

'Then may I enquire what you were doing?' he asked.

'I was making contact with the spirits of water,' I said with as much dignity as I could muster.

'And so when you make contact with the spirits of fire do you crawl into the nearest oven?' he asked. 'I dread to think of the stir you will create when you introduce yourself to the spirits of air!'

He was laughing at me and I was too young to enjoy being teased. To my dismay my lower lip began to tremble, and in another moment I might have disgraced myself by bursting into tears, but Cullen Beaumont came running towards us, my cloak over his arm, consternation all over his face.

'My Lord Duke, what happened?'

'Mistress Gida decided to take a swim,' the duke said, taking the cloak and bundling it about me. 'You should take better care of your sweethearts, young Beaumont!'

I opened my mouth to protest that I was nobody's sweetheart, but he clapped his squire on the back and walked off whistling.

'You had best come back to the tents, mistress,' Cullen said, 'or you'll catch your death of cold. River water can weaken the lungs, you know.'

I had never heard of such a thing, but I was already beginning to shiver, and so let him hurry me back across the field to the women's tent where I darted inside with a muttered word of thanks, pretending not to hear the gibe of a lounging archer who enquired if I'd been ducked for a scold.

The next day when we mounted up, the duke, winking at his wife, asked me if I planned to float the rest of the way. I hung my head, blushing, and during the next hour thought up several witty replies, none of which I'd have dared to voice at the time. I remember wishing that I was older, more beautiful, more sure of myself. I was tired of being fourteen and merely pretty.

We reached Kenilworth that same day. It was the most beautiful palace I had ever seen, with its high, square topped tower and the banqueting hall spread out below it. This hall had many windows, each mullion delicately and richly carved in a profusion of birds, beasts and flowers, the panes of glass reflecting the slanting light. There were great cannons set at each side of the wide, shallow steps that led up to the double doors, and within the hall shields and spears decorated the walls. Yet it was a home, much grander, than Marie Regina, much more comfortable than Windsor, but a place of great charm and loveliness, with everything in it chosen to complement its setting.

My own bed was in the women's quarters. They were light and airy, with a solar above that overlooked the lake, and the narrow staircase leading to the pleasance garden. The estate was vast, its deerparks, trout ponds, meadows and cornfields stretching, it seemed, to a limitless horizon. The stables and kitchens and barns were separate from the main house, interspersed by vegetables and fruit plots, by covered walks, by exercise yards where the squires trained, by tennis courts and a golf course, and arbours where fountains jetted water at the touch of a spring.

It was an enchanted world, created for a loved and loving wife. Yet it would have been an evil thing to grudge the Duchess Blanche one fountain or one spray of roses. She had been born to wealth and privilege, but wore both as lightly as a garland, and shared everything she had.

I eased my conscience before I had been long at Kenilworth in writing to the Abbot and to my brother. I told the Abbot that I was happily settled and hoped to profit from my service in the Lancaster household, and I told Godwin that I wished him well, which was true, and often thought of him, which was not. Then I took the letters to the duchess.

She was in her summer parlour, a piece of needlework in her hands, and the duke was reading aloud to her as she worked. He broke off and looked up as I hesitated in the doorway.

'I have letters to send, Your Grace, to my Lord Abbot and to my brother,' I said.

'I will see to the sending of them,' the duke said, holding out his hand for them. 'They are not sealed,' he observed.

'I have no seal,' I told him.

'Then we must find you one, eh, Blanche?

Something neat and pretty to suit a maid.'

'There are seals on the table over there,' she said. 'Choose one for yourself.'

I went over to the table and bent over the seals, turning them in my hand. Some of them were very pretty, carved into the shape of flowers and various birds and animals.

'That daisy is very neat,' the duke observed, coming to look over my shoulder.

I shook my head lifting up one on which a claw was depicted, each talon of rounded silver.

'My name is Falcon, sir, and this is like a falcon's claw,' I said.

'It is more of a man's seal,' the duchess objected. 'Would you not like something more dainty?'

'If your Grace please, I like this one,' I said,

'Then you may have it, my dear. John, will you melt some wax and show Gida how to use it?'

'I have sealed letters before,' I said. 'In the monastery of Marie Regina the monk used to let me seal documents for him. I was quick and neat, he said.'

'Which monk was this?'

'Brother Sixtus who illuminates the manuscripts there. He showed me how to mix the colours too.'

'The queen told me that you were clever,' the duchess said.

'I have always liked to study,' I said.

'Do you read French?' the duke asked.

'And Latin and English,' I said. 'I love reading.'

'Then you must read for the duchess when I am gone,' he said. 'For the next few months, until the child is born, she has to rest a lot.'

'I am perfectly healthy,' she protested.

'And must remain so, for the sake of our son. This time it will be a boy.'

'And if it is another girl?'

'Then I will beat you.' He crossed to where she sat and bent to kiss her cheek. To me he said, 'Do you not think she is a trifle pale, Gida?'

'A little ginger in hot water will bring back her colour, sir.'

'Ah, so now you're a herbalist too! Did they teach you that at the monastery?'

'I helped Brother Andrew in the infirmary, but it was my mother who told me about plants. There is much to learn.'

'There are many sick folk in the cottages on the estate,' the duchess said. 'Some of them come for help, and there is little one can do.'

'You do too much as it is,' the duke

chided. 'My home is cluttered with stinking peasants, all crying that they have sores and ailments and rheums and agues, and cannot work my land because of these manifold sicknesses!'

'Gida could help,' the Duchess said.

'And come back from some hovel with pestilence on her breath? It is too great a risk.'

'If one washes in wine the risk of infection is lessened,' I said.

'Wash in wine! I believed wine was for the drinking.'

'And it is well known that physicians seldom fall sick, or carry disease,' I said boldly. 'They build up a resistance to it in their own bodies, I believe.'

'An alchemist too! We have found ourselves a treasure in our new ward, my love!'

'Ward? Are you my guardian then, Your Grace?' I asked.

'For my sins. The Lady Joan persuaded me to it.'

'Which required very little persuasion at all,' the duchess said swiftly. 'We are delighted to have you, my dear.'

'And I to be here.' I dropped a curtsey.

'Her manners are as graceful as her face,' the duke said. 'I will carry a favourable report back to the Lady Joan.'

'I wish I could go with you,' his wife said wistfully, 'but I cannot risk a sea voyage at this time.'

'If it were possible for me to stay at home, I would,' he assured her, 'but Ned has asked for my support on his campaign.'

'And you must pay off your debts.'

Her smile made it clear that she knew his faults as well as his virtues and loved him the more for them.

'My son must not be a pauper,' he said, 'and Pippa and Bet will need dowries. They'll not go like beggar maids to their lords.'

'About dowries, Your Grace,' I put in.

'Yes? what about them?' He had sat by the duchess, his arm about her, and turned his head to glance at me.

'The Abbot told me that my father had saved money for my dowry. I wondered about the amount.'

'A thousand guineas, I think. Why do you ask?'

'She is in love,' the duke said, 'and wishes to know if she can afford to keep her bridegroom in the style to which she hopes he is accustomed.'

'I have no lovers,' I said, my face burning. 'I was thinking of my expenses while I am here. If Your Grace has debts — '

'John talks too freely about his debts.'

The duchess looked as nearly irritated as the sweetness of her face would permit. 'You must take no heed of it, my dear.'

'But I must cost a great deal to feed and clothe.'

'The Lady Joan pays a certain sum for that. Your father was her liege knight, and she naturally wishes to do what she can for his daughter. So you have no need to fret.'

'And you can be of immense help here,' the duchess said. 'Now that poor Katharine is gone back to her husband Pippa and Bet will need a companion. Dame Maud is too elderly to run about with them much. And if you are truly skilled at the impounding remedies, then you could be of assistance to my physician. He is a man who is always interested in new ideas.'

'So you have no need to feel conscience stricken by the vast sums of money your lodging here costs us.' The duke rose and stretched. 'We will work you off your feet, Mistress Gida!'

He spoke in jest but in the weeks that followed it came very near the truth. I found that my hours were full, so full that I'd very little leisure in which to gossip with the other women in the household. That troubled me not at all, for apart from Philippa de Roet who had been good-humoured and helpful,

I had little affection for other females. They seemed to care only for flirting with the guards, or trying out new ways of doing their hair, and their constant prinking and giggling made me scornful. Yet, to be fair, I must have seemed very odd to them too, for I spent so much time riding out to collect wild plants, and so much time mixing, pounding, blending and boiling them up into ointments and syrups. The duchess gave orders that I was to be given a chamber near the kitchens where I spent part of each morning hanging over what the duke called my 'hell-brews.' Yet he frequently glanced in to see what I was doing, advising me genially to try out my potions on the serfs first and not go killing off his household. In fact I did persuade quite a few of the cottagers to take my remedies, and some of them declared their ailments much improved.

My other interest lay in reading. The duke owned a library of more than fifty books, some of them covered in tooled leather, others in jewelled velvet. They were all most skilfully illuminated, and I loved to run my fingers over the patterned margins feasting my eyes on the vivid colours. I even begged some parchment and blended some inks, and tried to copy one of the psalms myself. It was not as successful as I'd hoped because the ink ran a little, but I presented it to the duchess who declared that it was the most beautiful thing she'd ever seen.

She was always generous and unstinting in her praise, and her sweet voice often took the edge off the duke's sharp teasing. It was no marvel that she was loved, or that her two little girls craved to grow up to be exactly like her. Pippa who was six insisted on wearing loose robes such as the duchess wore, and two year old Bet imitated her mother's faint lisp that gave her speech an added piquancy. I liked to play with the children and tell them stories, and sometimes I told them a story about a goblin maid who found an enchanted temple beneath a mountain and was changed into a princess. Dame Maud declared that I told that tale so well that it might almost have been true.

Two letters came for me. One, which had crossed my own, was from the Abbot. He wrote briefly but kindly, wishing me well in my new life, reminding me always to say my prayers and go often to Mass.

On the same day there came a much longer letter from Dorothy.

My dear Gida,
I think of you often, and see you in my mind with all the grand folk at Court. I

hope that your dresses are suitable for such a fine place. I suppose you will have grown some since you left Marie Regina. Ralph has grown too, but I cannot think these streets are good for children to grow in. They are so dirty and smell so foul. We go out whenever we can to the villages around where one may walk on grass instead of cobbles. But we must spend most of our days in the shop, for the wool has to be sold and the accounts kept. I am becoming a neat businesswoman and am helped in my labours by Jonathan Grey. He and his good wife have been as kind as country folk, and they have a little daughter, Petrella, who is just five and a playmate for Ralph.

It is not easy to find an honest servant here, for the apprentices will sneak away to brawl in the taverns and the maids think of nothing but pulling their bodices lower to entice the lads. But it is not a big house and I can manage much by myself. I suppose that you will remember it from the time you stayed there yourself.

The garden is small too, and there is a most pleasant seat under a pear tree. The tree has fine blossom, but it yields wormy fruit. Yet it gives good shade and so I let it stay.

There are many churches here. One could go to a different one every week. And there are stretches of common land where a body can breathe air instead of the smoke from other peoples fires. There is much poverty in the city. I never saw so many beggars or thin children in my life. At first I was troubled at such misery but now I turn my eyes away and hurry past.

There are many rich folk here too. I have seen fine ladies with their sleeves trailing on the ground, and young gallants with points so long on their shoes that they must needs scuttle sideways like crabs. The king and queen are much loved, as is the Black Prince and the Lady Joan. There is much talk about Alice Perrers. You will have met Alice by now and learned that she lived once at Marie Regina. You must have wondered why I never spoke to you about her.

The truth is that there was something about Alice I never liked even when she was little. She was sly and she followed people about, listening to them. It wasn't my place to say anything because your father had brought her to the castle, and I looked after her and made her liitle dresses for her own were all ragged, but I was pleased when the Lady Joan took her away to Court. Now they say that she is rich and sits next to the king at table, but I trust you don't follow her example, for you were gently bred and Alfreda was a lady, even if she did live in a wattle hut. So be a good wench and do not forget

Your loving
Dorothy.'

I read the letter through twice, then laid it down. It was strange but this message from Cheapside brought back the memories of Marie Regina in a way that the Abbot's letter could not do.

I could see Dorothy so clearly as she bustled from kitchen to hall, smell the succulence of the spiced puddings she used to bake, hear her scolding because I had ridden over to the monastery without telling her I'd be late for supper.

I would write to her, I decided, and tell her how happy and how busy I was. I told myself firmly that I was very happy and very busy, and put the letters away in the box which now held the Saracen ring, the carved rosary, the Abbot had given me, the book I'd found in the secret temple, and the seal with the falcon's claw.

Then I went to the Duchess Blanche's apartments. She had been unwell for a day or

131

two, but the physician declared that nothing serious ailed her, and the astrologer declared that excessive sickness during pregnancy was a sure sign that the coming child was a boy.

She was alone and she had been weeping. I knew the cause, for the duke set out on the first stage of his journey to Gascony on this day, and her tears meant she had said her farewells within the castle.

'Shall I read to you or send for the musicians?' I asked.

'No, no.' She wiped her eyes and gave a watery smile. 'I shall be better alone. Go down with the others to watch them leave. The duke has ordered me to rest here and not upset myself by seeing him ride away. It is very hard to watch someone one loves ride away.'

'I will come back and make a tisane for you,' I promised.

'Kind little Gida,' she said, closing her eyes as I curtsied and ran along the corridors and down the stairs into the great hall where the other ladies were gathered, many of them with favours to hand to their knights. It might be months or even years before the men came home again, and there were always some who would never return.

'Mistress Gida, I am pleased that you are

here to say goodbye to us.'

Cullen Beaumont came to my side, sweeping off his feathered cap. His pleasant young face beamed at me, for it was seldom I gave him the opportunity to seek me out.

'My lady mother has sent word to me that she will be most happy to have you visit her if the duchess permits,' he said. 'She will be happy to meet a friend of mine.'

'Yes, of course.' I smiled at him kindly.

'And when I do return perhaps you will allow me to — wear your favour?'

'Only knights are entitled to wear favours,' I objected.

'I may have gained my spurs by then,' he said eagerly.

'I shall hope for it,' I said vaguely.

'I do have the greatest admiration for you,' he said, stammering a little. 'Ever since you came to Windsor, I don't believe that I have looked with pleasure at any other maid.'

'Beaumont, get to your place unless you mean to stay at home with the women!' The duke, striding through the great hall, raised his voice impatiently.

We crowded after him into the courtyard where two ostlers held his powerful chestnut stallion. It was caparisoned in silver to match the cloak of silver cloth with its bands of white fur that he wore over his half-armour.

Mounted, with his squires pushing the ostlers away and handing up the short curved sword that buckled to his side, the other knights were mounting up, tying their favours to the points of their lances.

'Pass up the stirrup-cup, young Gida! I'll not leave without drinking to success,' he declared.

Dame Maud gave me the heavy silver goblet, and I stood on tiptoe to give it to him.

And it was all happening as it had happened before, so that for a moment I thought I was back in my dreaming again. The immense chestnut stallion rearing and snorting to be off, the gauntleted hand curving around the stem of the cup with the emerald bracelet clasping the wrist. Almost but not quite the same, for in the dream I had not seen his face. Now I saw it clearly, and loved him, and hated myself because I loved the duchess too.

6

The physician and the astrologer were both right. The duchess did recover from her bout of sickness and the babe was a boy named, Henry after her father, the powerful Duke of Lancaster from whom her husband derived his title. She went into Lincolnshire to bear the child, her medical advisers being of the opinion that the change of air would benefit her. I think she agreed because at Kenilworth the sense of the duke's presence was so strong that she could not forget her longing for him.

I was left with some of her other attendants and the two little girls at Kenilworth. Nobody thought for one moment that anybody else would be missing the duke and longing for his company with a pain that was almost physical. I was very young and much of my love was sprung from fantasy. I wove stories in my mind just before I went to sleep at night, stories in which the duke took me in his arms telling me that I was the most enchanting creature he had ever seen. The duchess never came into these fantasies at all, and I always fell asleep in the middle of them.

We heard occasionally about the progress of the campaign, but the news reached us months after the events happened and was generally garbled. However we did learn that the Black Prince and the duke had joined forces and crossed the Pyrenees in the depths of winter, losing more men from dysentry than wounds. But the final battle had been a victory with more than sixteen thousand Spaniards dead on the field, and the rightful king restored. But the gold he had promised his English allies stayed in his own coffers, and after months of waiting the Black Prince led his troops back to Bordeaux in time to greet his new son.

'The Lady Joan is past forty and nobody expected her to have any more children,' Dame Maud gossipped. 'Richard is his name after the Lionheart. The Black Prince will be happy for 'tis his first child.'

The birth of little Richard of Bordeaux meant that the duke's son moved a place down in the order of succession. I was surprised when the duchess on her return to Kenilworth seemed delighted at the news.

'Now my own babe is fifth in line and will move even further down if Prince Lionel's new wife has a son,' she said happily. 'My father often used to say to me that it was a fine thing to be a duke but a sad thing to be a monarch. So I am pleased that my child will not wear the heavy crown.'

Prince Lionel had married the heiress of Milan so that he could bring new allies to his brother, but not many months passed before we received news of his death. We were not only grieved but shocked at the tidings, for if the genial giant could be struck down by disease then our lives seemed more frail, our fates more uncertain. And if Prince Lionel could die then so could John of Gaunt. I might live out the rest of my life without seeing him again. I put my mind to other things but the childish fear of a dream unfulfilled lay dark beneath the ripples of my thoughts.

The long months dragged slowly into one year, two years, and then three. Season followed season, and I was growing out of childhood. The mirror told me that I was lovely; the glances of the pages and men-at-arms told me so, and I felt deep in my bones that the world was opening out before me into something rich and wonderful. I began to long for the duke to return, but it was an innocent longing. I swear it. My imaginings never went beyond the admiring glance, the graceful compliment. I loved the duchess and never, even in thought, did I betray her. I *swear* it.

But even I, in all my romantic dreaming, was aware that the campaign had begun to go very badly. In his absence the Black Prince's Gascon subjects had rebelled, refusing to pay their taxes, declaring that they wished to be the subjects of the King of France. And the rebellion was spreading through Aquitaine and Armagnac, Pitou and the Agenais. The prince was harried on all sides, and it was not possible for his brother of Lancaster to return to England while his support was still needed.

I marvelled that the duchess could remain so calm, never crying out her love and longing, never even writing to ask that she might join him. I asked her once why that was so, and she gave the faint, weary smile that had replaced her laughter since her husband rode away.

'The duke is occupied with military matters, my dear. He has not the leisure to spend with his family that we would wish. When the campaign is over he will return and find everything as it was when he left. That will be his pleasure to find those who love him unchanged.'

In the spring of thirteen hundred and sixty nine I was seventeen years old. The event passed, as usual, without comment. Only I was aware that I was no longer a half grown child, but a young woman eager for experience, with the man I loved so far out of my reach that he might as well never have existed at all. Yet I must still have been very young, for I believed love could be satisfied by looking and heartache eased with a smile.

A few weeks after my birthday I rode over to see Mistress Beaumont. I had kept my promise to go and see Cullen's mother. I found her a depressing and tiresome creature. She had nothing in her head beyond the latest fashionable ailment and her only pleasure lay in grumbling about the laziness of the servants, and in complaining that her sons neglected her.

'Always rushing off to fight in battles that they didn't begin. Sit down, my dear, and pour us both a glass of wine. Do be careful, for they are very delicate. My late husband brought them back from Italy. He did bring some very pretty things back for me, but he died before he went to Portugal. They blend some very fine wines in that country, but my husband must needs die before he set sail. I was never more disappointed in my life.'

I poured the wine and carried it back to her as she stretched out a languid arm from the day bed where she reclined. She was not like Cullen at all, being small and grey haired, with eyes like tiny black stones. Those eyes raked me now as I sat down, and I was glad I was wearing one of my more becoming gowns.

'Is the dear duchess well?' she began. To the best of my belief she had never laid eyes on Duchess Blanche, but she always spoke as if they were intimates.

'Very well,' I said.

'Ah, to be blessed with good health is the greatest boon woman can enjoy,' Mistress Beaumont sighed. 'I have been delicate since I was a child. My mother despaired of ever rearing me, and the physician was astonished that I managed to bear three healthy sons. The last almost killed me. I was four days in labour, my dear. Four days! Can you imagine what that does to a woman?'

I made some indeterminate noise which satisfied her for she went on talking. Her tongue was as energetic as Philippa de Roet and far less amiable.

'The queen is very ill, they say. Poor soul, to be thrust from her place by one such as Alice Perrers. They say the king dotes upon the woman and she appears openly with him at public tournaments. Men get worse as they get older, which is some consolation for being widowed young. But it has been a hard struggle for me.'

She glanced restlessly about her small parlour. In fact the Beaumont house was a fair sized manor and her acres impinged on the Kenilworth estate, but she always spoke as if she were fighting off starvation.

'At least your sons have good positions,' I said.

'Good enough, I suppose.' Her face remained discontented. 'They will be knights and that still counts for something, even in these days. They will have to make their own way in the world. I hope you have a sufficient dowry, my dear, for Cullen can expect very little.'

I gaped at her in astonishment but she went on unheeding.

'Of course you will be welcome to make your home here after you are wed. Cullen will be away for most of the time, and so you and I can bear each other company. You are so clever with your herb potions that you will be able to minister to me, and then you can read aloud so prettily. Oh, we will be very comfortable.'

'Mistress, you go too fast!' I protested.

'And you show a very natural modesty. I like to see that in a young girl.' She nodded her head approvingly. 'However, you need have no fears. The Beaumonts are not a family obsessed by their own importance, though my late husband's grandsire many times removed did come over with the Conqueror. My own line of descent is older still, pure Saxon, my dear. In fact it was always considered in my family that I had married a little beneath me, but in your case I do assure you that Cullen sets very little store by such things.'

'And my dowry would be compensation for my lack of gentility, I suppose?'

'You phrase it a trifle crudely,' she murmured.

'Then you must put the blame on my being low born,' I said, putting down my empty glass. I was so furious that I would gladly have thrown it at her.

'You have spirit,' she said. 'I was very spirited myself as a maid until ill-health forced me to moderate my pleasures.'

'Then I wish you good health and good day,' I said, briefly and bluntly, and marched out, snatching up my cloak as I went, and neglecting all the usual courtesies of leave taking. Outside I compounded my ill manners by whistling for the groom as if I had been a stable lad myself, and I set a furious pace back to Kenilworth.

The duchess was in the stillroom checking our supplies of honey which were still low after the winter. She raised her head as I entered, rebuking me mildly.

'Gida, is it necessary for you to erupt into a room in such a fashion?'

'I beg your Grace's pardon, but I have been to Beaumont Manor.'

'And have news of great importance that sends you rushing in here?'

'Mistress Beaumont seems to imagine that I am going to marry her son!' I exclaimed.

'Would that be beyond the limits of possibility?'

'Beyond the — ? Your Grace, you don't mean you knew of this scheme?'

'Cullen Beaumont did make his affections known to the duke before they left for Gascony.'

'Did he so! Well, he said nothing about it to me!' I began furiously.

'He acted very properly in first approaching your guardian,' she interrupted firmly. 'The duke considered that you were young enough, both of you, to wait. Cullen had his knighthood to gain and you were in my care. The matter was left in hopeful delay.'

'But I don't want to marry Cullen Beaumont!'

'That's unreasonable of you,' the duchess said, 'He is a fine young man, a most promising squire. Well-favoured too. What

143

have you against him?'

'Nothing. I like Cullen very well as a friend,' I said, 'but I cannot abide his mother.'

'My dear, you are not being asked to wed his mother,' she said, amused.

'It will amount to the same thing,' I said gloomily. 'Cullen will be away on campaign and I will be forced to deal with his mother. She is the most provoking woman I ever met who thinks only of her own sickness and her own needs and never spares a thought for anyone else. She actually told me that my dowry would compensate for my lack of breeding!'

'That pricked your pride.' She smiled at me. 'But Cullen is not like his mother. He is gentle and eager to please, and I think even she would be easy to manage if you set your mind to it.'

'I don't care to set my mind to it,' I said.

'Ah, well, there's nothing decided yet!' She turned aside her head and sneezed. 'God bless me! Some of these jars need dusting! I've been sneezing my head off this morning. Now we'll cease talking of wedlock and count honey pots instead.'

But she sneezed again as she spoke, and as my indignation faded I noticed that her usually pale skin was flushed unevenly, her eyes red rimmed.

'You have caught a chill, Your Grace. Shall I brew you a hot drink?'

'No, no I am perfectly well.'

'A spring chill is difficult to shake off. You ought to be in your own chambers, if only to avoid passing on the infection.'

'I'll rest for an hour then. Send Dame Maud to me. She has been complaining that the babe needs new caps, and I've not yet ordered the stuff for them. And you need new shoes yourself, so I will put them on my list too.'

'People with spring chills ought to rest,' I said.

'And young ladies ought not to scold their elders,' she returned. 'Go and fetch Dame Maud, there's a good wench. I must confess I will be glad to lie down. I feel most unaccountably dizzy.'

Dizziness, a blotched complexion, fits of sneezing. As the duchess left the stillroom I stared after her. Then I picked up my skirts and ran, not to Dame Maud, but in search of the physician.

Fear sometimes creeps like a thief into the mind, and sometimes it rages in, chilling the blood, jerking the heart, and making dreams horrible. In a few short hours all my small problems and anxieties were swallowed up in one word that was whispered from mouth to ear. Plague. Nobody knew how this outbreak had begun. There were always epidemics in the summer, but this disease with its symptoms of nausea, vomiting, delirium, with its black boils and putrid smell; this struck apparently at random and where it struck it usually killed.

My mother and the Abbot who had been burned had told me of the time the plague had first struck, in the time when my parents had been unwed and my father had only just come to Marie Regina. They had spoken of it as the Death, to distinguish it from other outbreaks. But at Marie Regina nobody had died.

'We smoked out the rats and killed them,' my mother had said. 'The Abbot believed that disease could be carried by the bite of a flea from a rat. He never believed that sickness was the punishment for sin.'

I remembered her words and, for the first time, believed her fully. Of all the folk at Kenilworth the elegant, gracious duchess was least in need of punishment but by nightfall we were told that she had it.

'The priests are here,' Dame Maud said. She stood at a distance, her veil across her mouth and nose.

'The priests flock like vultures in hope of a dying,' I said sharply. 'What are the physicians doing?'

'As much as they can. The duchess begs them to leave her and tend others who have greater need.'

'Are there others?'

'Two of the cooks, a stable lad, and one of the guards.' Beneath the veil her old woman's face contorted and she sneezed.

'And you?' I backed a step.

'I am old,' said Dame Maud. 'She bids you to look to the children now.'

I had forgotten the three children. They clung now about my skirts, the babe whimpering. He had been released from swaddling bands into petticoats and was confused by his new freedom. Bet sucked her thumb, her blue eyes wide. Nine year old Pippa drew a quivering breath and said, her voice hushed, 'What are we going to do, Gida?'

'We'll go to the old Dower house,' I said. 'Dame Maud, send one of the men to me. It's best we start out at once. The place is isolated and there's a good chance the disease has not reached there.'

Normally nobody would have dreamed of giving me such a responsibility, but the sudden illness of their mistress had caught

147

the household unprepared, and I was known to be skilled in the uses of herbs.

Within the hour the three children and I were mounted with two of the archers to accompany them. Both these men had recovered from previous attacks of the plague and I judged them unlikely to be carrying the infection now. I had changed my gown and made the children put on clean clothes, and in the courtyard I sponged our faces and hands with wine.

The old Dower house was a mile distant on the edge of a wheatfield with a stream rushing past it. It was used occasionally as a shelter for hunting parties if the weather changed before they could reach the main castle, and sometimes lovers used it as a trysting place. So it was kept in good repair though it lacked comfort, having been built in an earlier age when people had not grown accustomed to glass in their windows or a proper chimney.

I had brought clean linen on the packhorses, and wine, and a change of garments for the children, and a selection of my dried plants. The men would forage for food and keep other people away. It was a makeshift arrangement but the best I could devise under the circumstances. After the children had been tucked up, I went round each chamber invoking St Raphael and making faint pentagrams on the doors. And when I finally lay down I wove, not romantic fantasies about the duke, but tangled and desperate little prayers for the safety of the duchess.

They came the next day to tell us that she had died, and I am glad now that my first reaction was one of bitter weeping. It makes me feel less guilty about what happened later.

The children were to stay with me at the Dower house until it was safer to travel. We would be supplied with whatever we needed, but must await word from the king before anything further was done. Dame Maud was sick but expected to recover despite her age, and three more of the household had been taken ill. Red crosses were being painted on many doors to warn the unwary traveller and the chaplains were arranging a novena of prayer to rout the evil.

The messenger rode away again and there began the strangest period of my life. For that summer it was as if time had stopped and we hung suspended in a limbo where we saw few people and went nowhere we could not reach on our own two feet. Yet it was not an unhappy time. I allowed the children almost as much freedom as if they had been peasants, letting them play in the wheat and tickle trout in the stream. I kept fires burning around the building, and I made the children wash twice a day instead of every week as is customary.

It was a glorious summer, an ironically beautiful season when one remembered that the Death once more held England in its grip. But neither the children nor I fell sick, and by September the first, fierce stranglehold of the disease had slackened.

So we went back to Kenilworth, the children grown taller and sturdier after long days in the open air. Dame Maud greeted me affectionately, and set to gossipping at once.

'The king has sent word that the children are to be taken to Windsor. I am to travel with them, which will be a most pleasant change for me. It is many years since I was at Court, but I understand that some of my old friends are still alive. It will be wonderful to see them again. Not that I intend to have anything whatsoever to do with some people at Court. We will not name them for fear of spreading scandal, but we both know what an Alice is like, don't we dear?'

'She is not beautiful,' I said cautiously.

'And the queen was so very charming in her younger days,' Dame Maud sighed. 'She is near to death, I hear. Indeed it is a miracle that she has lasted so long, but then she has great strength of character.'

I was to remain at Kenilworth until instructions about me were received. I must confess that I felt a little hurt, as if I were an old dress tossed aside, but then I was not very important. I admitted as much to myself and then went away and had a good fit of crying because I disliked being neglected and I disliked even more the idea that I might have been left here as Cullen Beaumont's prospective bride.

That was a long and dismal winter after Dame Maud and the children had gone. I rattled around like a pea in the great palace, for I was not a member of the family and yet neither was I a servant. There were times when I longed to go into the kitchens, and tuck my skirt over my knees, and drink ale by the fire. But my skill at reading and writing, my knowledge of herbs, even my accent set me apart, and they were never quite at ease when I was there.

Out of boredom and the desire for company I was even driven to seek out Mistress Beaumont. She had been left unscathed by the Death, having lost not a single serf, and she behaved as if God had personally yielded to her will.

'For I informed my servants that I would not tolerate their falling sick, not with the late spring planting to complete and the thatching to be repaired. The lower classes have no right to indulge themselves in ill health!'

I endured her talk and her patronage because anything was better than sitting alone gazing down at the windswept lake. She had heard from Cullen who had been invested as a knight.

'So is now Sir Cullen Beaumont but you must not feel inferior on that account.'

'My own father was a knight,' I said mildly.

'Ah, yes, from Aquitaine or some such place, was it not? And he was taken prisoner.' She implied that to be taken prisoner was an inexcusable folly.

I always came back from Beaumont Manor quivering with suppressed indigination, but the humour of it struck me too, for it was foolish of me to let a stupid woman upset me when I had not the slightest intention of marrying her son. I wouldn't marry him even if he were granted an earldom, I vowed.

I returned from one such visit on a blustery spring day just before my nineteenth birthday, dismounted in the stableyard and ran up the winding stairs to the wing where my own chamber was situated. I had moved from the women's quarters into this apartment because here I could be private and alone. There were times, even when I was lonely, when I needed to be private.

I had just taken off my cloak and was putting my hair into place when the door was thrust open and the duke walked in.

I had pictured him coming home so often. I had imagined the bright armour and the clashing steel and the excited shouts of welcome, and I had imagined too his riding into the courtyard and looking down at me with startled admiration. I had never pictured him simply walking, without escort, into my room. He wore black against which his hair glowed reddish-gold, waving over his broad shoulders. There was a goblet in his hand and his eyes were overbright. I guessed that he had been drinking, but his speech was unslurred.

'Little Gida? You've grown up, my dear.'

'My Lord Duke, I wasn't aware that you were home.' My face flaming, I sank into a hurried curtsey, but he drew me towards him and kissed my cheek.

'I have business in the north before I return to France,' he said. 'I stay here for only one night and ride on in the morning.'

'If you had sent word — ' I began, but he held up his hand, smiling at me.

'I ride with a small escort. The time for pomp and ceremomy is not yet.'

'Then the campaign isn't finished?'

'No campaign is ever finished,' the duke said. 'There are always new battles to be fought. Will you have supper with me, child? I'm in no mood to eat alone.'

'We can eat here, if Your Grace wishes,' I said.

'Wherever you choose.' He looked about him vaguely, then sank into a deep chair by the fire. I had made the room and the sleeping apartment beyond as comfortable as I could, and some part of it seemed to touch him for he drew a long breath and said in warmer tones, 'Bring me something to eat then, there's a good wench, and tell the rest of the household I don't want to be disturbed.'

I hurried to do his bidding, my heart beating frantically. It was still difficult for me to grasp the reality of his presence. As I piled chicken and duck on a tray I found myself wondering if he had really come, or if I had merely conjured him up out of my own needs.

He was still there, long legs stretched out before him, his goblet half-filled. He looked up as I came in and put the food on the table.

'Draw up a stool and join me,' he invited. 'Did you bring any wine? I am more thirsty than hungry.'

'There's Burgundy here. You laid down many flagons of it before you went away.' I held up a bottle I'd brought.

'Pour some for me.' He put his goblet down on the table and nodded at me. 'Wine improves with keeping. A man may go for ten, twenty years and be certain when he returns that the bouquet of it is sweeter, the taste of it more mellow. But let him go away for ten years and he cannot expect to find people unchanged. He cannot even expect to find them still alive.'

'The duchess — ' I began, but he held up his hand again, his voice harsh.

'The duchess died nearly a year ago, and my lady mother has been buried these two months. The women I loved best in all the world, gone as if they had never been.'

'You have your son,' I ventured to remind him.

His face brightened slightly. 'I saw the little lad at Windsor,' he said. 'I'm told by Dame Maud that I have you to thank for taking good care of the children, for guarding them from the plague.'

'I wish I could have done something for Her Grace.' 'My lovely Blanche.' He gulped the Burgundy as if it were water and picked up a piece of duck, turning it over in his fingers. 'She was the fairest lady I ever knew and the only one I have loved. I found her death impossible to believe. It was a jest, I thought, a cruel, senseless jest that had no meaning. I found it impossible to believe until I came to Kenilworth and saw her presence everywhere and herself — where?'

'In Heaven, sir?'

'So the Church would have us all believe.' He gnawed the meat for a few moments, and tossed the bone away. 'They may well be right. If so, then Heaven is the richer for her presence.'

'She was loved,' I said, and felt small and inadequate, my words glib and shallow.

'And that's as good an epitaph as any. You're not eating anything.'

'I'm not hungry,' I said.

'No more am I.' He pushed the table aside and refilled his goblet. His high colour had deepened, but he was still far from drunk. After a moment he looked across at me and grinned. 'You've not asked me how Cullen Beaumont fares.'

'I've not much interest in Cullen Beaumont,' I said.

'He has asked my permission to pay court

to you,' he said. 'Are you unwilling to marry him?'

'I don't wish to be wed, my Lord Duke.'

'The cloister beckons you? I find that difficult to believe. You have too much spirit for a nun.'

'I don't wish to be a nun either,' I said.

'Then what are we to do with you?' he enquired. 'I am your guardian, my love, for better or worse. I'll not wed you to anyone against your will. I have that right, but I'll not force you to anything that displeases you. Blanche would not have approved of that, and I'll not go against her wishes. But Cullen is a fine young man.'

'I don't want him,' I said stubbornly.

'Then what do you want?' He spoke with something of his old impatience.

'To please you, my Lord Duke.' I leaned forward a little on my stool and saw him frown slightly and something flicker at the back of his eyes.

'I am going to be married again,' he said abruptly. 'Constanza of Castile lacks a mate and England lacks an ally. I will go back to Gascony to see how my brother fares. Ned is not well. He has bouts of dysentry that weaken him greatly. The Lady Joan is very anxious for him.'

'Married?' I looked at him. 'Do you want

to be married to this — ?'

'Constanza of Castile. My brother Edmund is to have her younger sister, Isabelle. Thus we gain a firm foothold in the south for our thrust into France. That is what royal marriages are all about.'

'But you loved the duchess!'

'We were bred to love each other,' he said. 'Blanche and I were pledged in our cradles and she was always true. It's over now.'

'You are not yet thirty,' I said.

'Just on thirty,' he corrected. 'And you are — seventeen, eighteen?'

'Almost nineteen, sir.'

'Has time run so quickly?' He blinked up at me. 'You were a youngling. Now you're a woman, a very beautiful woman. Take off your coif. Women bundle themselves up as if they were ashamed of their bodies and their hair.'

I took off the wired coif with its long ivory beaded pins, and shook my curls loose about my face.

'You have pretty hair,' he said slowly. 'And your eyes are blue. I met your brother out in Gascony. He is a coarser, rougher version of you. Men are coarse creatures on the whole. I have always preferred women.'

'Will Your Grace take something to eat now?' My voice was suddenly nervous, my hands perspiring, and I was not certain why.

'I'll take more wine and you will join me,' he said.

I poured it and we drank silently. The wine warmed me, but my hands were still damp.

'Can you pull off my boots or shall I call my valet?' he asked.

'I can pull them.' I knelt, tugging at the straps.

'You're a useful child,' he said indulgently, and his hand encircled by the emerald bracelet, pressed my head briefly against his calf. From the goblet in his other hand a few drops of wine splashed onto my neck, cool as rain or the tears that neither of us had shed.

'Tonight I'll sleep here. There are too many ghosts in my own apartments,' he said, rising and moving towards the inner room.

'As Your Grace pleases,' I whispered.

'Lock the outer door,' he said, 'and bring me the rest of the wine. Bring yourself too — but only of your own free will. I'll not force you to any alliance, either with Cullen Beaumont or anyone else.'

I stood, staring after him. It had never happened like this in all the dreams I

159

had woven as I drifted into sleep. It was happening now and I was not ready. All my experiences had been gleaned from books and the giggling comments of other women.

The duke had come home but home was become an empty place now that the duchess had died. Soon he would make a loveless, political marriage with a foreign princess. In the morning he would ride on again. But I had this one night.

Slowly I slid the bolt into its socket and began to unlace my bodice. I was used to dressing and undressing myself, and as I stepped out of my skirts and pulled my shift over my head I was pleased for almost the first time, that I was not really a fine lady.

'I need more wine,' he called from within.

I picked up goblet and bottle and walked, the rushes pricking my bare feet, into the bedchamber.

'I have wine here, sir,' I said. 'Is there anything else you need?'

His eyes raked me slowly, and when he spoke his voice was slow and reflective.

'I need wine,' he said, 'I desire — something else. But I'll not take what isn't offered willingly.'

'It is offered most willingly, sir,' I said.

'Put down the wine then. We'll drink later. And leave the candles for a while.'

I did as he ordered and moved towards him. This was a new dream, more bright and beautiful than any I had ever known. It filled the emptiness and bridged the years of absence, and I was not even jolted back to reality when, at the moment of our mutual climax he called me Blanche.

7

Two months after the duke rode away I was forced to admit as a fact what I had begun to suspect. I was with child and if my reckoning was right the babe would be born in November. There was nobody in whom I could confide, for if I did, there was every possibility of my being married off to Cullen Beaumont without further ado. And yet it would be impossible to bear the child all alone with no woman to help me.

I decided that my only recourse was to go to Dorothy. I had not heard of her in years nor written to her myself, but childishly I pictured her as unchanged and I was equally certain that she would welcome me though I fully expected a scolding when I confided my plight. However a scolding from Dorothy was infinitely preferable to a lifetime spent with Mistress Beaumont as my mother-in-law!

I left Kenilworth early in June, having made my preparations with care. The duke, I told the servants, had left word that I was to join my old housekeeper in London. I am not sure if they believed me or not, but I was not much concerned. Two of the men were to accompany me, I said firmly, and such was my air of authority that one of the stablelads actually recalled the duke saying something of the same to him.

The Death had run its course, and people were saying the outbreak had not been as severe as the one twenty years before when a third of the population, and in some districts, a half, had died. But to my inexperienced eyes the devastation wrought had been fearful. We passed through whole villages where only lean yellow dogs ran out to bark at our heels, and fields where the grain grew wild for lack of ploughing and reaping.

The roads, despite that, were crowded. Begging friars and pilgrims on their way to Canterbury, soldiers who had turned to begging when they were too old or infirm for active service, furred merchants with their apprentices, stewards and journeymen, even serfs with leather collars about their necks walked and rode along the rutted roads to London.

It would have been a simple matter to turn aside into Kent, and I longed to be in Marie Regina for just a little while, but the Abbot would surely hear of my coming and I was not certain I could keep my secret from his sharp eyes. So I said nothing and we kept on the main London road that grew steadily more congested as we approached the outskirts of the city.

I had been a small child when I had last visited Cheapside, but its clatter broke upon my startled ears with the same impact. My two escorts, provided with gold from my purse, parted company with me on the corner of the street and rode off, no doubt in search of the nearest tavern, and I rode on, my belongings strapped to the packhorse behind.

I found the tall, narrow house without difficulty and dismounted hitching the two ponies to the rail. There were bales of woollen stuff displayed in the bulging lower window and, as I hesitated, Dorothy came through the open doorway.

'Good morrow, mistress. Will you step inside, for you'll not be able to appreciate the texture of the cloth until you feel it for yourself?'

'Lord, Dorothy! Don't you know me?' I enquired, laughing.

'Gida!' She gave me one incredulous look, then hugged me. 'I never would have recognised you until you spoke! Ah, but you've grown into a fine young woman! Come indoors, do! You're staying with me for a spell?'

'If it's not inconvenient,' I said, letting her lead me within.

'How could you think such a thing?' she reproached. 'There's a room spare next to my own. I can shift Ralph's belongings up to the attic.'

'No, don't do that. I'll take the attic room,' I interrupted.

'Ah, well, we'll arrange it later. Come up to the parlour now. Ben!' She raised her voice as a tousle haired lad came from the back. 'Ben! Take the two horses round to the stable and bring in the bags. Look sharp now! He was bound apprentice a year ago,' she continued as we mounted the stairs. 'Ralph will be home soon. He goes for lessons every day to the priest. You'll find he's grown up a lot these past years. Sit down and I'll get you something to eat. I do keep a servant but she's young and a mite careless.'

Excitement had quickened her tongue and brought a sparkle to her eyes. I sat down in the parlour and let her fuss around me, bringing bread and ale and cheese. 'Dorothy.' I broke in upon her talk, clenching my hands under my cloak. 'Dorothy, I need a place to stay for about a year, until after my child is born.'

She stopped short, the smile on her face fading a little.

'You're not wed,' she said at last. I shook my head, and she sat down heavily and gazed at me.

'Will he wed you?' she asked.

'He cannot. He doesn't even know about the babe.'

'You don't know yet. When is it due?'

'In November, if I've not miscounted. Can I stay?'

'You don't need to ask,' she said, looking hurt.

'Thankyou, Dorothy.' I spoke humbly, grateful that she had not asked the name of the father.

'Won't your neighbours gossip?' I asked her.

'Gossip never hurt,' she said shortly, 'and I never paid it any heed anyway. Eat your food. You'll need to take care of yourself now.'

So I came back to Cheapside and at first it was strange. I kept expecting, when I woke in the morning, to see the lake beyond the window, and every morning I felt the same shock of surprise when my eyes rested on whitewashed walls and low beams and narrow windows that looked down into the cobbled street along which the iron-railed wagons began to roll at first light.

Dorothy, despite her grumbling about the

inconvenience of city life, had adapted to it well, and though she would not have admitted it I believe she enjoyed running the business. She spent most of the day in the shop and kept the accounts very neatly, adding up the columns of figures in a series of small books.

'One third of what we take each week is for living on, one third buys new stock, and the rest is saved for Ralph,' she told me. 'Everything will be in order when he is of age to take over. He'll have to serve an apprenticeship first with another merchant before he can get his Guild Licence. They bent the rules a little bit for me and let me take over his father's licence until he's qualified to apply for one of his own.'

She had refused to take anything from me for my keep, but agreed to let me help in the shop, and I became accustomed to greeting customers and persuading them to buy. In my plainest gown with the seams let out to accommodate my widening girth, and my hair tucked beneath a coif, I looked like any respectable young matron.

The only people with whom Dorothy was on anything approaching social terms were the Greys who had befriended her when she first came into the city.

Jonathan Grey was a pleasantly spoken

167

man with a wry sense of humour and a thin little wife forever nibbling sweetmeats. They were both devoted to their ten year old daughter, Petrella, who ought to have been marred by their indulgence but was a lively, happy child with pretty manners. She and Ralph were excellent friends, and I guessed that the Greys encouraged the relationship in the hope of an eventual marriage.

The Greys accepted me without question, never referring to my lack of a wedding ring. They were kindly people and I liked them.

I liked them, and I was grateful for the home Dorothy had given me but there was never a moment when I didn't think of the duke and yearn for the peace and spaciousness of the countryside. In summer the house was airless, the streets thick with the flies that swarmed over the dungheaps and piles of stinking refuse that cluttered the ditches. In the evening, when the shop had been locked up, I used to go into the long, narrow garden at the back. The pear tree was still there and I remembered how Dorothy had told me in her letter that it bore bitter fruit, and I thought too of my mother sitting there beneath it just before we went back to Marie Regina and found that everything had changed.

Sometimes when I had been to Mass on

Sunday I would ride out with Ralph at my side and go as far from the centre of the city as we could get. I wanted to feel grass beneath my feet and see trees and flowers spreading themselves across the land with no cobbled yards or high walls to interrupt the beauty. Ralph was a stolid boy, his hair dark as his father's had been, his chunky frame already slightly bent as if he were practising for the day when he would bend over his accounts book. He had accepted me and my coming babe with a complete lack of interest and I suspected that our rides together bored him a little though he was too polite to complain.

By the end of summer it was no longer possible for me to ride, lest the jolting bring on a premature labour, and I was confined to the house and garden and to such walks as I could take in the district. I went sometimes to meet Ralph when he was coming from school, and if I was early I would sit in the porch and wait for him.

Father Bonaventure was a harassed little man who had a little more learning than most clerics of his station, and regularly taught a dozen or so boys for a small fee. He was a conscientious soul, so bashful that he scarcely ever raised his eyes to my face, and so innocent that he assumed automatically I was a widow struggling to bear my babe in a hostile world. His one vice, if vice it is, was a passion for following the comings and goings of his betters and in speaking about them a little too freely. So from Father Bonaventure I learned that the king, now that the poor queen was dead, lived openly with Alice Perrers, decking her in his late wife's jewels, installing her as Lady of the Sun at a great banquet. I learned too that the Duke of Lancaster was still trying to raise an army and sufficient funds to maintain it, that Prince Thomas had been finally wed to the Lady Eleanor de Bohun, and that one of the king's squires had written a poem about the death of the fair Duchess Blanche. It was being copied and circulated as swiftly as possible, and it was said to be a pretty piece though its author had chosen to write in rude English.

It was strange to hear their names spoken by a man who had never met them and had no idea of my connection with any of them. I listened and said nothing, but the image of the duke troubled my mind. The night we had spent together was more vivid than anything else that had ever happened in my life.

My pains began on the eve of All Saints, earlier than I had expected, but Dorothy said that a first child was often in a hurry to be born and that such births were often easy. My own labour seemed very hard and painful to me, but within three hours it was over and I heard Dorothy saying cheerfully. 'Thanks be to Our Lady! It's a fine healthy boy.'

I named him Maudelyn and Father Bonavanture baptised him for me when he was a week old. He was a small baby with a fuss of light down on his head and wide open eyes that were blue at first but darkened to green. And he was a good baby, seldom crying except when he was hungry or soiled.

I was a little disappointed to find that, though I recovered very quickly from my confinement, I was unable to feed the child myself. Fortunately Mistress Grey found a wetnurse for him, a clean and buxom woman whose own babe had died and who agreed to come in to feed Maudelyn. Certainly he thrived on her milk and by New Year was laughing and gurgling whenever anyone bent over his crib.

But it was obvious that I couldn't stay with Dorothy for ever. Sooner or later someone would remember me and send to Kenilworth and then enquiries about my whereabouts would begin. It would be wise for me to return and wait there until the duke came home again. It was equally obvious that I couldn't take Maudelyn back with me. Too many tongues would wag if I returned to Kenilworth after so long an absence with a strange baby in my arms.

It was Dorothy who came to the rescue, without asking any questions.

'You must leave the babe here until you're settled. I can easily manage a small child, for I've plenty of energy left even if I have lost my back teeth. And you cannot go jaunting up and down the countryside with a baby!'

I agreed, because it was better for Maudelyn to stay with her at least until he was weaned, but I had not realised, until he was born, how much I would love him.

'How will you travel? You cannot possibly ride alone,' Dorothy said.

'I was hoping Master Grey might be able to hire an escort to take me into Warwickshire,' I said.

'I'll enquire for you, but this is a bad time of the year for travelling,' she doubted.

'Any time of the year is a bad one for journeys,' I told her. 'Two stout apprentices will be sufficient protection.'

'One hopes so. There are many runaway serfs on the move these days, demanding more money *and* demanding the right to work where they choose. So many perished in the Death that labour is scarce and the peasants take advantage.'

'I'll be perfectly safe,' I countered firmly. 'I'll leave money with you for Maudelyn and when he's weaned I'll come and fetch him.'

I wished Dorothy were free for then I could have taken the risk of installing her and the baby in the old Dower house, but she had the task of rearing Ralph and taking care of the business. It was very good of her to agree to have Maudelyn at all, and I told her so.

'When you were born,' she said, 'I helped at it. I never had children of my own but I helped to care for you and Godwin, and there were times when you seemed like my own. You more than your brother. So there is every reason, short of actual blood kinship, why I should take care of Maudelyn too.'

And then she flashed me a shrewd look and said, 'Great men often honour their bastards. Don't leave it too long before you tell him.'

I was in haste to be gone now that I had made the decision for every day that I stayed made it harder for me to leave Maudelyn. Soon he would begin to recognise me and then it would be even more difficult.

One morning I rode out beyond the city. My mount needed exercise after being winter stabled, and I judged it prudent to take her on gradually increasing distances to prepare her for the journey ahead. It was a fine, clear morning with a snap in the air and I felt my own energy bubbling forth again. The common was almost deserted and I gave Silver her head letting her gallop across the short turf.

'Gida! Gida!'

I heard the voice above the thudding of the hoofs, and pulled up short as two figures trotted towards me.

'Philippa de Roet!' My own voice rose in pleasure.

'Philippa Chaucer now. Geoffrey and I have been wed these three years,' she said.

'Master Geoffrey, you look as if marriage agrees with you,' I smiled, leaning to clasp hands. He was as plump and placid as ever, his eyes twinkling.

'We thought you at Kenilworth,' Philippa bubbled.

'I am visiting my old housekeeper,' I evaded. 'I return to Warwickshire soon.'

'Without calling on us!' Her voice was reproachful. 'Why, I never thought you would neglect old friends.'

'It has been so long,' I excused myself, 'and we have not even written.'

'I leave writing to my lord and master,' she dimpled. 'His poem about the death of the

174

Duchess Blanche has been most favourably received.'

'I was a great admirer of the duchess,' Geoffrey said modestly.

'And what is your news?'

Philippa moved her pony alongside my own and leaned towards me, her sharp nose jutting. 'The duke is your guardian, is he not? I thought he would have found a husband for you by now.'

'I don't want a husband,' I said coolly.

'My dear, we nearly all of us say that, and we nearly all of us end up with a wedding ring!' she exclaimed, laughing. 'Geoffrey, do ride ahead. How can we gossip with a great man leering at us?'

'There is a tavern over there,' he pointed. 'Shall I go and order some refreshment for us all?'

'Yes, do. Find a quiet corner!' She flapped a hand at him and turned again to me. 'It is the greatest good fortune that we met, Gida! You are the one person who might be able to help me.'

'In what way?'

'When you were at Court,' she said, 'you were mightily skilful at concocting remedies. I remember how once, when we feared a tournament would be rained off, you conjured a wind and the rain never fell.'

'I was boasting,' I said.

'Boast or not, it didn't rain,' she insisted. 'Meeting you today brought the memory back. Do you still conjure — just a little?'

'Why do you ask?'

'Because I know someone who would dearly love to bear a child,' Philippa said and blushed scarlet.

'Then she must find a man,' I said lightly.

'Oh, there is a man,' she assured me. 'A child would make her happiness complete. You see the man is — is not inclined that way towards her.'

'So you would need something to rouse his ardour?'

'So that a child might be born. It is not wrong, is it, to wish for a child?'

'You and Geoffrey — ' I began.

'I fear I am barren,' she said in a desolate tone. 'But we were speaking of my friend.'

'Yes, of course.'

'Can you help her?' she asked eagerly.

'If I had something of hers and something of his,' I said cautiously.

'I know that already,' she said with slight impatience. 'One of the serving wenches went to old Mother Jennet, and she told her what to do. I was going to go to Mother Jennet myself, but I don't want Geoffrey to find out. Cannot you take the things from me, and say the words? You do know what words to say?'

'I know some words.'

'And you'll do it? I — my friend would be so grateful!'

I nodded slowly and she fumbled in her sleeve and drew out a small packet wrapped in black, leaning to press it into my hand. From the doorway of the tavern Geoffrey called, 'I've ordered ale and some oyster pie.'

'Good! I'm starving!' Philippa put her finger to her lips in a swift gesture of warning and allowed herself to be lifted from the saddle.

The tavern was clean and quiet and the pie delicious, the crust flaking, the oysters smothered in cream flavoured with ginger. The ride in the fresh air had made me hungry, and while we ate Philippa chattered on in her old fashion.

'You should see the airs and graces that Alice Perrers puts on! She is the haughtiest person I ever met in my life! The king cannot refuse her anything. He hangs upon her words like a fly on a spider's web and is as tightly enmeshed. She loads her person with so many furs and velvets and gold chains 'tis a marvel she can walk a step! His Grace will

177

make no move without her approval.'

'Keep your own disapproval in a lower key, my love,' Geoffrey murmured.

'I only say what the Lady Joan is saying,' she pouted.

'The Lady Joan? Is she in England then?'

'Two weeks since. The Black Prince came with her, and they stayed for a few days at Windsor and then went to Berkhamsted. He is a very sick man, his legs swollen and his face puffed out, but the Lady Joan is lovely. So gracious and charming. Even Geoffrey declared her to be so, and he is not usually complimentary about ladies.'

'I love them all,' he said, 'but they afford me a great deal of amusement! My darling wife fulminates against Mistress Alice's jewels, but give her the opportunity and she'd load her own person with twice as many!'

'Pay him no attention,' Philippa said, 'You know that the Duke of Lancaster is to be married again, of course? Don Pedro has given both his daughters to the king's sons, but neither seems in any hurry to join his bride.'

'They are trying to raise money for the wars, my love,' Geoffrey said patiently. 'I did try to explain it to you.'

'And you explained it very cleverly,' she

178

returned, 'but I never did understand politics.'

'Economics,' he corrected.

'Whatever you said. It is all a waste of time in my opinion, all this marching and fighting and making and breaking treaties,' she said.

'Tell me what other news you have,' I invited.

'The Duke of Lancaster's two daughters are betrothed,' she said, 'Lady Philippa is to wed Joachim of Portugal and Lady Elizabeth is promised to the Earl of Pembroke's son.'

Eleven year old Pippa and seven year old Bet to be married! I remembered how they had played in the wheat and how Pippa had squealed when Bet found a long worm and chased her with it. They had been children then and they were children still, but already they were pawns in the marriage game.

'What of Henry, the boy?'

'The duke wants to marry him to little Mary de Bohun, but her parents declare she is to be destined for the cloister.'

'She's only a babe!' I said indignantly.

'And what of yourself?' Geoffrey interposed. 'Have you no ambition?'

'Not for marriage bed or convent,' I said firmly. 'The duke is a lenient guardian and allows me much freedom.'

'So you ride unescorted and visit where you choose. I envy you, for Geoffrey is so careful of me that I cannot stir a step without falling over him,' Philippa sighed.

'Lest some other man snatch you away from me,' he retorted.

'Fie! How you do run on!' she cried. 'Keep your pretty words for your poetry. Gida, we ought to go. I am in attendance on Eleanor this evening and I have a dress to finish before then. Do you remember how much she hated the thought of marrying Prince Thomas, and what a disagreeable boy he was. Well, he is worse now and she likes him no better, but they are married for all that.'

'Shall we ride back with you?' Geoffrey asked. 'No need. I know my way.' I rose, kissing them both, unwilling that they should come back and catch sight of Maudelyn who looked so much like me already that they must surely guess. I wanted no sympathy, no friendly curiosity from Philippa.

When I was mounted she hurried forward to clasp my hand again and to whisper, 'You will not forget? It means so much to me.'

'I promise,' I said, and waved as I gathered up the reins.

I said nothing to Dorothy about my meeting, but much later that day, when she and Ralph were asleep and the babe settled for the night, I slid the bolt on my attic room and took out the black packet, unwrapping it carefully. A shabby little purse with a plain silver ring inside it fell onto the pallet. I wrapped them up again binding them seven times round, and then, in a round copper bowl I kindled rose petals and lavender and dittany of Crete, and let the blue fragrance rise up into the air. Then I took the book I had found in the underground temple, and by the light of the candle I read out the words of the binding spell.

'Till the end of time be these two bound, as foam to water, as smoke to fire, as earth to root, as breath to wind. Let these two be bound. In the name of all the powers of love and light may they be bound and may their union bring forth a fine child. As foam to water, as smoke to fire, as earth to root, as breath to wind. Amen, amen, amen.'

I passed the packet seven times through the smoke for seven is the number of Venus, she who is mistress of all passion and glows brighter than the moon when the night is clear.

Philippa had no child to bless her marriage. When I had extinguished the smoke I put book and packet back into the box again and blew out the candle. Then I lay down on my pallet, pulling the covers up about me, drifting into sleep. I had done what I could. I hoped that it had been sufficient.

I dreamed that night of the Lady Joan. She looked exactly as she had looked during our brief meeting in the hut, her golden hair rippling about a rosy face, her eyes blue shadowed. But she did not sit reflective, chin on hand. She danced, slow and sinuous, her arms moving in patterns of colour behind veils of brilliant light. There were other figures in the dream. My mother was there, and my father, and the Abbot who had been burned. I saw them clearly and then the veils of the Lady Joan spun before me, faster and faster, obscuring everything, and I heard the Lady Joan laughing so infectiously that I began to laugh too and woke laughing though my face was wet.

That morning when I bent over the cradle Maudelyn looked at me, really looked at me, and I could have sworn that he recognised me. As I turned away he began to wail softly, and I knew that it would be cruel to him and to myself to stay longer in Cheapside.

As soon as Ralph had set off for school, and Dorothy was occupied with a customer in the storeroom, I slipped through the front door into the street and hurried round to the stable where, a few minutes later, I succeeded in rousing a lazy ostler to saddle Silver.

I had decided, after some thought, that before leaving London I would indulge myself with one peep at forbidden things. The duke was still in England and I wanted to see him, to imprint his face upon my memory lest long years passed before he returned.

Dorothy had mentioned a few days previously that a joust was to be held at Smithfield. It was not the season for such festivity but the king wished to please Mistress Alice Perrers. Among the crowd I hoped to see without being seen.

The fields about Smithfield were already packed. Stands had been erected for those with money to pay, others must press close against the wooden barricades. I wedged my horse as near as I could get to the canopied stand where the royal family would sit.

It was another fine, cold morning and the chestnut sellers were already doing a brisk trade. I bought some for myself and munched them as I waited. My hood was drawn close over my face and there was no chance of my being recognised.

The trumpets were sounding, the halberdiers clearing the way for the horses and litters that swayed towards us along the highway.

The cheering was loud, more, I suspected, out of sheer high spirits than anything else, for as Alice Perrers was handed down I heard muttering and hissing around me.

She was clad in scarlet and gold and her face was painted as thickly as a mask, but I saw the narrow eyes and the great sapphire on her hand, and I felt the old anger at her betrayal. The king sat close to her and he had changed too. He had grown stooped and his greying hair was almost white, his mouth slack, his eyes fixed dotingly on his mistress. He looked, I thought, like the ruin of a king, and I felt anger rise up in me against him too.

The king's granddaughter, Philippa, as tiny as her father Lionel had been gigantic, was there with her burly husband, the Earl of March. I thought that she looked tired and pale and very much in awe of her husband. Near to her Prince Thomas scowled at the crowds and said something under his breath to Eleanor who shrugged, looking as ill-pleased with his company as he was with hers.

And then the cheers grew loud again and the duke stood in his stirrups, raising his hand to the crowd. He was magnificent, like a lion with his mane of red-gold hair like an eagle with his sharp profile. I closed my eyes briefly, remembering the smell of his flesh, the long muscles moving under the tanned skin. One night was all I had enjoyed, but I would enjoy many more. I vowed it, my eyes flickering open to gaze upon him hungrily. He would come back to Kenilworth and I would be waiting for him as my mother had waited for my father.

'Mistress Gida.' The voice was a strange one and came from a guard in the Black Prince's livery.

I gaped at him in foolish dismay.

'The Lady Joan wishes you to attend her at Baynard's Castle early tomorrow morning,' the man said. 'You are to come to the water garden, through the side gate.'

'But I don't — ' I began, but he had turned and was moving away into the crowd again.

My eyes had been filled with the duke and I had not seen her mount the royal stand. I saw her now, wrapped in a cloak of deep blue velvet. There were pearls twined about her neck and in her bright hair, and she was as I remembered her.

The heralds were crying Largesse! the horses snorting and rearing, the banners rising. I took another long look at the duke, and edged my horse away, fearful that he might recognise me as the Lady Joan had obviously done.

I rode back to Cheapside where I found Master Grey, waiting to tell me that he had hired two men to escort me back into Warwickshire.

'Good fellows, both of them. They are merchants going north and will take you with them without fee. I know them both and can vouch for them.'

'You're very kind,' I said gratefully.

'Mistress Dorothy would not be easy in her mind unless you were well guarded,' he said. 'I have a daughter, Mistress Falcon, and I tell you frankly that it would fret me to death to have her ride alone as you do.'

'I am well able to take care of myself,' I said, smiling to show that I was not being rude.

'I wish you a safe journey,' he said at last, pulling at his beard as if he were not sure whether to approve of me or not.

Dorothy cried a little when I told her that I was leaving, and then blew her nose and said crossly that I should have given her more warning because she would never be able to get my gowns packed or any bread baked for the journey.

'I'll send for Maudelyn,' I said, my voice quick and bright. 'You'll guard him well?'

'I promise you that I will guard him as if he were my own,' she said gravely, and then fell to scolding again as she bustled around, declaring she would not rest easy in her bed until I was safely married with a rich husband to protect me, and that she had no doubt at all I would not write for years but would turn up again like false coin when it suited me. And then she hugged me fiercely, declaring that she never would forget me.

It was hard to leave, much harder than I had realised. There is a bond between mother and babe, especially when that babe cannot carry his father's name. But the duke would acknowledge him. I was certain of that.

'When you come back I shall be a man grown and wed to Petrella,' Ralph said.

I smiled at his round serious face with the tuft of hair sticking up at the back. His life was planned out for him and he would live happily, never wishing for more than he had been given.

For all my dreams and spells, you see, parts of the future were hidden from me. Had I known then what was to be I'd have snatched up Ralph and taken him to Warwickshire with me, or conjured up a wind to blow a certain ship to the bottom of the ocean. And probably none of it would have been any use. We are all, struggle though we might, condemned to weave our destined part of the tapestry. So Ralph Aston had to grow up in Cheapside and the ship had to sail, and I had to go back to Kenilworth to wait for the duke to return.

But first, very early in the morning, I had to make my way to the water garden at Baynard's Castle to see the Lady Joan. I fell asleep at last that night, wondering what she wanted of me.

8

Before dawn the next morning I was mounted on Silver, my luggage strapped to the packhorse behind a cloak shielding me from the cold. Maudelyn was still peacefully asleep and I let him lie, but Dorothy had cooked bacon and oat cakes and practically stood over me while I ate them.

I was to meet my escorts at St. Paul's, and so, disregarding Dorothy's protests that it was too early to start out, I left, promising to write to her, resisting the temptation to go back for another look at the sleeping child.

I had seen the great, frowning bulk of Baynard's Castle on my rides through the city, and hoped I would find the water garden without too much difficulty. It was wierd, threading my way through the maze of dark streets where only the flaring torches at the corners illumined the cobbles. I dismounted at the arch and looked about, wondering what to do next.

There was the rattle of metal behind me and I swung round. The Lady Joan, wrapped in a cloak of some shimmering stuff, beckoned me from within the high barred gate she had unlocked.

'Your Grace.' I tied the horses' reins to the bars and followed her within. The garden sloped down in a series of terraces to a landing stage beyond which the river flowed. The sky was that strange leaden colour just before dawn comes, the colour that drains the rosiness out of the prettiest face.

The Lady Joan's face had grown plumper now that I saw her close, but even her lack of colour could not detract from the beauty of her long lashed eyes.

'Philippa Chaucer told me that she had seen you,' she said in a low voice. 'I warned her to tell nobody else for I guessed you were in London without permission.'

'Yes, Your Grace!' I hoped that she wouldn't ask me any more questions, and her mind was evidently on other matters for she drew me down the slope to where a bench was set.

'You have used the key,' she said. It was a statement.

'I found the temple,' I said. 'I found a book there, hidden deep in the wall.'

'You have it safe?'

'Yes, my Lady.' As I spoke she drew a long sigh of relief.

'What did you make of it all? she asked, after a moment.

'I cannot tell,' I said slowly. 'I was told that my Lord Abbot was burned because he was a devil worshipper, but there were archangels painted on the walls. I think perhaps he was a man who knew many truths that others have forgotten.'

'You have the heart of it,' she cried softly. 'There are mysteries of time and space known only to the ancients, suppressed by the Church authorities who fear that such knowledge would be dangerous, for it teaches men to think for themselves instead of being told by the priests. But those mysteries are not lost. Through the centuries they have been kept, handed down by generations, from the lost shores of Lyonesse to the acolytes of Egypt and Greece, the Druids who held safe the western tradition, the Knights Templar who went to the east and studied the wisdom of India.'

'Isn't all that — heresy?' I whispered.

'So the Church tells us, for the Church seeks to confine men's minds and shackle their tongues. Oh, for the mass of people that way is right, for they could not cope with such power, or they might seek to do harm. But for the few, the chosen few, the knowledge is there. I received it from my own mother who was friend to the Abbot.'

'And my mother? She was one of the few too, wasn't she?'

'As was your grandmother. The king too, in his younger days. And you were destined to follow in their footsteps. You were created for that.'

'Created?' We were seated on the bench and I looked at her sharply.

'From time to time a child is conceived within the temple,' she explained. 'Such a child is born, if the ritual runs aright, with many gifts of seership and healing. I hear that you are skilled at herbal remedies.'

'My mother taught me,' I said.

'Dear Alfreda! I was very close to her once. She was a good woman,' Lady Joan said.

'She loved my father.' There was both challenge and question in my voice.

'And he loved me,' she said, 'or thought he did. Oh, I think that he loved your mother too, though he neglected her to serve me. I knew that, and never tried to alter anything. I accepted his devotion without question. Men have always fallen in love with me. Even the king desired me once.'

Looking at her in the strengthening light I believed her, for her skin was as unblemished as a girl's, her teeth white, her hair curling thickly about her temples.

'Did you know that you look a little like

me?' she asked suddenly, and laughed. 'No, Alfreda was your true mother! But you look like me all the same. I find that strange, very strange.'

'And my brother? He is my twin.'

'Godwin is an able squire, but he is not the same as you are,' she said. 'My lord prince left him at the Gascon Court with a handful of others to await the Duke of Lancaster and his army.'

'I heard that it was not easy for him to raise troops,' I said.

'Parliament will grant very little money,' she said with a flash of indignation. 'My husband is a sick man, his health ruined by the last campaign, and we are deep in debt because he could not rest until his men were paid. And the Commons will not see how necessary an extra tax is. We have even petitioned the king, but that does no good, for His Grace has nothing in his head beyond his desire to gratify Alice's every whim.'

'She wears the Abbot's ring,' I said tightly. 'It was Alice Perrers who betrayed him.'

'She will suffer for it,' Lady Joan said. 'Have no fears on that score. She will not enjoy her present position for long. The king cannot live for ever and when Ned succeeds to the crown he will give Alice short shift.'

'The duke supports her,' I said sadly.

'The duke pities her, I think. It is one thing upon which he and Ned disagree. Now, tell me something of yourself these last years since we met in Marie Regina.'

'There is little to tell,' I said cautiously. 'I was taken to Kenilworth after my father died, to serve the Duchess Blanche. I've been visiting Dorothy.'

'And without permission if your guilty expression is anything to go by.'

I said nothing, but dropped my eyes modestly, hoping she would not enquire further into my disobedience. Apparently she dismissed the subject, however, for she patted my hand kindly, saying, 'We'll not tell the duke. Have you escort back into Warwick? A maid cannot ride alone as she chooses up and down the land.'

'Not even a — Temple child?'

'There was a time, not many years ago, when many went to the rituals,' she said. 'There were ceremonies at which non-initiates could pay honour to the forces of Life and partake of cakes and ale. Now we must be more cautious, for the Church declares all magic to be evil. And for you it will be very hard, for you must keep the rituals and disciplines alone, confiding in none. Only pass on what you have learned to a female child. She must have your blood though she need not have been born of you, and she must be born after her own mother has died.'

'Your Grace, that makes no sense!' I protested.

'It makes none to me either,' she agreed, 'but I dreamed of it long ago. I used to dream true. Of recent years my vision has been clouded.'

'I dreamed of Your Grace dancing in the temple,' I said slowly. 'There were veils all about you, tossing as if there was a wind but you moved slowly like weeds under water.'

'I danced in the temple the night you were conceived,' Lady Joan said. 'It seems that you also can dream true.'

Her voice was sorrowful as if she spoke of times long past. I no longer hated her because my father had neglected my mother on her account, for I guessed she was as innocent as the flame into which moths flutter.

'You don't keep the rituals yourself?' I ventured.

'It has always been difficult for me,' she said, 'for my three husbands have been what the world calls devout Christians, and so I have to keep that part of my nature hidden from them. Oh, in former times when the king came to the rituals it was much,

much easier. Those who were of our temple respected me and those who suspected could do nothing for I enjoyed the protection of the king, but times are changed now. And my husband is a sick man. He has the dropsy, his physicians say, and neither their arts nor my own can cure him. When he dies, I will have to guard my son for Richard will be heir to his grandfather's throne.'

I stared at her, seeing not her face but a boy's face, a weakly handsome one with red gold hair and a golden crown upon his head. And then the face began to change, skin shredding from flesh, flesh peeling from bone, eye sockets empty. And the crown slipped and fell.

'You see something! What is it that you see?' The Lady Joan's voice jerked me back to the bench on which we sat and the river that ran beyond.

'I see — nothing,' I said at last. 'Forgive me, Your Grace, but I have to leave now. The merchants who are to accompany me into Warwickshire will be waiting for me.'

She did not attempt to detain me further but there was apprehension in her eyes when we parted at the side gate, and I glanced back as I mounted Silver and saw her still watching me, one hand pressed to her mouth.

The two merchants were, as Jonathan Grey had assured me, respectable men, travelling north on business. Their apprentices were with them, cudgels at the ready, and I guessed that under their robes the merchants had sharper weapons concealed. Certainly there was little cause for me to be nervous. And we were fortunate in the weather, for it stayed dry and crisp, and the inn where we stayed overnight was clean and warm. We parted company amiably at the gates of Kenilworth, my invitation to enter being refused as they wished to press on. So I rode alone up to the main gates and, though the servants greeted me pleasantly, hurrying to make my rooms ready, it was a cold coming. I wished that the duke had been there or was expected soon. Without his presence the great castle echoed with emptiness. The merchants had promised to give Dorothy word of my safe arrival as soon as they returned to London, so there was no point in my writing even if I could have found somebody to take a letter. I missed my baby, and what made it worse was that I couldn't even talk about him to anyone. When he came back to me he would be weaned and out of swaddling clothes into petticoats, and I would have missed the time between. I comforted myself with the knowledge that I had left him in the kindest hands and that the duke would acknowledge him as his own when he came home again.

I used to picture his coming back, his hair glowing under a blue sky, his cloak flowing over broad shoulders. He would be married again soon but I never thought of his bride as a living woman. She was a signature on a treaty, a Spanish princess who must wed for her country's sake. I was young and heedless then despite all that I had learned and all that had happened to me.

I went often to the old Dower house, spending whole days there sometimes. My mother had taught me how to cook and clean and sew, it being one of her maxims that a lady should be able to do whatever she expected of her servants. I used to pretend the Dower House was mine and I laid sweet smelling rushes on the floor and sewed new covers and hangings for the beds. I took food there sometimes and cooked it for myself, and I hung bunches of dried herbs from the ledges of the windows. I used to pretend that the man I loved was not Prince John of Gaunt, Duke of Lancaster, but an ordinary man, a merchant or a squire. He would come home each night to the meal I had prepared, then when he had played for a while with our son, he and I would sit by the fire and talk about the small events that had made up my day, and of his ambitions for the future. It was such a happy, contented picture that I painted in those long solitary days, and I painted it so vividly that it became like reality.

In the late summer we received word that the Duke's little son was to be brought back to Kenilworth and reared there during his father's absence. Mistress Swynford had been widowed and was reappointed as governess.

I was pleased that I was to have the company of Philippa de Roet's sister, though I scarcely remembered her from our brief meeting at Windsor. And to have Lord Henry near to me would be like having my own babe here. I went to particular trouble to make her apartments welcoming, for though it was generally known that Katharine Swynford had disliked her husband, I felt pity for her. She had borne two children and was left with very little money.

They arrived with a considerable escort, and there was a jealous little hurt in me, because the duke had taken such pains for his son and heir, and had never even sent to ask how I was. It was foolish to be like that because I was only his ward and men think more of boys than girls anyway. So I choked back such feeling and went out gaily to greet them.

Katharine looked pale and quiet, her widow's barbe and mourning robes emphasising her large eyes. Her own two children clung to her skirts and she pushed them forward.

'Mistress Falcon, this is Blanchette, who is four years old, and this is Tom who is nearly three. You must make your bows to her for she cared for Lord Henry when he was a babe, and his lady mother was dying.'

They were plain children, poor mites, with big noses and wispy hair and I wondered if they resembled Hugh Swynford, and if their mother loved them less on that account. She treated them tenderly but I thought she paid more attention to Lord Henry, who was a sturdy, square-faced child with red hair that sprang up from his brow in vital waves and grey eyes that darted about as restlessly as his tongue ran.

'Why cannot Pippa and Bet be here? Why cannot I have a room to myself? Why cannot I have a sword, a *real* sword, such as my lord father has?'

'Your lord father is bringing your sisters here before he returns to France. You must share a room with Tom until you are breeched, and when you are breeched you may have a sword and be taught how to use it.'

Katharine answered his questions patiently, but I had caught only the first sentence properly.

'Is the duke coming to Kenilworth?' I asked.

'With the Lady Philippa and the Lady Elizabeth,' she nodded. 'They are both wed, of course, but they are too young in His Grace's opinion to be wives, so they are to come home and finish their education.'

'It will be good to see them again,' I said, and hoped that she had not noticed the bright blush that suffused my face. Fortunately she took it to be a sign of my pleasure in the children's return for she said, 'It will be most agreeable for you to have them home again with you, will it not? They told me how good you were to them when the Duchess Blanche died.'

'I did what I could,' I said, a little shortly, because though I liked Katharine Swynford I'd no real desire to share my memories with her. She looked a little hurt but said nothing, and a few minutes later was urging the children to sponge their hands and brush their hair before supper.

The duke returned at the end of the week, and not until I heard the familiar hoofbeats and clashing steel of his escort did I allow myself to believe that the long absence was over. He looked as strong and handsome as he had always done and I fancied that his voice dropped to a more tender level when he clasped my hand and drew me up from the formal curtsey into which I had sunk.

'My dear Gida, it had been such a long time since we met.'

He passed on then to Katharine, asking her how she did, kneeling to coax her small children towards him. Pippa and Bet flung their arms about me and then hugged Katharine tightly, which was natural for she had been their governess long before I came on the scene.

'You are not to rush away and marry anyone else now that you are widowed!' Bet cried imperiously to her.

'I will stay as long as I am need,' was Katharine's quiet reply.

She was so different from her lively chatterbox of a sister, but there was strength in her gentleness that was attractive despite her lack of surface charm.

We were a strange party at supper that evening. I put on my best blue gown with its oversleeves of silver thread and let my hair hang loose from a coif of white lace. When we were sat at table I had a moment's guiltiness because I saw Katharine in her widow's weeds and hoped she wouldn't think I'd put on a fine gown in order to point the contrast between her state and my own. She seemed not to notice however, but sat, addressing a remark to the children now and then. Her own were obviously awed by their surroundings and picked at the food on their plates, but Henry ate like a little trencherman, demanding more meat and soaking up all the juices with his bread as if he had not eaten in a twelvemonth.

'He puts me in mind of my ancestor, Henry the Second,' the duke said. 'He was a great Plantagenet who ate heartily, so they say.'

'They also say that he used to eat carpets when the mood was upon him,' Katharine said. 'I hope you don't wish me to rear your son to those habits, my lord?'

There was a sly humour in her voice of which I had not thought her capable. The duke however answered gravely. 'Rear him to be a good man, Mistress Katharine. I will not expect more.'

One thing had troubled me a little. I feared the servants might mention my long absence from the castle, but evidently nobody said anything, for he never mentioned the matter to me, and, perversely, that gave me a moment's anger. It was so like a man to go off on campaign and come home in the sure expectation that his woman would still be exactly where he had left her. And the duke had not even been on campaign. He had been ranging up and down the countryside, collecting men and money, and never bothered to send any word to me.

'Why do you scowl at your plate so?' he was demanding. 'Is the meat not to your taste?'

'It's well-spiced, but a letter would have given me more appetite,' I said boldly.

'A letter? Do you mean from myself?' His eyebrows rising, he stared at me.

'Not a word in more than a year, my lord,' I reproached.

'Is it so long?' He frowned slighty, then patted my arm consolingly. 'I have been occupied with so many matters. As it is I can spare only a few days before I set sail. I ought to have been gone months ago, if Parliament had the wit to grant me sufficient funds. Those petty squires think themselves equal to their betters these days!'

He was launched on what was obviously his main grievance. I could understand how he felt but I could also understand how weary the common people must be to have to pay more and more money, and fight in longer, more savage wars, and to see no return for their sacrifices. I suppose I could dimly see both sides of the issue because my father had been of gentle birth and my mother had lived in a wattle hut.

'Why cannot I go with you, my Lord father?' Henry demanded.

'To war? You must grow taller and broader and be able to write clearly,' the duke said.

'Then he could write to me,' I said with icy sweetness.

'You've grown claws, little Gida. They ought to be clipped by marriage,' he retorted.

'Marriage, my lord.' I was suddenly very still.

'Cullen Beaumont is still hoping,' he said.

'Then he must content himself with hope,' I said lightly.

'I'll not force you,' he said briefly, 'but one day you must wed somebody, you know.'

'When I can no longer avoid it,' I said, 'but you'd not want me to walk up the aisle praying for an early widowhood, would you?'

'You'll stay here then while I'm gone, to help Mistress Katharine with my brood?'

'My old housekeeper, Dorothy, lives in Cheapside now,' I said, 'and I would like to visit her.'

'By all means, if you can get escort.'

'I would ask too for leave to visit Marie Regina,' I continued.

'The place where you were born? It's in the Lady Joan's lease, is it not?'

'She would allow me to stay for a while in the castle,' I said.

'Very well then.' He patted my arm again and smiled, kindly but indifferently. My heart sank a little, but then I saw Katharine's eyes flicker towards us, and I allowed myself to feel more cheerful because it was clear that he could not possibly allow the true nature of our relationship to be suspected. I was, you see, very foolish despite my education.

I retired early and sat up till after midnight waiting for him to come, but no knock sounded on my door and I fell asleep at last, my joy at the duke's return curiously muted.

He had much to oversee and arrange during the next days. There were wages to be paid to the labourers, repairs to the battlements, supplies to be ordered for the coming winter, a dispute to be settled between neighbouring yeomen, books, inks and pens for the children's lessons to be unpacked, a guard set to watch castle, possessions and inmates while the duke was away. He was up at dawn and not until supper time did we see him. And then the children and Katharine were there.

I tried to pretend that this was my own home, that the five children were ours, that we had been married long years, that Maudelyn was sleeping in the next room. It was only a pretence and it never became more, though I sat up night after night waiting for him. He never came, and I was too proud to tell him how unhappy I was, how much I longed for private passion to console me for public neglect.

'Tomorrow you leave us, my lord father,' Pippa said as we rose from supper one evening.

I had known when he would leave but I had made myself forget, pushing the knowledge to the back of my mind. Now I stared at him mutely, willing him to look at me with some hint of the desire he had shown me when he had come alone to Kenilworth.

'I'll leave at dawn, if any of you are minded to see me go,' he said teasingly, and his three children crowded about him, declaring they would all rise at cockcrow. Over their heads he smiled at the two Swynford children and I thought then how his love for children was one of the finest facets of his nature. Surely he would acknowledge Maudelyn as his own when I revealed the truth.

'I will bid you farewell now, little Gida,' he said.

'Now?' I gaped at him foolishly.

'I will have very little time in which to make long farewells,' he said. 'I dislike them anyway. A man should ride away with a light heart, not turning about in the saddle to see his family gathered weeping.'

'We won't weep!' Bet cried indignantly. And he laughed, sweeping her up until her small face was level with his, kissing the tip of her nose, telling her she was a brave little wench. Nobody noticed when I quietly turned and left the hall.

In my own apartment I stood irresolute, running my hands up and down the smooth silk of my gown. To leave so soon with no private word or look, with nothing to tell me that he even remembered, was too cruel for me to bear. I was certain that if I merely waited tonight as I had waited before he would not come.

Perhaps a small voice whispered to me, he keeps away because he feels he is to blame for your seduction. He is a man of noble principles and the memory of that night fills him with guilt. He knows he must make a political alliance and cannot offer you marriage, so he holds back.

I had not thought of it in that light before,

and my misery lifted a little. If that were true, then I would go to him and make him understand that I felt no shame at our union, no desire to live in what the world regards as an honourable estate. I must make him understand that before he went away.

I waited now, not for him to come to me, but for the household to retire for the night and the great castle to sink into slumber. The long summer evening drifted into darkness and I heard the barked commands and tramping of feet as the guard was changed. The children would be tucked up now, the dogs set loose to roam the grounds, the fires damped down save for the one in the kitchen where the men servants slept. I waited until I had seen the last bright star glitter into the expectant sky.

Then, having unbound my hair and exchanged my tight waisted houppelande for a loose robe, I took my courage and my longing in both hands and opened the door.

The long corridor stretched ahead, its corner illuminated by a flaring torch. I went down it and began to ascend the narrow steps that led to the apartment where the duke slept. He usually dispensed with a guard when he was at home, and I was glad to see that no sentry leaned against the wall.

I lifted my hand to knock, then realised the door was slightly ajar, so I pushed it wider.

Voices came to me from behind the carved screen that excluded the draught. I stopped on the threshold, disappointment striking through me as I heard Katharine's quiet tone.

'Then what are we to do, my lord?'

And the duke's deeper voice, equally hopeless. 'There is no remedy. I am too far committed now to draw back. It is necessary for me to wed Donna Catharina.'

'The same name as myself. There is bitter irony in that. Don't you find it so?'

'I find it damnable,' the duke said.

'But I will not ask you to be forsworn,' Katherine said. 'I have not that right. You must go away and forget me. You must forget me.'

'As well as ask me to forget my own right arm,' he said. 'You have drawn the sting of Blanche's death out of my life and sweetened it for me again. I fell in love with you against my will, you know.'

'And if you could,' she asked softly, 'would you have these past weeks wiped out as if they had never been? Would you?'

'I would not cancel a single hour,' the duke murmured. 'Katharine, dear, lovely Katharine!'

I couldn't bear to stay and listen to any more of this murmured conversation. One part of my shocked mind retained the wit to move very quietly, pulling the door close. And I went very softly down the twisting steps, holding up my skirts so that they would not rustle over the stone.

The duke and Katharine Swynford. The most powerful man in England after king and Black Prince and the widow of an obscure knight. It was impossible, but it had happened. Impossible to believe but I had heard the words, the tone in which they had been spoken.

In my own apartment I sat on the edge of the bed, my hands over my ears as if by so doing I could shut out the echo of those loving voices. I sat, without tears, until the stars faded, and dawn began to lighten the sky and make clear the outlines of wall and gate.

I was very cold, the fire in my room having died into ashes long before, and my face was stiff and painful. My limbs were cramped and when I rose quivers of pain tingled through my muscles. I walked up and down, rubbing my hands to try to restore the blood to them. I was so tired I wanted to sleep for ever, and so unhappy I never thought I would ever sleep again.

There was noise below, and I moved to the window, and looked down into the courtyard, and wished that I had not. The duke was mounted on his big chestnut stallion, armed and cloaked, his hair gleaming under the pale sky. Katharine Swynford, the stirrup cup in her hands, stood at his side, reaching towards him. I saw her face, pale and tense within its black hood, and I saw his fingers clasp hers as he took the cup, and then I moved back and stood in the centrre of the room, shaking my head from side to side as if to deny the truth of what I had just seen.

I don't know how long I stood there, but at last I heard a tap on the door, heard myself say, 'Come in'

Katharine Swynford entered, closing the door behind her and standing with her back against it. She looked drained and ill, but her voice held the usual firm calm quality.

'The duke is gone. It may be many years before he comes to Kenilworth again.'

'Yes.'

'I noticed you at your window,' she said. 'You have found out the truth of it, I think.'

'You and the duke?' I nodded slowly.

'I have loved him for a long time,' she confided. 'Even when my own husband was alive — even then, God forgive me! But John loved his wife and my own love for him was the love of a friend.'

'That isn't true!' I said sharply.

'No, it isn't true.' She gave an odd little laugh and moved her hands in a rueful fashion. 'I used to think it was like that but I know now that I was deceiving myself. But I never dreamed that he could ever feel for me as I felt for him. Shall I tell you something?'

I didn't want to have her tell me anything, but I had to hear it.

'I stole a ring belonging to the duke and put it with one of my own, and then I gave them to my sister, to Philippa, and asked her to get old Mother Jennet to work a spell. Oh, it was foolish, but I loved him and I wanted so much to bear his child. Simply to bear his child! I have prayed for that, Gida.'

'And did your prayers work?' I asked lightly.

'Either that or Mother Jennet's spell,' said Katharine. 'I am with child, Gida. I am certain of it.'

'Does — have you told His Grace?'

'He has to make a political marriage,' she said. 'I'll not hold him back from that by telling him. When he comes home, then he will know. He is very fond of children, very kind to them, and he will be pleased.'

'Your own reputation —— '

'Is of no importance,' she said simply. 'I shall live here, teaching the children, waiting for his return. Who is going to trouble about a widow who bears a child? I see no difficulty.'

'You are very brave,' I said, and I smiled at her, the cramp in my joints tightening into hatred. Hatred not only for this plain young woman, but for my own stupidity. I ought to have left well alone and not meddled with my arts in the lives of others, for I had succeeded all too well.

'I had to tell somebody,' she said, 'because I will need help in the months ahead. If anything were to happen to me, I want someone to know the babe's true father so that he may be acknowledged.'

'He will be a bastard,' I reminded her.

'Great men often love their bastards with a very special affection,' she said.

'So I've heard.' I wished she would go away, but she went on standing there, talking about the duke and her love for him, looking at me with her candid eyes as she said, 'I am so happy we are to be friends, Gida. The duke thinks very highly of you and so do the children. We will be good company for one another in the months to come.'

And I agreed, clasping the hand she offered, the flesh on my own fingers shrinking and shrivelling, and I went on smiling while the sickness rose up in me and the day grew brighter.

9

Katharine's child was a boy. Throughout the long months of her pregnancy I was torn in two directions. Part of me felt pity for her state because, loving the duke myself, I could understand how she felt too, but there was another part of me that watched her with hatred, praying that she might die. She did not, of course. Her confinement was an easy one and the boy was healthy. She named him John giving him the surname of Beaufort, and none of the servants said anything, though they must have guessed the father for the baby was John of Gaunt in minature. The other children accepted him without bothering about his beginnings and even I had an impulse of affection towards the mite when I held him, for he looked at me with the duke's eyes and I could trace in the chubby baby face my own lover's strong features.

I still pretended to myself that he was my lover, but I knew very well that what had happened between us was no more, on his part, than the need of a lonely man coming back to the house where his wife had died.

He had been wrong to take me on that night, but I must take my share of blame, for he had given me the chance to refuse.

Katharine wrote to the duke, telling him how the children were, telling him too that she had borne a child. She showed the letter to me and, reading its formal phrases, I pictured the duke smiling as he recognised the hand, pictured the surprised delight as he realised the new child must be his. And I knew that I could not do myself the violence of staying at Kenilworth until his return.

The baby was almost a year old when I wrote to Dorothy telling her I was returning for a visit. A pedlar on his way south had called in, offering to take any letters for the household, and I took the opportunity of giving him mine. Katharine had sent her own missive by the official post rider, but such means were expensive. I knew my dowry was still untouched, but for my ready use I had only a few gold coins and I must hoard them against need.

Katharine would have demurred at my going, but she knew the duke had given me leave to go visiting and she had no authority to prevent it. I was one and twenty, and considered myself to be an independent woman. I have heard it said that we renew ourselves every seven years, so that I was not the person I had been at fourteen, and when I thought of myself I thought there was truth in the saying. Although I felt myself to be the same I knew I was changed in many subtle ways from the young girl who had ridden down from the monastery and met the Lady Joan in the wattle hut by the river.

For one thing I no longer believed that the impossible might come true and that the duke would fall in love with me. There are some joys that can never be and it did no good to blame Katharine whose love had brought her nothing but the anguish of separation. In many ways we were in like case she and I, and I forgot that I hated her and regarded her with a sympathy that had its roots in common misfortune.

Before I left Kenilworth word came that Mistress Beaumont had died. She had been claiming to be an invalid for so long that her death seemed no more than an intensification of her normal condition, and I certainly felt not the slightest grief, for since my refusal to consider Cullen as a husband she had issued no invitations to me. However good manners demanded that someone from the castle attend the funeral, and I agreed to go.

The poor woman had had few friends, probably because her complaining nature had driven them away, but there was a sprinkling of neighbours and the household servants were there, in neat, black garbed ranks. I took a place near the back of the church during the requiem Mass, bowing my head at suitable moments, listening with inward cynicism when the priest extolled her virtues as a devout Christian weighed down by the burden of constant ill-health.

The funeral over, I slipped away, having done what convention demanded of me, and was about to mount Silver when someone hurried up, speaking my name in accents of such delight that I turned, smiling.

'Mistress Gida! You were not going to ride away without speaking to me, were you?'

'Cullen! I had no idea you were in England!' My own voice was warm with pleasure for he was, after all, a friend.

'I came home the day before my lady mother died. A sad chance that I should be here to wish her farewell, but she died as she had lived, bravely, uncomplainingly.'

'You were very fond of her,' I said, and wondered if my own son would be blind to my faults.

'My brothers are settled in France and have found wives there,' he went on.

'And you are a knight! You have your spurs now.' 'And a shoulder wound that has weakened my sword arm and is not expected to heal properly for the next six months. You will come into the house for some refreshment?'

I hadn't the heart to refuse, and it is, in any event, very flattering to meet an old admirer, so I mounted and we rode together through the green parkland and up to the manor house. Straw was laid over the cobbled courtyard and there was black crepe on the knocker. Not until we were seated in the small parlour at the side of the hall, with wine and cakes before us, did he look at me again, delight in his honest eyes.

'To see you again after so long a time! It makes me — like a boy again, not knowing what to say.'

'Tell me about yourself,' I invited. 'Will you go back into the duke's service when your arm is healed?'

'No, I intend to stay here and farm. My brothers have no interest in the place, and I cannot let it go to rack and ruin. I have had my fill of campaigning.'

'So you will live here then?' I imagined him riding over the estate, discussing the price of crops and the iniquities of the latest tax. He would grow a beard, and put on a little weight, and change his short gown for a long one. And he would fit into his new life easily and happily.

'It is a good house,' Cullen said, as if I had argued the fact. 'My father had this parlour built onto the hall so my mother would have a pleasant room where she could rest quietly. The kitchen is well away from the main house so we are never troubled by smoke or cooking smells, and the midden is in the other direction entirely.'

'It's a fine house,' I said politely.

'And I have always thought of you as — living here,' he said. 'No, don't say anything yet. Hear me first. I know that you and my lady mother were not the best of friends. It is often thus, I'm told, between ladies. But now that she is gone — '

'Please, you really mustn't speak in that way,' I interrupted.

'No, this is the wrong time. It is very ill of me to speak of such matters on this day, but I have not seen you for years.'

'Nor remembered me much, I'll wager,' I said lightly.

'Then you would lose your wager,' he said. 'I have remembered everything about you. Oh, my lord duke told me you had no leanings towards marriage, so I have not wearied you with letters. But I never ceased to hope that you would come to care for me, that we might be wed. I am twenty-five years old and have remained a bachelor for your sake.'

'And are like to remain one,' I said. 'I still have no inclination to wed, and the duke has said he will not force me.'

'Nor would I,' he said earnestly. 'I would persuade you to it. You need not love me, for I would have affection sufficient for both. Gida, if you would allow me to see you, to pay court to you — we live but a mile apart!'

'I shall be happy to have you visit me,' I said formally, 'but I am going south to visit an old friend of mine very soon. Dorothy was the housekeeper where I used to live in Marie Regina. She lives in London now.'

'Then you must accept my escort,' he said promptly.

'No need. I have escort and you will have your hands full with the estate for the next several months,' I said hastily.

He didn't press the point but gave me more wine and poured some for himself. When he next spoke it was cheerfully, as if he had put the problem of marriage to one side for the moment.

'My Lord Duke is much occupied with the campaign. It goes badly even though he signed a treaty with Spain.'

'He wed the Infanta,' I said.

'Who presented him with a daughter just before I sailed for England.'

'A daughter.' I echoed the word, wanting to laugh and cry at the same time. Political or not the marriage had been consummated, it seemed. Perhaps the Spanish princess was not unattractive. Perhaps she was charming and gentle and the duke had fallen in love with her and forgotten not only me but Katharine Swynford too.

'It is being whispered that the Black Prince will not live to succeed to the throne,' Cullen said, lowering his voice. 'He is broken in health, and when he dies the heir will be Prince Richard. A child cannot wield power, so the real ruler of the kingdom will be my Lord Duke. No man had such power before, and he will face great danger from those who resent his privileges. I am determined in my own mind to be loyal to him.'

'Very creditable of you,' I said lightly.

'Do you place loyalty at such small account?' he asked, and his voice betrayed disappointment. Then his face cleared and he said, 'But there, Mistress Gida! You're a woman and women don't see things in the same light as we do. Now we'll talk of other things.'

'On another day, I fear. I promised Mistress Swynford that I would ride home early.' I rose, hoping to avoid another declaration of love.

'I would like to escort you,' he said, 'but I must sup with the priest and arrange for Masses for my mother. I have paid for a hundred to speed her soul out of purgatory.'

Privately I doubted if a thousand would achieve it, but I said warmly, 'She'll be obliged to you for that. And I'm obliged to you for your good wishes.'

' 'Tis more than that. It has always been more than that. For many years, ever since I first saw you at Court, it has been more than good wishes.'

'We'll speak of it at a more convenient time,' I said.

'And you are not offended at my speaking thus?'

'I am deeply touched,' I said sincerely. 'I can appreciate personal loyalty, even if as a woman I cannot understand public affairs.'

'I meant no criticism,' he assured me, flushing deeply.

'I know you did not,' I gave him my hand, feeling a little sad because I liked him so very much and could never love him.

A few days later I took my leave of Katharine and the children and set out for London. It was two years since I had taken a long journey and the prospect pleased me, for at the end of it lay a reunion with my son. He would not remember me, of course, but I hoped that Dorothy had spoken of me. One day I would tell him about his father and make him understand that he had been born of love, even if that love had only lasted for a night.

'You will take care of yourself?' Katharine had questioned earnestly as we parted. 'I will miss your company, Gida.'

'The duke will be back soon then you'll have company enough,' I had smiled back, and then I had hugged the children, and flanked by two squires, ridden down the curving drive between the tall oaks.

I had no intention of returning to Kenilworth until Maudelyn was of an age to be told about his father, and when that would be depended on the boy himself, for some are of a stomach to stand the truth before others are reached to that maturity.

We reached London without incident and, having paid the squires who had given me their promise to return without roistering in every tavern on the way, I pressed on towards Cheapside. It was midday and I was conscious at once of the smell of rotting sewage and emptied pisspots. There were laws, I knew, meant to keep the streets sweet, but in high summer the alleys were stinking and the risk of plague high. I wondered how long I would be able to endure the close confines of the city after the spaciousness of Kenilworth.

Outside the Aston shop I dismounted and stopped, for a very small boy in a wool smock sat on the front step, straight fair hair dangling over his brow. He was playing with a brightly coloured wooden soldier, making its jointed legs move backwards and forwards, and as I moved forward he looked up, fixing me with an intent, greenish gaze.

'Maudelyn? Are you Maudelyn?' I dropped to one knee, speaking softly lest he be nervous, but he went on gazing at me solemnly.

'Is that your soldier?' I asked.

He nodded, held it out for my inspection, and said in a piping voice, 'Dotty gived it to me.'

'Where is Dotty?' I asked. He pointed over his shoulder just as Dorothy herself came to the door, wiping her hands on her apron, exclaiming with joy at the sight of me, demanding that I come indoors out of the sun at once, hoisting up the child to her ample hip while she declared that he was growing taller and heavier by the minute.

Nothing within the tall narrow house had

changed in my two years absence. The round table in the parlour, two high-backed chairs, the sweet smelling rushes, the copper and pewter pans against the whitewashed walls, were all as they had been. But it was clear that my arrival presented difficulties, though Dorothy would have bitten out her tongue rather than admit it. Ralph, being now twelve, had taken over the attic where I had slept. Maudelyn still had his crib in Dorothy's bedchamber, and my coming inevitably meant an upheaval in her arrangements, for it entailed despatching the serving girl from her bed in the corner to a pallet in the kitchen. The apprentice had a bed in the store room at the back of the shop, but all the household sat down together and there was no disguising the fact that an extra place meant crowding for the rest.

I had expected to have to spend some considerable time in making myself known to Maudelyn, but he seemed to accept me at once, not with any great emotion for he was a stolid, serious child who occupied himself quietly in corners. The one thing upon which his affections seemed set was the wooden soldier. He carried that toy around with him everywhere, even propping it at the end of his crib when he was put to bed. A woodcarver had made it for him and I wished to thank the man for his kindness, but Dorothy made so many objections to my going that in the end I ordered her to tell me exactly what was wrong.

'He is a Jew,' she said at last with great reluctance.

'I thought they had all been driven out of England!' I exclaimed.

'There are still a few left, but they attend Mass to keep the authorities happy,' she explained. 'I was sorry for Joseph. Joseph Benacre is his name.'

'How did you come to meet a Jew?' I asked in astonishment.

'Hush, do!' Dorothy begged. 'I saw some wood carvings he'd done up for sale and I ordered one.' She nodded towards a small carved dish in which she kept fruit. 'He was very grateful, for he gets few orders, it seems. When I went back the next week, for I'd my eye on some other things he'd made he gave me the soldier for Maudelyn.'

'Then I will certainly thank him,' I said firmly.

'He lives at the back of Lombard Street,' she said reluctantly.

I went a few days later riding through the streets on Silver, but with far less pleasure than I had galloped over the countryside. This city was too dirty, too ill-kept, too crowded. There were times when I felt stifled by so many people, so many high buildings. And the entry in which I found Master Benacre's house was so narrow that two horses, could not possibly have passed each other.

There were some carvings in the window and a thin woman with a face the colour of old ivory admitted me into a low ceilinged room with a big window at the back through which the rays of sunlight slanted onto a table littered with wood shavings and small blocks of wood. An elderly man, with a leather apron over his long gown, rose from a stool and bowed, a question in his eyes.

'I am Mistress Gida Falcon,' I said, offering my hand. 'You made a wooden soldier for my little boy.'

'For Master Maudelyn. Yes, I remember the little one. An unusual child with green eyes.'

'I came to thank you,' I said. 'Perhaps I will order a carving from you for my own use.'

'I shall be glad of the business,' he said. 'Forgive me, Mistress Falcon, will you not sit down. Rebecca, bring some wine.'

'Thank you.' I sat down on the stool the woman lifted forward and looked about me.

The room was large and low ceilinged,

the floor covered not with rushes but with wood shavings. The furniture was sparse but most intricately carved with bunches of fruit and flowers. Everything in the apartment was neat and most beautifully fashioned, and the man who had greeted me had the same neat, patrician aspect.

The woman poured wine into two goblets, dipped a curtsey, and withdrew. There was a grace in her bearing that told me the Benacres had once been very wealthy. I would have liked to know more about them, but the man, though he smiled at me hospitably, waited silently for me to open the conversation.

'I have been in Warwickshire these past two years,' I said, 'in the household of the Duke of Lancaster, and it has not been possible to have my son with me.'

'His Grace is a very powerful noble,' Joseph Benacre said.

'With much to occupy him.' I stopped, puzzled because I had an overwhelming desire to talk to this man, to tell him of the contradictory feelings that swayed me like gusts of wind. I wanted to confide in him, and I have often thought of that since, and tried to understand why. I suppose it was partly his tranquil air, but also it was my own realization that we were alike, for he, like myself, was an alien among others, separated from them by his beliefs.

'You are troubled, Mistress Falcon,' he said.

'About my son. He is very dear to me.'

'Yet you left him.' He made the statement with no hint of accusation in his voice, but my cheeks flamed.

'I am unwed,' I said. 'It was necessary for me to leave the boy with my old housekeeper, Dorothy. But I am more or less my own mistress now, so I came back to London.'

'And like it not.' Again he made the statement without expression.

'It is no place to bring up the son of a — gentleman,' I said.

'Does the boy's father take no interest?'

'He does not know. One day I will tell him, but now is not the time. I need advice.'

'So you come to me?' He frowned slightly. 'You ought to consult your priest.'

'Any priest would rail at me for a light woman.'

'As would any religious authority,' he interrupted. 'Chastity is honoured in all faiths, and purity of women is an ideal — '

'Which is seldom realised.' I rose impatiently, kicking aside the curling bits of wood. 'It is of the child I wish to speak, not of my own shortcomings. When I saw the soldier you had carved for him I hoped you were a man who understood children, who might show sympathy for a child without a father.'

'My own child grew up without a mother,' he said. 'Rebecca is a good maid, a Christian now as the Law demands, but she will never have a suitor, husband, child of her own. Her birth is against her. Your son has a mother and is Christian born.'

'And is bastard.'

'Too late to consider that now. Boys are not blamed because their parents were not wed. There is something else troubling you.'

I hesitated, then took off my glove, and drew off the ring that Lady Joan had given me years before, and handed it to him.

'Where did you get this?' he asked, a sharpness in his voice.

'It came from the East, from the land of the Saracen. I thought a man of your race might know — '

'I know nothing,' he said. 'I know nothing at all. You forget that Jews who wish to remain in this country were required to accept Christian baptism.'

'Few did so,' I said, 'But you and your daughter were baptised and go now to Mass. That could mean one of two things. Either you were a man of little faith, and this, having met you, is not the truth, I'm sure, or — '

'Or?' he echoed.

I took a deep breath and said, 'Or you believe as I do that all religions spring from the same Source and all gods meet in the heart of man?'

'Are you a spy for some priest?' he asked. For answer I gave him the secret sign by which one Templar recognises another.

'So!' He repeated the sign, his face expressing deep relief. 'So, you too are of the Mysteries. It is a very long time since I spoke to one of my fellows. In our own tradition women are not admitted to the inner sanctuaries, but I have passed on some of my own knowledge to Rebecca though in the city we dare not practise the Rites.'

'And should I tell my son?'

'Has nobody given you advice on that point?' he asked.

'Advice that makes no sense. I am to pass on my knowledge to a female of my blood born after her mother has died.'

'Then you must wait for that which makes no sense, and bring up your son to be a good Christian. Not all are privileged to enter the upper room.'

'We could meet again at the Equinox,' I suggested.

'It is better that we do not,' said Joseph Benacre. 'We are still watched, Rebecca and I, very closely. It would arouse suspicion if you came here often.'

'Then I will order a carving,' I said, taking back the ring and smoothing on my glove. 'Can you make me a prayer stool, a very solid one, for I wish to give Dorothy a Yuletide gift.'

'Then I shall be happy to make it, and to discuss the design if you wish to call again. Rebecca, come and bid our guest goodbye.'

The young woman glided from an inner room, and curtsied, her dark eyes downcast modestly.

'I am glad you came, Mistress Falcon,' he said. 'I am glad you honoured me with your confidence. I am only sorry that I was not able to be of more help.'

'You told me to find my own way and to stop feeling sorry for myself,' I said. 'Good-day, Master Benacre. Mistress.'

I went out into the alley, feeling more light of heart than I had done for years. I felt, for the first time since I had talked with the Lady Joan in the water garden of Baynards' Castle, that I was not alone in my beliefs and practices, that others too knew the ancient wisdom and were not afraid of walking alien through the world.

Cramped as we were I resolved to stay longer with Dorothy. The narrow house, the garden with the pear tree, the stable where I kept Silver and the pack horse, Maize, all these represented security, the familiar. I sank back into it as if I were a child again. I could almost imagine that my parents were still alive and would come home soon. I would sit under the tree and see myself as a child again standing at the door, and then I would see my own child come trotting out, holding his wooden soldier by its arm, telling me that Dotty had made some march-pane. He loved Dorothy, and I was glad of it for there was always the chance that the duke might send for me.

That was my secret dream, but it faded as the months stretched into a year, two, three. The pear tree had blossomed, and given forth its hard, bitter fruit three times, and the duke had not sent for me. He had come back to England more than once and travelled into Warwickshire. That much I learned from Master Grey, who went often into the city and kept his ear close to the ground.

'It is rumoured that the duke has a mistress. Katharine Swynford, his own children's governess! She has borne him two sons and they say she is with child again. I know he is your guardian, Mistress Gida, but I find it shocking that great men should so behave. The king himself is worse than any of them. A white bearded dotard who drools over Alice Perrers.'

'We must not talk of such things,' his wife said, snatching nervously at a candied nut. 'We must not talk thus of our betters.'

'Half the world talks of its betters,' Jonathan Grey said impatiently. 'The other half listens, my dear. That is the way of the world.'

'Then the world has some very odd habits,' Mistress Grey said, taking another sweet. 'These are matters that ought not to be discussed when ladies are present. I hope, I hope very much, that our dear Petrella never learns of such things. I will be glad when she and Ralph are safely wed and out of temptation.'

'Not until she is seventeen,' Master Grey said firmly. 'When she is seventeen she will make a lovely bride.'

'Ralph is eager to take her as his wife now,' Dorothy said, abandoning the subject of royal immorality with relief.

'Ralph is a lusty lad but a little deprivation will do him no harm,' said Master Grey firmly.

Certainly Ralph appeared to be much in love with Petrella, but then they had been brought up with the idea that one day they would marry. I liked Ralph very much. He was a good humoured boy who had begun his apprenticeship in the wool trade and would, as soon as possible, obtain his licence. And the question of his marriage brought my own situation to mind. When Ralph wed he would expect to bring his wife to live with him and there would be no room then for Maudelyn or me. I put the question to Joseph Benacre for I had fallen into the habit of visiting him and Rebecca from time to time.

'When the time comes you will know where to go,' was all that he would say.

I thought that if the duke had sent for me, I would have returned to Kenilworth long since. But John of Gaunt had more pressing matters to occupy his mind than an obscure young woman who had been wished on him as a ward and whose brief seduction he surely wished to forget.

Parliament, aware at last of the squandering of money upon the abortive campaigns of the past years, of the corruption in high places that left ordinary folk destitute and decked Alice Perrers in silk and jewels, ordered an investigation. Alice Perrers

237

was accused of misappropriation of the king's funds and three of his ministers were called to account for the embezzling of taxes.

Like most women I find these political matters almost impossible to understand. My opinions have been shaped by my personal experience of people and larger issues have meant very little, but I was pleased that Alice was to be called to account. I never could forget that she had betrayed the Abbot, and I never will understand why the duke supported her and stayed her friend. But then I cannot understand why he fell in love with Katharine Swynford either.

'Latimer has employed his agent to keep a percentage of all taxes to his own benefit, and the two rascals are hand in glove with the royal mistress,' Ralph said. 'The Black Prince supports the Commons, and is coming from Berkhamsted to give evidence at the enquiry, and the Duke of Lancaster has undertaken to defend Alice Perrers.'

'The prince is a dying man!' I exclaimed. 'He has been ill for years, ever since his last campaign.'

'He is coming in a litter,' Ralph said, 'I had it from Master Grey when I called upon Petrella this morning. The prince knows that his father is in his dotage and he fears that his own son stands to inherit a corrupt government.'

'But if Prince Richard becomes king before he is grown,' Dorothy said, wrinkling her brow, 'will not the duke be his guardian?'

'The duke will be good uncle to his nephew,' I said warmly, 'even if he does not agree with the prince's championing of the Commons.'

'There is a knight who speaks for the Commons,' Ralph told us. 'His name is Peter de la Mare and they say he is most eloquent, for he has been elected as their official Speaker.'

'To argue against the Lords? I didn't think such a thing was allowed,' I said.

'Everything is changing,' the boy said with enthusiasm. 'The merchant classes are no longer content simply to vote money when the great nobles desire it. They demand the right to know how that money should be spent, to frame the laws and not merely to approve them. What do you think of that?'

'I think it's all a great nonsense,' Dorothy said firmly. 'How could the Commons ever hope to govern us when they are ordinary folk like ourselves? You will be telling me next that serfs can vote.'

'Not serfs, but merchants who bring profit to the land ought to have the right to make the laws. I feel very strongly about these matters.'

'You are too young to meddle in such things,' Dorothy said.

'In a few months time I'll be wed, and in a year or two I'll be admitted to the Guild,' he argued. 'Anyway I'm going with Master Grey into the City tomorrow to see the Lords going to Parliament. There will be crowds there.'

'A good reason for staying away,' Dorothy said. 'You'll have your purse snatched or bring home some disease.'

'Or be robbed and tipped into the Thames. Cease fretting!' Ralph ordered, giving her a brief hug before he swung out of the parlour and clattered down the stairs into the shop.

'He is sixteen. You cannot keep him penned like a child,' I said.

'Will you go to see the Lords?' Dorothy asked.

I shook my head.

'Have you no wish even to see him?' she asked.

'I am not a child either,' I said.

'No. You are neither maid nor wife either,' she said with sudden frankness. 'You ought to be wed.'

'To give my son a father? He manages well enough.'

'Oh, we all *manage*!' she said with scorn. 'But that is not living! And hiding from the duke will accomplish nothing, Gida Falcon.'

The next day the temptation to ride out and see the duke was almost overwhelming, but I resisted it. Seeing him again would bring me nothing but pain. My life had settled into the busy routine of the shop, with lessons to be given to Maudelyn, the weekly Mass, visits to the Benacres, rides out to the fields of Chelsea. I had trained myself not to think of the duke, nor even the life upon which I had turned my back when I rode away from Kenilworth.

Ralph came home after dusk, brushing aside Dorothy's anxious enquiries, eager to tell us his news.

'The streets were packed. Cheek by jowl as we stood to watch the Lords pass. The Black Prince was carried in a litter. He is dying, he truly is dying. The people cheered him, but they hissed the duke.'

'Why? Why did they dare to do that?' I asked indignantly.

'Because he came to speak on Alice Perrers' behalf. He had troops with him, not just a simple escort, but halberdiers and axemen and an entire company of archers! He took no notice of the hissing but rode on, looking neither to left nor right. One might have thought that he came, not to defend, but to accuse.'

'What was decided?' Dorothy asked.

'The Commons won!' Ralph said, flopping down into a chair and stretching his legs to the fire. 'What do you think of that? The entire Commons voted for Latimer to be dismissed and Alice Perrers sent from the king's bed.'

'And how did the duke take it?' I asked.

'He did not quarrel with his brother over the verdict,' Ralph said. 'The duke rode at the side of the litter when they came out of the Commons, and they seemed amiable.'

'So Alice Perrers is banished,' Dorothy said. 'I'm glad of it, for I never liked her even when she was a child.'

'She will come back,' I said and wondered why I spoke with such calm certainty.

10

The Black Prince died less than a month later and, within another month, the duke had seized control of the Commons and upended all its decisions.

'The duke packed Parliament with his own armed retainers and they voted unanimously to restore Latimer and to allow Alice Perrers to return to Court. Peter de la Mare has been flung into Nottingham Gaol on a charge of sedition, and William of Wykeham has been charged with malpractice.'

'But he is Bishop of Winchester. One cannot accuse a Bishop of malpractice,' I said in bewilderment.

Joseph Benacre, in whose house I sat, gave a shrewd, unsmiling glance.

'One can even burn an Abbot, if it be politic,' he reminded me.

'The duke never liked the Bishop,' I remembered.

'He likes him less since Wykeham preached against his scandalous association with the governess of his children. He has a wife in Spain and a daughter, the Lady Catalina.'

'That was a political marriage.'

'Which does not excuse him from his duties,' the old man said.

'Life is not so simple,' I said, irritated by his unyielding manner. 'It is not simply black and white, but many, many shades. The duke may love Katharine Swynford.'

'And as a measure of his love he makes a harlot of her?'

'We cannot judge,' I said weakly.

'But we need not condone,' Joseph said. 'Rebecca is a chaste young woman, but she has a heart as other women have. Yet I would not expect her to give way to passion and forget her duty.'

'Then it is you who condemn all women,' I said lightly.

'No, Mistress Gida. I condemn men who misuse their powers in order to bend others to their will, or to deceive women who love them. And I condemn women in equal measure when they seek to ensnare men.'

'As Alice Perrers cozened the king? I knew her once when I was at Court. She was a hard young woman even then, and Dorothy says she was the same when she was a child.'

'Perhaps she gives comfort to the king,' said Rebecca.

She so seldom entered into the conversation that I glanced at her in surprise. Her smooth olive cheeks flushed slightly, but she held her ground, meeting my gaze steadily.

'The king is old and they say his mind is confused,' she said. 'This woman may give him comfort.'

'Not the sort an honest woman gives,' Joseph began, then held up a rueful hand. 'I grow old and crotchety,' he said. 'I sit here and pass judgement even though I pretend that I don't. You too see shades, Rebecca, when my eyes can measure only black and white.'

'The king will die soon,' I said. 'When he dies a child will sit upon the throne. And the Lady Joan — '

'Will need friends,' Joseph said. 'It must be many years since you have met her, Mistress Gida?'

'I have seen her only twice in my entire life,' I said. 'I thought her very beautiful.'

'They say she is still comely,' said Rebecca gently, 'though she must be near fifty. I pitied her when the prince died.'

'They say she was a true and faithful wife,' Joseph approved.

'To three husbands,' I could not resist saying.

'And you and I, Mistress Gida, have not one husband between us,' Rebecca said with a gleam of humour in her dark eyes. 'Perhaps we ought not to grudge Alice Perrers what she tries to obtain and hold. This is a sad world for women.'

'Rebecca, you are a better person than either of us,' I said, kissing her. 'Master Benacre, I have to leave before it gets dark.'

'It is not safe, even in the light, for a lady to ride through the streets without escort,' he said.

'The streets are full of the duke's men,' I said in amusement. 'There will be little danger from footpads. But I am used to being alone — unprotected, as you call it.'

Used to it, but not entirely reconciled. As I rode down the alley into the main thoroughfare I thought that in a few months I would be twenty-five years old, an age at which most women had a husband and family or were in some convent or other.

I rode alone through the narrow streets, cloaked and hooded to avoid possible molestation. My guardian had apparently forgotten my existence for I had heard no word from him in years. Even Cullen Beaumont had never come in search of me, and for all I knew my twin was dead on some foreign battlefield. So I was thinking as I rode and surely some instinct brought Godwin into my mind for, as I turned into

Cheapside, I heard Maudelyn's excited shout, and he came panting up to me.

'Lady mother, my uncle is come home from France! He is in the parlour now.'

My son generally displayed so little emotion that it was clear Godwin had made a considerable impression on him. I dismounted, calling to the apprentice to stable Silver, and was tugged indoors by Maudelyn's eager little hand.

Godwin sat by the fire, ale at his elbow. It was long since I had seen him, but there was still much of the boy I had known in the tall, fair haired man who rose to greet me. He was well dressed, a sleeveless tunic of black velvet covering a shirt of lime silk, the hanging sleeves lined with the same dark green as the hose. His hair waved almost to his shoulders and his face was my own set in a masculine mould.

'Gida, you're a comely woman!' he exclaimed in unflattering surprise. 'But what the devil are you doing here? I thought you up in Warwickshire with the duke's leman! And how came you to have a boy? Dorothy will tell me nothing.'

'Dorothy has nothing to tell,' I said, returning my brother's kiss. 'And I had the boy in the usual way.'

'With no wedding ring?' He caught at my

hand and threw it down again, exclaiming impatiently, 'Sister, you're a fool! Does Cullen Beaumont know?'

'Nothing, and you'll not tell him. Cullen is farming his land in Warwickshire and is very likely wed by now.'

'As you should be, but you always went your own way even when you were a child.'

'We have not been close,' I said, regretting it.

'I dislike close ties,' Godwin said. 'A wandering life fits me better.'

'But you will surely settle now that you are back?' Dorothy set meat before him.

'Not to merchant life. It would kill me to live as young Ralph lives. Counting one's profits, scolding the apprentice, grumbling about the Staple, that is no life for a real man.'

Ralph, who sat at the table, shuffled his feet uncomfortably, and said, 'I like it well enough.'

'At your age you should be enjoying yourself,' Godwin said.

'Ralph is to be wed in June,' Dorothy interposed. 'You met his sweetheart going out as you came in.'

'The wench called Petrella? She was well enough,' Godwin said indifferently.

'She is a charming girl,' I said firmly. 'You

would do well to find yourself such a wife.'

'Like you, sister, I'd liefer take my pleasure between unhallowed sheets,' Godwin said airily.

'There'll be none in this house,' Dorothy said crossly.

'I shall be the perfect guest,' Godwin promised. 'Will you let me share your chamber, Ralph? I don't snore or scratch or belch, and if I come in late I take off my shoes.'

'If you come in late the door will be locked,' Dorothy threatened.

'You take much upon yourself,' Godwin said, and the coldness of his eyes startled me for a moment. 'It is time Ralph was freed from petticoat rule.'

'Me too,' Maudelyn said.

'You too, my fine rascal,' Godwin assured him. 'Gida, is there more meat? A knight home from the wars needs good, red meat.'

So he considered himself to be home, and in the weeks that followed he made no mention of going away again. He had been the Black Prince's liege man, but was now, I supposed, free to offer his sword arm where he chose.

He chose, however, to stay with us in Cheapside, giving Dorothy a generous sum of money every week to pay for his keep.

I suspected that he had made a lot of money during the long campaigns, for he dressed well and bought gifts for us, an expensive necklace for me, a silver dagger in a velvet scabbard for Maudelyn, a new coif of starched lace for Dorothy to wear to Mass. He spent most of his day out and about in the City, and in the evening he sat with us and told us tales of the campaigns.

'I went everywhere, I can tell you!' he exclaimed. 'Mountain ranges with snow on them even in the summer. Freezing at one moment, baking at the next. Sheer hell when we were on the march, for the joints of our armour rusted and when the snows melted the horses skidded into the mud and had to be pulled clear, and so we wasted more time.'

'Poor beasts!' Dorothy exclaimed.

'Poor knights you should rather say!' he retorted. 'I lost two good mounts in that way and had to pay good gold for a fresh one each time. I envied the footsoldiers for they marched without the encumbrance of steel or chain mail. And yet they too had sickness, with the bowels turning to water. The Black Prince himself could not stand against that, nor against the treachery of his Gascon subjects.'

'And now he is dead,' said Ralph. 'It is a

tragedy, for he had the good of the commons at heart.'

'The commons seek to rise too high,' Godwin said moodily. 'Unless they are checked one day they will overwhelm the throne itself.'

'Too many ape their betters,' Dorothy agreed. 'But they will be loyal to the prince's son surely?'

'He is to be presented to the Lords there to be acknowledged as rightful heir to the throne,' Ralph said. 'There is to be a grand Yuletide procession.'

'I want to see it,' Maudelyn piped.

'And so you shall!,' Godwin cried before I could make answer. 'We'll make up a party and all go together. You can bring that wench of yours, young Ralph.'

Even Dorothy was agreeing that it was a good idea, and I had perforce to nod agreement too. There would be so many there that I thought it unlikely anybody would notice me, but I shrank still from the pain of seeing the duke again. Yet one day I would have to find the courage to present Maudelyn to him. I would do so, I had vowed, in order to claim some kind of recognition for my child. But I had no desire to be seen before it was time.

In the end it was decided that we

would all go. There would be stands erected outside Westminster, and Godwin, with the lavishness that seemed typical of him, offered to buy places for us all. The Greys disliked large crowds, but had agreed to allow Petrella to come. Despite myself a little spark of excited anticipation was kindled within me. I had lived so quietly, so obscurely in the cramped quarters of the shop that any change was a treat. And I felt that Maudelyn ought to be given the opportunity, even if he was not aware of it, of seeing his royal relatives.

You know, it's a strange thing but it never occurred to me then that my son was not only bastard but the son of an incestuous union, for the duke was my natural uncle, the king being my grandfather. I never thought of that then, not until very much later, and by then it really didn't seem to matter.

We set out early on the morning of the presentation, Maudelyn in front of Godwin, Petrella riding pillion behind Ralph. We had arranged to stable the horses part way and continue on foot, but within a few yards of Cheapside the crowds grew so thick that it was obvious we would make better time afoot.

'Or by river,' Godwin said. 'I was a fool not to have thought of that before. Go down to the bank and hire a boat, Ralph. I'll get someone to take the horses back and join you later. The little lad can come with me.'

Dismounted, we continued on foot, Ralph shouldering his way through the press of people. There was not too much difficulty in hiring a boat once we had agreed to pay double the normal fare. The river was usually choked with craft of all kinds and on this day there were so many that it was almost possible to jump from deck to deck without touching water. Dorothy, who distrusted boats even more than she distrusted horses, settled herself cautiously, crossing herself fervently. It was not long before Godwin, with my small son atop his shoulder, hailed us from the bank.

Before noon we were in our places in the high stands, a red carpeted space below roped and guarded. The people were milling against the barriers, calling to one another, waving small banners, shouting and cheering or mocking as the Members of the Commons arrived and went within the great stone edifice of the ancient Hall.

'The king can no longer sit his horse,' Godwin said to me. 'He will come in a litter, they say.'

And it was with Alice Perrers. My own mouth dropped open in surprise when I saw her, for I had not imagined that even she would have the impudence to appear with him in public, and yet there she was, as slant eyed and thin lipped as ever, her coif glittering with diamonds. Hissing broke out covered only by a thin layer of cheering as the king was helped down. He looked round in a bewildered fashion, stroking his long white beard. Then Alice took his arm, saying something to him, and he smiled at her, patting her hand. I remembered then how Queen Philippa had told me about Abishag who had warmed King David's bed in Biblical times, and for some reason I couldn't hate Alice any longer

'The duke is coming!' Godwin said loudly. 'The crowds hate him but they will cheer for the sake of Prince Richard and the Lady Joan.'

Unobtrusively I drew a corner of my veil across the lower part of my face and leaned forward, watching intently, a pulse in my throat beating irregularly.

He was cloaked in purple as if he thought of himself as king, and his head was bare, golden-red under the wintry sky. He ignored the crowds, turning to help the Lady Joan for whom a loyal cheer rang out vociferously. She was in widow's weeds still, her face carefully painted within its white hood.

'Is that Prince Richard?' Petrella was asking.

Her small face was flushed with pleasure and excitement, and she wrung her hands together, her voice growing shriller.

'He's a brave lad! A beautiful lad!' Dorothy cried, waving her scarf.

He was tall for his age and very slim, his features delicate as a woman's, his hair bright as his uncle's but softer and finer. He was enveloped in cloth of gold so heavy that it required four pages to lift its hem from the ground and so relieve the weight on the slight shoulders, but he held himself very proudly.

And I saw again that same face grow older, youthful prettiness becoming weakness, the golden coronet dissolving into a crown that tipped and fell.

The three of them moved slowly out of view, but the mist was still all about me and the noise of the crowd was muted.

'Are they coming out again soon?' Maudelyn asked.

'In an hour or two. Do you want to wait, or shall we go and have something to eat? They're setting tables in the inns and in the fields,' Ralph informed us.

'Indoors. It's too cold to sit in the fields,' Dorothy said.

We made our way with some difficulty from the high stand, for the procession was still winding below, and the crowds were pressing forward, snatching at the red carpet, for a piece of cloth on which a royal foot had trodden would cure many ailments.

Ralph took Maudelyn's hand and he and Godwin cleared a narrow path through which Dorothy, Petrella and I squeezed with the crowd closing in behind us. There were muttered comments about the folk who had not the manners to wait for the end of the show but must needs disturb everybody else, but there was nothing to explain the sudden feeling of terror that assailed me as we pushed our way through. Sweat broke out on the palms of my hands and on my forehead, and my mouth was so dry that it was hard to swallow.

'Do hurry or every table will be taken!' Godwin was saying.

'I want a big mug of ale!' Maudelyn was demanding, his normally quiet little voice shrill with excitement.

'You'll have a small beer and like it,' Dorothy was beginning.

Then her voice changed, rising into something like panic.

'Godwin! That noise? What is that noise?' We had all heard it at the same moment and the people around us were moving back, talking, pointing, questioning. Shouts, the thudding of hoofs across the fields, the clash of steel, I heard it as they did. The sounds grew louder, drowning the cheers from nearer the roped enclosure.

'Riot! Dear God, it's a riot!' Some woman shouted out the words and there was an immediate scramble as those who heard tried desperately to get out of the way of whatever was coming.

' 'Prentices! 'Prentices!' The cry was sent up, and echoed in panic as the realization spread that something had happened. I found myself struggling to keep my feet as I was pushed this way and that.

I had heard of the occasional outbreak of violence that flared up from time to time among the apprentices, but I had never experienced one, and I looked round questioningly, wondering what had caused it.

' 'Tis the duke!' a man said loudly. 'He has moved the Staple for his own enrichment, and the apprentices are demonstrating against it.'

'But this is a public occasion,' I heard myself mutter foolishly.

'They are trying to present a petition to the king,' someone said, 'but the duke will not have it so.'

The shouts were growing louder and men on horseback were pushing their way into the centre of the crowd, laying about them with the flats of their swords. They wore the duke's livery. That much I saw and then I was carried along, despite myself, as the crowds broke rank, and began to run aimlessly trying to escape into the narrow streets that radiated out of the square. I was running with them, filled with the same unreasoning panic. I caught a glimpse of Ralph, with Maudelyn on his shoulder, and then their heads bobbed from view again as the crowds swept back, trapped between the duke's men and a mob of leather aproned apprentices armed with swords and cudgels.

I was running with the rest, screaming with the rest, my coif half torn off, my veil lost, my skirt dragging over the cobbles. I had lost sight of the others, but there was neither time nor space to seek them. A kind of madness had possessed the crowd. It seemed to me, in this blurred, disorderly scene, that many had seized the opportunity to settle private quarrels. I saw two men flailing at each other with their fists, and a woman belabouring a cowering man with a saucepan. I still can't understand what anyone was doing in that crowd with a saucepan. It made no sense then and it makes none now. But it stayed in my mind.

The shouts were growing fainter. I paused, my hand to the stabbing pain in my side, and leaned against the wall. I could distinguish shouts and individual, running footsteps. The violence was fading, growing in another direction as if the mob had found a new focus for its anger.

I was near to the river and I suppose the sensible thing to do would have been to hire a boat and go home, but in such moments we are not always sensible. I had lost sight of the others completely and could only pray they had not been trampled in the rush of fleeing spectators.

The noise was growing louder and I flattened myself against the wall as the apprentices streamed past, some carrying the banners of their Guilds. A few were mounted, but most of them ran on foot, their faces set and stern. I had no way of knowing how far the rioting had spread or if it involved anything more serious than a few broken heads. I had known there was discontent in the city but I had not guessed it would flare up into violence on such an occasion as the presentation of the heir to the Commons.

It seemed that everywhere I looked were

groups of struggling, fighting men. I hurried as best I could, stopping from time to time to call Ralph's or Dorothy's name, but nobody took the slightest notice of me.

A man was haranguing the crowd at a corner of a square and I stopped, drawn by the rough, deep, passionate voice.

'The king is old and leans upon his jewelled whore, and Prince Richard is but a lad. Where then shall we turn for help? The duke is a hard man, lining his own pockets, with a mistress of his own to keep. Shall we turn to God then? Will God bring back the Staple and help us to set fair prices? Not so, for the Church forgets that Christ was an apprentice too.'

I had never thought of that but the idea fascinated me, though I could not connect it with the events that were making the streets ugly. I suppose I had always regarded injustice as a fact of life and cared little for the wider issues involved. Now, for the first time, I wondered uneasily what would happen if ordinary, decent people rose up to agitate for justice and increased profits and an end to the strict monopolies on trade held by the Crown and the great nobles.

The ceremony was over. The old king and Alice had evidently been hustled away, for when I came to the roped space I found the ropes cut and the carpet hacked to pieces. This was customary but the fighting, brawling mass of men at arms and apprentices was not. There would be windows broken and looting before the end of the day. An archer in the Lancaster colours was running towards me, swerving as he came. I caught at his sleeve, calling above the noise, 'What of the duke?'

'Ridden to Kennington with the Lady Joan. The riot is spreading!' He shook himself free and ran on again.

'Spreading where?'

'Everywhere. The 'prentices are on the march,' a woman said. She was a plump female with a pocked complexion who looked stimulated rather than afraid.

The stands were being torn down, though whether for fuel or to provide weapons I couldn't tell. I was cold and hungry and more than a little afraid, for I had not yet seen mob violence, and I feared more for the duke than for myself. I knew that he had never troubled to court popular approval but rode proudly, ignoring the opinion of the Commons. If he had gone with the Lady Joan however he had probably been unworried by the riot, or perhaps he had been more concerned about her safety than the possibility of danger for himself.

'Are you hurt, mistress?' A man in a smock marked with the Fishmonger's Sign paused to ask the question.

I suppose, with my dishevelled gown, I must have looked like some victim of the rougher elements in the crowd.

'I was separated from my family in the excitement,' I told him, trying to straighten my coif.

'They'll likely be home now. Where do you live?'

'Cheapside.'

'Then you'd do best to make your way there, but avoid the main road. They'll be crammed and the taverns are already packed. The boats are all taken or I'd advise that. This will all come to nothing, I promise you.'

He touched his forelock and hurried on, whether to join his fellow 'prentices or to return to his own home I don't know.

That long walk was a nightmare. Every street seemed to be filled with struggling, running people. Not all of them were apprentices either, I'll swear. There were soldiers who yelled that they hadn't been paid for nigh on six months, women whose painted cheeks and curled bare heads proclaimed their trade, even a few clerics with their gowns tucked up and the light, not of prayer but of battle, in their eyes.

I passed groups of rioters quarrelling over goods pulled out of broken shop windows, and in every tavern men, some of them in royal livery, staggered out, catching at my cloak, spilling ale and laughing. I hated the city then and all the people in it. I hated the way a pleasant occasion could turn in an instant to quarrelling, and I hated myself for having been fool enough to agree to go in the first place.

I was relieved, as I came into Cheapside, to find the street comparatively deserted with the shutters up in every building. Dorothy, who was looking down from the upper window, waved her hand and hurried to draw the bolts.

'Maudelyn is safe with me,' she gasped out, pulling me within. 'Ralph went over to the Greys to see if Petrella made her way home. We lost her in the crowd. Godwin is out searching too. I have been fretted out of my mind!'

'Where's Jem?' I asked, referring to the apprentice.

'Not back yet. I've no doubt he's run mad with the rest.'

'They are protesting against the removal of the Staple and Court monopolies,' I said.

'And rioting is no way to go about it,'

Dorothy said crossly. 'Breaking windows and stealing and frightening innocent folk to death! That won't please the duke very much. Come upstairs and we'll have a bite to eat. No sense in starving because the rest of the world has gone clean off its head!'

Maudelyn greeted us at the top of the stairs. 'If I'd had my dagger I'd have killed them all,' he said, receiving my embrace with childish indifference.

'It was no place for a little boy,' I said absently.

'Prince Richard was there,' Maudelyn argued.

'Because he is to be king,' Dorothy said. 'Did you not think him a beautiful boy, Gida?'

'Beautiful,' I said, and thought again of the falling crown.

'And the Lady Joan wears well,' She carefully did not mention the duke.

We ate a hurried meal punctuated by the complaints of Maudelyn who had hoped to eat in a tavern. The little maidservant — I cannot remember her name, but then I don't recall Dorothy ever calling her anything but 'wench' — was in such a state of nerves that Dorothy ordered her to go and lie down and washed the dishes herself.

Halfway through the afternoon Ralph

arrived, hammering for admission, his gown torn and dirt streaked.

'The duke's men took me for a rioter and the 'prentices tried to get me to join them, so I was caught between the two, has Godwin come back? The Greys have not seen Petrella, but Master Grey set off at once. Mistress Grey is having hysterics. No, I'll just have a slice of pie. Dorothy. I must go out again directly.'

'To run like a chicken without its head? You'd do better to call the Watch and have her cried through the streets,' I interrupted.

'The city is packed with citizens trying to get back to their homes. It would be hopeless to find the Watch. They were setting barricades when I got back, to try to split up the rioters so that the duke's men could ride among them more easily. Every Guild seems to be joining in, and there will be real danger if the trouble spreads across the river. The duke's palace of the Savoy might be attacked.'

He was eating as he spoke, swilling the pie down with ale.

'Petrella will come to no harm,' I said. 'I found my own way without harm.'

'You're accustomed to riding about the city alone,' Ralph said. 'Petrella has always been carefully guarded, and she is scarce sixteen. The world is full of rogues.'

He spoke like an elderly man though he was only a year older than Petrella himself, and I could not help smiling to myself at his gravity, though I too was anxious for the girl.

He went out again almost at once and we settled to wait. I would have gone out myself but no woman would be safe on the streets now for the riot would, in all probability, have degenerated into a series of private battles, drunken rapes and unorganised vandalism.

And it had all begun, I thought, as a pleasant day, a royal occasion to cheer, a few moments for me in which I could watch the duke. It was spoiled now, and there was danger ahead, not now perhaps, but in the future. It was so palpable that the ends of my fingers tingled.

'Godwin is here!' Dorothy who had never moved from her vantage point by the window, called out.

I ran down to let him in, clutching at his sleeve. 'Where is Petrella? Did you find her?'

'She's safe at home. I met up with her hiding in a tavern.'

He had obviously visited a few taverns himself, for his breath stank and his face was flushed.

'And you're not hurt?'

'By a mob of fools? Not one of them would stand up against a trained band of archers or foot soldiers!'

'They wanted to present a petition.'

'To whom? The king is well nigh senile and the prince is only a child. The duke has no sympathy with agitators. The apprentices may scream all they please about their wrongs, but they are leaderless and have no hope of bettering their condition.'

'I pity them,' I admitted. 'Have you seen Ralph?'

'He was at the Greys. We met him at the door. He had been running to and fro, looking for Petrella in one place after another, but never the right one! Are you going to keep me here all night, or are you going to offer me supper?'

'Dorothy has something ready. Was Petrella hurt?'

'Frightened out of her wits, poor maid! I had to pour a couple of mugs of Burgundy into her before she would venture into the street.'

He gave me a cheerful grin and ran up the stairs, swinging Maudelyn into the air and declaring he was a brave fellow to have protected the womenfolk.

'Ralph is staying over at the Greys until

tomorrow,' Godwin was saying as I went in. 'The duke will be back by then, I'll swear, to clear the taverns of the remnants of the riot. They will have gained nothing save stricter controls.'

'I shall be glad when it is all over,' Dorothy said. 'I am too old to bear these foolish alarums and I will never grow accustomed to these new fangled notions. In my day apprentices knew their place and left the fighting to their betters.'

'The duke will put them down with a firm hand,' Godwin said. 'You know I have a mind to seek service with him, I'm my own man now that the Black Prince is gone, but I cannot sit here for ever. I'm accustomed to a life of action, not of counting profits and stacking bales of cloth.'

He sounded restless all at once, the good humour dying out of his face, his lower lip drooping as if he were still a sulky boy.

'You'll stay for the wedding? It's to be in June.'

'I'll make a point of dancing at it with you alone, Dorothy my sweet.'

'I'd be better pleased,' she said, 'to dance with you at your own, or at Gida's. 'Tis time you were both married.'

I turned abruptly and went out to the

landing. Dorothy was upset after the events of the day, but I wished she had not spoken of my marriage. I knew that I would never marry without love, and I knew I would never love any man but the duke.

I would leave Cheapside after the wedding, I decided. I would go back to Kenilworth to see Katharine Swynford and the children. Her two sons by the duke were still little lads, but his three children by the duchess would be growing up fast. And there was the child he had fathered upon his Spanish wife. Surely, in all that brood, there would be room for Maudelyn.

I risked going downstairs and into the garden, for the night air was cool and fresh, and the sounds of riot had died.

In the garden I went to the pear tree and leaned my head against its trunk. At this season it bore neither blossom nor fruit, but was as bare as the years that stretched ahead of me. I was nearly twenty-five years old and I could not think of one man who loved me as I had imagined love could be. Even Cullen Beaumont had not seen fit to leave his manor and come in search of me.

I wanted to cry, but if I did, Godwin and Dorothy would notice. So I patted the dark trunk of the tree and bit my lip hard to give myself an excuse for the tears in my eyes.

And then I went back indoors again to put my bastard son to bed.

11

Ralph and Petrella were to be married in June, a concession to the eagerness of the younglings for Petrella was scarce sixteen and her parents had hoped to keep her with them for a year or two longer. But Ralph was, they agreed, a pleasant, steady youth and marriage would prevent him from even beginning to sow those wild oats upon which the older generation speculated with great disapproval.

Dorothy threw herself into the preparations with as much enthusiasm as if Petrella had been her own daughter. Mistress Grey seemed happy to leave the arrangements to her, and long hours were spent discussing the colours of the bride's gown and the prettiest flowers for her wreath.

'A very pale green, my dear, with a hip girdle of darker green and gold and a wreath of white rosebuds would suit your dark hair beautifully.'

'As you please, Mistress Dorothy,' Petrella said docilely.

'Not as I please, but as you desire,' Dorothy said. 'This is your wedding, not mine.'

'I have no preference,' the girl said, in a tone of such despondency that I looked at her sharply.

She was paler than usual and there were dark rings under her eyes.

'Are you feeling well?' I asked.

'She is nervous,' Dorothy consoled. 'Wenches are often terrified before they marry. I was myself. But you have no cause, Petrella. Ralph is young and as deep in love with you as you are with him.'

'You do love Ralph, don't you?' I asked suddenly.

'Of course she loves him! What a question!' Dorothy scolded.

'I always have,' Petrella said gently. She sounded sincere, but her brown eyes slid away from us and her hands plucked nervously at her skirt.

I found myself wishing that the marriage was safely over. I had made up my mind to return to Kenilworth as soon as the wedding had been performed. Katharine Swynford had borne a third son, and the duke had acknowledged all her children as his own, no longer troubling to hide the fact that she was his mistress.

The riots were over, the apprentices dispersed, and the city was in the grip of the duke's men, a fact for which most merchants were grateful.

'We cannot have sedition,' Master Grey said. 'Trade cannot prosper where the servants seek to instruct the masters. And it sets an ill example to the lower classes. Soon we will have the peasants demanding privileges.'

'Not so. The peasants have no man to speak for them,' Godwin declared. 'They have not the wit to organize themselves.'

'I am sorry for them,' Ralph said. 'They have many grievances and few rights at all.'

'You speak foolishly,' Master Grey said, frowning slightly. 'But you're still very young indeed. You'll come to wisdom through maturity.'

'The King cannot last many more months,' Godwin said. 'The tale goes that Alice Perrers sticks close to his side, gathering every jewel that she can lay her hands on. The duke has supported her, but he cannot continue to do so after his nephew comes to the throne.'

'Such a beautiful child, but he will have no power,' Dorothy said sadly.

'Is it possible that the duke might seek to depose his nephew and take the throne for himself?' Ralph asked.

'The duke is completely loyal and would entertain no such idea!' I exclaimed.

'Why should he, when he has all the power already?' Godwin said cynically.

I opened my mouth to protest and closed it again. There was no profit in arguing, or in stating my own convictions too fervently.

When the marriage was over I would simply return quietly to Warwickshire. And I would present Maudelyn to the duke. I like to think now that it was because I longed for some recognition for my son, but if I am to be honest I must admit that I did feel a very personal hurt at my guardian's complete neglect of me. He had used me and thrown me aside, and though I did not resent it nor love him the less, part of me did whisper, 'Let him know that every action has its effect. Shame him, just a little, and reveal to him the existence of yet another son.'

Godwin would not be remaining for the wedding. He was bored and restless after his months of inactivity, chafing against the restrictions of the quiet domestic life we led.

'I had meant to seek service with the duke, but I may chance my sword arm abroad for a time,' he said cheerfully. 'I intend to make my fortune, you know.'

'You'd better make it swiftly then,' I said tartly, 'lest you grow too old to enjoy it.'

'Well phrased, my spinster twin.' He gave

me a displeased grin. 'When I grow rich shall I buy you a husband?'

'Gida never had any call to the married state,' Dorothy said loyally.

'Despite — ?' He raised his eyebrows and nodded in Maudelyn's direction.

'That's my private business.'

'As is my own life. Remember that, sister dear!' He softened his words with a hug, but watching him swagger through the door I was forced to admit to myself, that had he not been my brother, I would not have liked him very much.

His manner of leaving was typically casual. He came downstairs one morning, kissed Dorothy, pressed a leather bag into my hands, clapped Ralph on his shoulder, tweaked Maudelyn's fair hair and was gone, riding down the narrow street with his feathered hat pushed to the back of his head and his cloak splashing turquoise over the saddle.

'I am going to move my things up into the attic,' Dorothy announced. 'Ralph and Petrella will be more comfortable in the main room. I think we will clean and freshen the chamber.'

'I'll move my own things too,' I offered. 'It will only be for a month or two, then you'll have it to yourself.'

'Until the babes start arriving.'

She looked pleased at the prospect though she was all of sixty and cannot have relished the idea of nights broken by the crying of an infant. 'But you don't have to leave, Gida. This is your home now.'

'Dorothy, I love you!' I put my arms about her ample frame and kissed the tip of her nose. 'I'm going over to see Master Benacre and Rebecca. Is there anything you want?'

'Nothing, unless they're giving it free. I wish you didn't go so often to Lombard Street. I've heard rumours from Mistress Grey that since the riots there has been suspicion directed against the Jews.'

'But they had nothing to do with it,' I said.

'They lend money at interest, and that is forbidden by the Church.'

'Joseph Benacre carves wood and his daughter keeps house. They attend Mass regularly, and they neither borrow nor lend.'

'I was only asking you to be discreet,' Dorothy complained.

'I'm always discreet,' I said wryly, and went to saddle Silver.

It was a blustery afternoon and a salt breeze blew in from the river. Spring was in the air, and I felt the restlessness that always troubled me round about the Vernal

Equinox. The city was at its best, the cold winter past and fly-bloated summer still to come. The windows and doors stood open, and housewifes were engaged in clearing out piles of grubby rushes and beating the year's dust out of their tapestries.

The Benacres were at home, for Rebecca seldom went far save to buy necessities. As far as I could judge they ate mainly fish and cheese, Joseph Benacre having remarked, 'I cannot get used to eating non-Kosher meat, Mistress Gida. So I avoid beef whenever possible, and I still cannot bring myself to eat bacon, though Rebecca and I were baptised so long ago that it seems quite natural to go to Mass like a good Christian.' Rebecca opened the door to me and from the expression on her face I knew that something had happened.

'Is your father sick?,' I asked in alarm.

'No, no. He is well enough. Come in, Mistress Gida. My father is in the back yard, but we do have another visitor.'

I had glimpsed her already and exclaimed, cutting Rebecca short, 'Petrella! What are you doing here?'

'She came in great trouble of mind,' Rebecca said.

'But I had no idea she knew where you lived,' I said.

'I heard you telling Dorothy once,' Petrella said. She had been crying and spoke thickly, dabbing at her eyelids with the ends of her sleeve. 'I found myself near and it seemed like a sign.'

'A sign of what? Petrella, what in the world has happened?'

For answer she put her face in her hands and burst into a fresh storm of weeping.

'Mistress Gida! I am happy to see you!' Joseph Benacre, his voice full of lively relief, hurried in, a pile of freshly cut logs in his arms. He let them fall into the hearth, and greeted me with an outstretched hand. 'I was on the point of sending to you, for this is sorry business.'

'I have not told Mistress Gida yet. She is only just come,' Rebecca said.

'I know nothing,' I said. 'I have no idea what Petrella is doing here.'

'She is with child,' said Rebecca.

'With child?' I gaped foolishly. 'Petrella, are you sure?'

'Three months gone,' she sobbed, raising her head briefly, then lowering it again.

'She came here because she believed that we being Jews, would not scruple to help her to get rid of it,' Joseph Benacre said.

'But I never gave her any such impression,' I said.

'I thought Jews knew about such things,' Petrella said.

'Master Benacre and Mistress Rebecca are Christian converts, but they would not have done such a thing even before that,' I said crossly.

'I had nowhere else to go,' Petrella said.

'Silly wench! You must go to Ralph and tell him at once. The wedding can be brought forward.'

'You don't understand!' The girl's voice rose into a wail. 'Ralph is not the father. It was Godwin, your brother, Godwin!'

'Oh, no, no,' I sat down heavily on a stool and shook my head to and fro.

It was the day of the riot, the day we went to see the prince presented to the Commons,' Petrella said. 'I was lost in the crowd, and I was so frightened with people running up and down shouting! I went into a tavern and hid there, and much later Godwin found me. He said the streets were still unsafe and it would be wiser to rest for a while before we set off home again. He gave the innkeeper some coins and we went up to a room. I was crying, and I was so pleased to see him, so grateful — ' She broke down again.

'Women were always frail,' Master Benacre said gloomily.

'Godwin must marry you,' I said. 'He must

be told of what has occurred and be made to marry you.'

'He knows,' Petrella said. 'When I was sure I told him. He said he was pleased, he said that it would be better to marry quietly, so that it could not be undone when we confessed it. He promised to take me with him to France. When he left a week since he was going to obtain passage for us and a licence to wed. It was arranged for us to meet, and I slipped out of the house at noon and went to the Nag's Head. The landlord said there was a message for me. A letter, he said.

She was holding it out to me and I took it, the few words leaping up.

'Dear Mistress Petrella,
My hearty regrets but I fear that marriage is not a state into which I have the inclination to enter. I pray you to think of me kindly and remember your obedient servant,

Godwin Falcon.'

'If women are weak-willed,' Rebecca said, 'then men are brutal.'

'My own brother.' I read the note again, anger was rising in me as I pictured how the girl must have felt upon reading it, of her pitiful shock when she realised he had gone.

'I didn't know what to do,' Petrella said. 'I walked and then I saw I was in Lombard Street and I remembered something you had once said about the Benacres living near and I thought — I was so frantic, so full of despair.'

'It was very wrong of you to seek help of that kind,' I said. 'I had a child out of wedlock, and I have found great happiness in his company.'

'You are different, Mistress Gida,' Joseph said. 'You were always strong I think, able to take care of yourself. Mistress Petrella is a child.'

'You must tell Ralph,' I said. 'You must beg his forgiveness and ask him to accept the child as his own. Ralph is a good lad, a kind lad, and he loves you.'

'I cannot.' She quailed, her mouth shaking. 'I cannot face him. Cannot you tell him, Gida? Cannot you please tell him?'

'It is your burden,' Joseph said sternly.

'She has not the nature to bear it,' I said.

'Then you will tell him?' She rose and came over, kneeling at my side, her hands clutching at mine, 'Please, Gida. Tell him that I was forced, that I love him truly, that

281

I would never offend again!'

'I'll do what I can,' I said wearily. 'We'd best go home now, before your parents miss you. Master Benacre, I must apologise. Petrella was overwrought else she would never have come here.'

'You and she are both welcome,' Joseph said, 'but these are troubled times. Rebecca and I live in the midst of suspicion. There is so much unrest in the city. We are thinking of leaving, of finding somewhere quiet to live. I have a little money saved, and it might be possible to buy some land.'

'But we will see you before we make our final decision,' Rebecca said in her gentle manner.

I hoisted Petrella up to the saddle and led Silver back to Cheapside. I was angry with her for her foolishness, and sick at heart when I thought of Godwin who had come back after so long and disrupted our lives so cruelly.

'If I tell Ralph,' I said, 'it may be possible to hide part of the truth from your parents. Not for your sake but for the child. Ralph may agree to accept blame for anticipating your wedding. That is a very little sin, and it is unlikely the Church will demand a fine as you are both officially plighted.'

'I can get down here,' she interrupted. 'My

lady mother is always resting at this hour and my father will be out. I'll go to my room and say that I have a headache.'

'You do still wish to marry Ralph?' I asked in sudden anxiety. 'You were ready to go to Godwin only today.'

'I have to be married,' she said with childlike logic. 'I wanted to marry Godwin, but he lied to me. I see that now. Ralph is good and kind, and I've always known I would marry him one day.'

It struck me as I helped her down that Ralph would be getting a very silly wife, but Petrella was young and frightened and I could not expect a spoiled, cossetted child to behave with courage in such a situation.

'I will tell Ralph at once,' I said. 'You may expect him to call round later this evening.'

'I'm very grateful, Gida,' she said, and sped away.

I went on more slowly, forgetting the beauty of the spring, thinking only of my brother's dishonour. He had not even the excuse of ignorance to explain his departure.

Ralph was in the store room at the back, marking off a bale of cloth. He looked up as I came in, his face pleased.

'You're in time to tell me if this cloth will make a good cloak for the wedding,' he said.

'For yourself?' I fingered it absently.

'I thought it might be too warm for June, but the weave is fine.'

'Never mind the cloth now. Come into the garden, Ralph. I have something to tell you.'

'Is anything wrong?' He straightened up and looked at me in puzzlement.

'Come into the garden,' I said, 'I want to talk privately to you.'

He opened the door and I went into the long, narrow plot where the herb beds scented the air, and the pear tree waved its blossoms in the wind.

'What is it? Is anything wrong?' he repeated. I sat down on the bench and looked up at him. I could vaguely recall his father who had borne the same name and had been like him in feature. I could recall my mother saying that Ralph had been a soldier of fortune once, and had given it up and settled into business as a married man. Ralph had been bred for the same quiet, domestic life. Now I was about to shatter it and I hated the task more than anything I had yet done.

'Ralph, it's Petrella,' I said at last.

'Is she sick?'

'No, no. She's quite well. I was with her just now, and she was quite well.'

'Then what is it? What ails you?'

'She is with child,' I said, deciding on bluntness.

'That's not possible,' he said quickly and blankly. 'I have never touched her in that way.'

'Not you. It was Godwin. On the day of the riot when she was lost, Godwin found her and forced her. Petrella has been out of her mind with guilt and fear.'

'Forced her?'

'Aye, in the tavern where she was hiding.'

His face had altered. Looking at him I knew how he would look when he was old.

'Was there no landlord there? Could she not have cried out?' he asked slowly.

'Perhaps she was afraid,' I said.

'I met them at her house when he was bringing her back,' Ralph said. 'She was distressed, by the riot, but if she had been forced, she could not have kept such a matter to herself. She was a willing partner.'

'Perhaps she was seduced,' I said. 'Does it matter what happened exactly? She loves you, Ralph, and she needs your help.'

'She needs a father for her child.'

'That too, but she needs a husband more. If you have any affection for her — '

'I'll take no man's leavings,' he interrupted.

'Petrella is young and in great trouble,' I

persisted, 'She will be a good and loving wife to you, Ralph. I would guarantee it.'

'I need no guarantees from such as you,' he said tightly. 'You had a bastard for yourself, so I assume you take these matters lightly — as does your brother. I was not reared to wink at immorality.'

'Ralph wait!' I had risen but he flung away, scowling and banged the door on his way through to the front of the shop.

'What's going on? 'Tis not like Ralph to lose his temper.' As I entered the house Dorothy came to the head of the stairs.

'It is bad news,' I said frankly, going to meet her.

'Why, what's caused such a stir?' she asked.

I ushered her into the parlour and closed the door.

'You'd best prepare yourself for a shock,' I began, but she interrupted, her plump face flushing.

'What's amiss? I'm no child to be fobbed off with pretty tales.'

'Then I'll not give you any. Petrella is with child by Godwin and Ralph is angry, very angry.'

'Dear God!' She sat down heavily and stared at me.

'It's a bad business,' I agreed, 'but if Ralph

will accept the babe as his own then good may yet come. If he allows himself to cool down he may soon come to a better view of the matter.'

'Ralph is obstinate,' Dorothy said. 'He can be most stubborn. And he is very proud, though you might not think it. I can see no happy outcome.'

'Godwin knew about the child. That's why he went to France in such haste.'

'He learned bad ways in Gascony,' she said. 'Ralph will never forgive him for that.'

'I will never forgive him myself,' I said grimly. 'But Petrella is the one to be considered now, she and the babe. If Ralph will agree to be known as the father of the babe, then she will spend the rest of her life making it up to him.'

'It's for Ralph to say.' She put her chin in her hand and sighed.

'Ralph went out in such a rush,' I said, 'that I cannot believe him capable of reasoned argument.'

'Then we must wait for him to come back.'

'I wish Godwin had never come back,' I said. 'He brought nothing but trouble, as I brought trouble when I came here to have my bastard and left you with the care of him.'

'I was pleased to have you come and

delighted that you trusted me with Maudelyn,' she said firmly. 'You must not think for one moment that I set your circumstances against Petrella's.'

'I was more foolish,' I said. 'I knew that my lover would never marry me, but it meant nothing. I don't believe the thought even crossed my mind. I am so sorry for Petrella, so angry with Godwin!'

'We can only wait,' Dorothy said, folding her hands together. 'I'm old enough to know that troubles never last for ever. I know that.'

'But while they're upon us they're heavy enough in all conscience,' I said gloomily. 'Dorothy, whatever happens now you must see that I cannot remain here. I will go back to Kenilworth with Maudelyn at once.'

'You have no escort.'

'Then I'll hire one,' I said impatiently. 'Ralph will not endure my presence here for I would only remind him of Godwin. It's best for me to leave.'

'At least wait and see what has been decided,' she begged.

'I cannot wait here. I'll go over to the Greys.'

'You'd do better to stay here,' she said, as firmly as if I were a child. 'Ralph will do better without you there. If he does cool down, there's no reason why the Greys need ever know the two fathers of the child.'

'We'll wait then,' I said briefly, and took up my sewing.

The day dragged on. I found it impossible to concentrate on the tunic I was making for Maudelyn, and Maudelyn himself was in a teasing, complaining mood. It was with a mixture of relief and dread that I heard Ralph's step below.

Dorothy was on her feet at once, her voice anxious. 'Ralph, Gida told me. Have you and Petrella — ?'

'I'll not have her name spoken,' he interrupted. 'It's over between us, finished.'

'Did you go to her parents?'

'I told them how she had deceived me. There will be no wedding.'

'But what of Petrella?' I asked.

'She no longer exists,' he said.

'I had not thought you so unforgiving!' I exclaimed. 'Surely you can forget one mistake!'

'Not when a child will be born to remind me of that mistake.'

'You're very young.'

'But old enough to refuse to be a cuckold,' he returned. 'Now we'll not talk of it again. Dorothy, will you start supper?'

'Ralph, you must see reason,' I ventured.

'I see truth,' he said. 'I see my betrothed turned harlot and the man I welcomed as my friend her seducer. And I see you, Mistress Gida, living here shamelessly with your own bastard!'

'Not for much longer.' In the face of his unyielding attitude my own temper rose. 'I am riding back to Kenilworth tomorrow and taking Maudelyn with me, so you'll not be troubled by my presence.'

He said nothing but hunched himself over the fire, his face averted.

'You'll not leave so soon,' Dorothy began, but I hushed her and went upstairs.

My packing was soon done for I was not one to accumulate possessions. The leather bag Godwin had pressed upon me at his going had contained a hundred gold sovereigns. I wondered now if that had been a gesture to his conscience. Maudelyn hung around me, not asking questions as I had anticipated, but watching me as I packed. He must have sensed that there was trouble as a child does sense such things, and he kept silent but I saw his green eyes flicker from me to Dorothy and back again.

Ralph had gone out again when I went downstairs and I ate a solitary supper. Dorothy and I said very little, partly because Maudelyn was still there, partly because there was nothing to be said that could alter the situation. Godwin had come back and his dishonour stained us all.

I retired early, slept fitfully, and rose at dawn. Rather to my surprise Ralph was in the parlour when Maudelyn and I came in. His voice was apologetic but there was no yielding in his face.

'I spoke harshly to you, and I'm sorry for that because I know you to be a good woman and I have an affection for Maudelyn, but I cannot alter my mind. I will neither see her nor marry her nor speak of her. She deceived me and it is over.'

'And Godwin?'

'I have sworn to kill him if I ever see him again,' he said.

'Then I pray he stays in France!' Dorothy said tearfully. 'I pray it fervently.'

'I am going to bid farewell to the Benacres,' I said. 'I can hire escort there. You will take good care of yourself won't you?'

'You also, my dear.' She put her arms about me and kissed me, and then I took Maudelyn by the hand, and went downstairs to where the horses waited with Jem at their heads. I gave him a coin and mounted, lifting Maudelyn in front of me.

At the Benacre house I knocked softly, prepared to go away again if nobody answered, but the door was opened at once and Rebecca beckoned us within.

'Mistress Petrella is here again,' she said. 'What!' I stared at her in consternation.

'I had to come,' Petrella said. 'Oh, Gida, my parents are so angry! They say I have disgraced them for ever and no man will want to marry me now! Ralph went to them and told them that Godwin and I had deceived him, and they would not even listen to my side of the tale. My father says I am to be put in a convent and when the babe is born it's to be taken away from me. He locked me in my room but I climbed out of the window, and I didn't know where to go so I came here. I shall die if they put me in a convent. I know I shall die.'

'I came to bid you and your father farewell,' I said to Rebecca. 'It seems that some men are brutal and others unforgiving. Ralph will not stomach a Falcon in his house now.'

'He has been greatly wronged,' Joseph Benacre said sternly, 'but this girl is no more to blame than a rabbit caught in the gleam of a snake's regard. Certainly she will be no asset to the religious life.'

'And a mother should be with her child,' Rebecca said. 'The poor babe has done nothing.'

'I could go into Sanctuary,' Petrella said,

looking from one to the other of us in a hopeful manner.

'To live with murderers and thieves? Then you would certainly turn harlot if you were not murdered for your silliness first!' I said.

'I won't go into a convent,' she said wildly. 'I'll throw myself in the river first.'

'Hush, let me think.' I bit my lip aware of Maudelyn's inquisitive little face.

'She can come with us,' he piped. 'Petrella can come with us.'

'To Kenilworth? The duke would find out eventually and send her packing to her parents. He's scandal enough of his own to worry about.'

'Must you go to Kenilworth?' Joseph Benacre asked. 'You told me once about the place in Kent where you were born.'

'The castle at Marie Regina. Lady Joan leases it from the monks.'

'Cannot you go there for a while? I cannot think that the Greys would seek their daughter there.'

'To Marie Regina? But the abbot would find out about — ' I broke off, glancing at Maudelyn.

'Would that be so terrible?' he questioned. 'He has no legal jurisdiction over you, and you have nothing to lose but his good opinion.'

'It is more than ten years since I went home,' I said slowly.

'You think of it as home?'

'My roots are there,' I said. 'My mother was born and reared there as was her mother before that. It's a quiet place with the river running through it and the castle.'

'Who lives there now?' Joseph asked.

'Why, nobody save a few retainers, I suppose. The Lady Joan no longer goes there, but I have leave to visit the place whenever I choose.'

'Then we will come with you,' he said. I was so startled that I gaped at him wordlessly, but Rebecca's quiet face glowed.

'Would it be permitted?' she asked eagerly. 'Would we be safe there?'

'Safer than in the city where we are constantly under suspicion,' he said calmly. 'And Mistress Gida cannot travel without escort.'

That was true but I had not envisaged the escort to be an elderly woodcarver and his spinster daughter.

'Could we make ready in time?' Rebecca asked.

'I have no attachments, physical or mental, in this place,' he said. 'We would need to purchase two extra horses, no, three, for the journey. I can do that myself this morning.'

'I can pack what we need,' Rebecca said. 'I am so tired of the city, father. There is no room to breathe, and we have no friends.'

'There would be little work for you in Marie Regina,' I said wearily.

'I have sufficient saved to pay our way,' Joseph said. 'And both Rebecca and I will be willing to make ourselves useful.'

'We could work the Rit — you know.' Rebecca nodded her head meaningly.

I think that settled the matter for me. To visit that great, underground chamber and see the archangels glow into life as the ancient words ascended into the echoing incense filled me with a quivering joy.

'What is to become of me?' Petrella wailed.

It's strange, but I had almost forgotten about her plight. Now she stood, her face tear-streaked, and gazing at us imploringly.

'How soon will your parents miss you?' I asked.

'Not until this evening. My father said I was to be left alone to think about my sins.'

'Then we must be out of the city by then. Master Benacre, can you truly be ready so quickly?'

'By midmorning.' He hesitated for a moment, then said, 'You know it is not my usual habit to help foolish young maids to defy their parents. Honour is due to one's father and mother even when they act unjustly. But to force a girl into a convent is a very great sin. I could not, in conscience, stand by and allow such a thing to happen.'

'I will wait until the babe is born and then find out from Dorothy if their anger has cooled,' I said. 'It may be possible to arrange a reconciliation.'

'I never want to see them again,' Petrella said sulkily. 'I want to go away and never come back.'

'Then sit down and be quiet,' I said with scant sympathy. 'I'll help you, Rebecca.'

'We have little to take,' she said tranquilly. 'My father and I will simply lock up and ride away. We have no roots.'

There was a sad acceptance in her voice that moved me more than Petrella's tears. There was even a sneaking respect in me for Godwin who had refused to be trapped into marriage with a fool.

'We cannot ride openly through the streets!' Rebecca, in the midst of folding linen, looked at me in concern. 'Someone may recognise Mistress Petrella and then her parents would have every right to claim her back.'

'We can wait until dusk or go hooded in pilgrim garb. Then we'd be safe enough.'

'I want to get away,' Petrella said, starting to cry again.

I was becoming more and more impatient with her. I think now that in a sense I was angry because her behaviour reminded me of my own when I had yielded to the duke. Yet surely I had never been so foolish, so clinging!

'Are we really going to Marie Regina?' Maudelyn asked, tugging at my skirt.

'Yes, yes, we're all going there.'

'Will we see my father there?' he asked.

'Your father? Why what put that idea into your head?' I demanded.

It was the first time I could ever remember his mentioning a father or questioning me.

'Will my father be at Marie Regina?' he persisted.

'No. No, I don't expect so. Do get from under my feet.'

I wondered, hearing the snap in my voice, if from now on I could expect nothing but curiosity about his beginnings, and how long it would be before I was forced to answer.

12

We rode into Marie Regina in mid-afternoon, and I pointed to the monastery crowned tor with a feeling of pride as if I had created the place myself.

'I used to have my lessons there, and I helped in the infirmary and watched the scribe illuminate the manuscripts. All the land hereabouts belongs to the Order. The lay brothers work in the fields and keep the cattle. The Abbot is a strict and narrow man, but a just one.'

'Is that the river?' Rebecca demanded.

'Aye, and in full flood!' I laughed to see the spray dashing against the supports of the bridge. 'In the summer it is lazy and calm, but at this end of the year it rushes past. My mother's hut used to be among the trees on the other bank. She lived at the castle after she was wed but she used to go down to the hut sometimes. I went with her and she would pick the plants and show me which ones were good for eating. The castle is three miles further on. I hope someone there will remember me.'

I had no letter of admittance but we were a

respectable, though travel-grimed little party, and I saw few difficulties in our settling in.

'Is it a big castle? Is it as big as the king's castle?' Maudelyn demanded.

'No more than a fortified hunting lodge,' I said. 'The Lady Joan's father leased the land in the beginning. Look, you can see the top of the main tower just above the trees!'

I was as excited as any child and I saw Joseph Benacre smile into his beard, but it was a fine thing to return though I knew, deep beneath my pleasure, that I had put off the garments of childhood long before.

The oaks arched over us as we left the road and approached the gate. It was open and unguarded, the courtyard deserted, and when I raised my voice to shout a lad in a grubby smock lounged out of the door and stared at us.

'Is there nobody at home?' I dismounted and frowned at him.

'There's Bessie and Alfie and me,' he voluntered.

'Who might you be?' I demanded.

'I'm Edward,' he informed me.

'But surely there are others here! Where is the guard?'

'Dunno.' He lifted thin shoulders.

'I am Mistress Falcon,' I said. 'Mistress Gida Falcon. I am come back to live here.

You are to feed and stable these horses. Have you feed?'

'I reckon I could find some,' he said indifferently.

'Then do so. And see you rub them down thoroughly or I'll have the skin off your back!'

It was not often I spoke so roughly to a servant, but I was tired and the pleasure of my return was souring into disappointment. I went with the others into the great hall and stood, staring in consternation, at the matted straw, the hearth with its piled ashes, the table and benches foul with mouse droppings.

'Bessie!' Remembering the name the lad had given me I called it loudly as I strode through to the kitchen. Dorothy had always kept it spotless, but now it was in chaos with pans and copper green with rust and a slatternly looking woman drinking ale at the unscrubbed table.

'Was someone calling?' she asked.

'I was. Stand up when I speak to you. Is there nobody else here?'

'Alfie's out back,' she said, jerking her head.

'Bring him in, and sober up! This place is going to be cleaned from top to bottom by nightfall. I am Mistress Gida Falcon, here on the authority of the Lady Joan. We'll require supper too, but not on those dishes.'

'It's a fine castle,' Rebecca said in her tranquil manner. 'I can help, you know, to get everything straight and neat. What other rooms are there?'

'Two in the tower, and the women's chamber next to the kitchen. I am sorry to bring you to all this, but I truly thought it would be as it used to be.'

'It will be again, mistress.'

Joseph Benacre had joined us, and his voice was calm too as if it were quite a usual thing for him to arrive at a place gone to rack and ruin.

'Petrella must rest,' I said, thinking rapidly. 'She'd best have the tower room and I'll take the one above with you, Rebecca. No, it's better for your father to have that room, then we can take the women's quarters.'

'Petrella will sleep with me, and you, being mistress, will take the tower room,' Rebecca said as firmly as Dorothy could have spoken.

Mistress. I mouthed the word in my mind. It could mean so many things. Wife, lover, head of the household. Well, at least I could be head of the household, I thought wryly, for nobody else seemed to have any interest in the place.

But it was a disappointing homecoming, and I wished it could have been different. I wished my mother had been alive and happy instead of so often forlorn as I remembered her. I wished that I had never gone away or that Godwin had never come back. I wished so many things, but I had to make do with reality.

It was almost a week before the castle was in a condition that satisfied Rebecca. She worked miracles, on her feet from dawn to dusk, never shouting at the servants, never losing her temper, yet bringing order out of chaos. The whole place was scrubbed and scoured, new rushes cut and laid, the copper cleaned and polished, the covers beaten and the tapestries mended, the hearths swept, the horses groomed. We all of us worked except Petrella who sat weeping, declaring that she was quite sure someone would come seeking her and lock her up in a convent where she would never see her poor baby.

At the end of the week I took my courage in both hands and rode over to the monastery. And it was as if I had never been away, as if only a few days had passed since I had gone there for my lessons.

The Abbot extended his hand and awarded me a cool little smile.

'Gida, my child, you are well grown and

comely,' he approved, 'but you ought to have written to us. We have had no news of you for many years.'

'I am well.' I said stiffly.

'But troubled.' He gave me a shrewd glance and indicated the stool. I sat on it, feeling like a child about to be scolded, and Brother Simon came in, so little changed that I felt even more like a child.

'I have a son,' I said abruptly.

'A son? My dear Gida, I had no idea you'd married!' the Abbot exclaimed.

'I am not married. The child is — Maudelyn is a love child,' I said. 'He is nearly seven years old and very bright for his age. He's a good boy and I've tried to rear him properly. I really have tried, my Lord Abbot!'

'We don't doubt it,' the Abbot said. 'And it is too late now to impose penance for your sin, but I confess that I am disappointed. I am very disappointed.'

'Who is the father, my child?' Brother Simon asked. 'He too must bear the responsibility.'

'The father is not important,' I countered. 'He knows nothing of this. I don't want him to know. I came back to Marie Regina to live here quietly, but there are people with me.'

'Oh?' He glanced at me enquiringly.

'Joseph Benacre and his daughter Rebecca

are friends of mine from London. They're good people, my Lord Abbot, very good people.'

'Their names are Jewish,' he said.

'They're Christian converts according to law. Good people who don't want to be followed, questioned, spied upon. Master Benacre is a wood carver. I was hoping there might be work for him in the monastery, something he could do. He has a little money, but not much.'

'It might be possible.' He gave me another shrewd glance.

'We have a girl with us, a distant cousin of the Benacres.' I told my prepared story glibly. 'She is a widow and with child.'

'Poor soul!' Brother Simon looked sympathetic.

'Her name is Petrella Benacre, and she is very young. I fear that she is not strong and may need a physician when her time comes.'

'One can be brought from Maidstone,' the Abbot said.

'I'm grateful, my Lord Abbot.'

'So you came to the castle. Nobody has lived there for a long time,' Brother Simon observed.

'Only three servants who idled their time away,' said the Abbot.

'They don't have much time for idling since Rebecca Benacre took charge,' I said. 'The place is scrubbed and sweetened now.'

'You have permission to stay there from your guardian, the Lady Joan?'

'The Lady Joan sold my wardship to the Duke of Lancaster. He gave me leave to travel.'

'I am sorry he should be your guardian,' the Abbot frowned. 'He lives in open fornication with Katharine Swynford who has borne him three sons. And he is known for his anti-clericalism, for his support of the king's whore.'

'But tell us of yourself,' Brother Simon interposed. 'What of your brother, and Mistress Dorothy, and the child Ralph?'

'Ralph is seventeen now and near to obtaining his Guild Licence. Dorothy keeps house for him. My brother visited us briefly and now is in France again.'

'And you have come back to Marie Regina with a son.' Brother Simon shook his head at the swift passing of time.

'Nothing has happened here,' the Abbot said, 'Brother Philip died. You remember poor old Brother Philip? A holy soul, if a little wandering in his wits.'

Looking at them both, glancing about the austere parlour, I could readily accept their unchanging quality of life, and when I rose to take my leave, in some obscure way, some of my own troubling thoughts had been dissolved.

In June the old king died and ten year old Prince Richard was proclaimed as the second monarch of that name. People declared there would be a new golden age but I confess I saw few signs of it when I rode about the district. Most of the cottagers lived in abject poverty, for the prohibitions on hunting were strict and their own land highly taxed. There was a sullen discontent among them and I wondered what would eventually kindle it into violence.

And we were at war still. It seems to me that all through my life I have heard of nothing but battles and campaigns, as if men were created to fight one another to the death. Those who were not fighting were either bound to the land or struggling to make a living in trade. And those who were not doing any of those things were churchmen.

'Raking in the profits,' Joseph Benacre said. 'These monks sit in comfort while others work. They sell salvation at a price.'

'There are good clergymen too,' Rebecca said mildly. 'The laybrothers of Marie Regina work very hard in the fields and they have been most helpful in providing labourers for this land.'

That was true. We now had about a dozen serfs working the neglected acres around the castle and I had taken the precaution of hiring a couple of stout retainers, men of middle age but considerable experience, to protect the household. My hundred sovereigns wouldn't last for ever and in order to survive we would have to work the land. That it was still in the Lady Joan's lease might have presented difficulties but the Abbot agreed to sublet it at a peppercorn rent, and I guessed that if the Lady Joan did hear of it she would not object.

July and August were making their slow way into a cooler September and everything was in readiness for the babe's arrival. We had sewed swaddling clothes and Rebecca had spun a shawl. I had even found the birthing stool and the cradle in which Godwin and I had been rocked. Only Petrella took no interest in the coming child. Indeed there were times when I felt it would have been much more sensible for her to give up the baby and go into a convent. She spent much of her day lying on her bed sleeping, or pretending to sleep. I had begun to build up my store of medicines from the herbs and flowers growing around, and I gave her soothing draughts of rosewater and rosemary but they seemed to do very little for she remained tense and withdrawn, so that in the end I quite lost patience with her and concentrated instead on teaching Maudelyn his letters. He was clever for his years, and I knew that in a year or two the Abbot would expect me to send him to the monastery for instruction. But Maudelyn had no liking for long hours at his books. He learned his lessons quickly and well and then went off to ride Silver, or to practise with the bow and arrow that Joseph had carved for him. He practised with the dagger that Godwin had presented to him as well, slashing and slicing the empty air. He would have practised with a sword if he'd been given the opportunity to lay his hands on one. Certainly he would make a fine soldier one day, but I wanted him to be educated in the duke's household. I wanted him to have his rightful place in the world.

He had not mentioned his father again but I sensed him watching me, and I knew that sooner or later he would ask about him. He must have guessed that he was bastard and that I had never been married. I wanted to make him understand that I had loved his father and that he was the son of a great man, but I needed to find the right moment and the right words.

I was in my own chamber after supper one evening when I heard Rebecca calling me from below. Her normally placid voice was raised to a higher pitch than usual, and I picked up my skirts and ran down the spiral stairs into the hall and through to the women's quarters.

Petrella was bent over, groaning and retching, and Rebecca, her face pale, straightened up, her voice falsely bright.

'Petrella has begun her labour, Mistress Gida. It's a bit early but that means the babe will come easily and quickly, doesn't it?'

'Generally, you should keep on your feet for as long as possible.'

'It hurts,' Petrella moaned, rocking to and fro.

'I'll make some rosemary tisane, and that will soothe the pain,' I said.

'I'm going to die,' Petrella whimpered. 'I know I'm going to die.'

Her small face was greenish white and her eyes were terrified.

'Of course you're not going to die,' I said firmly. 'Rebecca, help her into a clean shift and I'll make the infusion. Is your father in his room? I think Maudelyn should sleep up there tonight.'

I spoke confidently, firmly, but my stomach

was churning. I had no notion of what to do in childbirth, and it was hard to recall exactly what Dorothy had done when I was having Maudelyn. He had been born so quickly and the pain of it was faded from my mind.

Maudelyn went to bed with his usual docility. He was an obedient boy, more obedient than most children, but his eyes had an adult curiosity.

'We will take turns to sit up with you,' I said bracingly when I went back to Petrella.

Rebecca had persuaded her into a clean white shift and tied back her curly brown hair with a ribbon, but she refused to walk about, huddling on the bed instead and crying.

'I think she is having regular cramps every few minutes,' Rebecca said in a low voice. 'I have no experience of these matters, I fear.'

'Go to bed I'll take first watch,' I said.

'You will wake me?'

'I promise. Go to bed now.' I gave her what I hoped was a reassuring smile, and turned my attention back to Petrella.

I have known long nights, but that was one of the longest. By the time I was due to wake Rebecca it was clear, even to me, that Petrella was in great pain. She moaned and twisted, sweat pouring down her face, her hands rubbed raw on the rope I'd looped to the bedpost. Rebecca had gone to my room to sleep, but she woke by herself and came in, a candle in her hand.

'If it's not here by dawn,' I said, drawing her to one side, 'I'll send someone to the monastery to see if the physician can be brought'.

'She looks so swollen,' Rebecca whispered. 'Her ankles and wrists are puffed out, and there's a blue tinge about her mouth. Is she supposed to look like that?'

'I don't know,' I said honestly. From the bed Petrella called out sharply, her eyes half-closed, her face so contorted that the veins stood out like cords in her face.

'Perhaps we should help her on to the birthstool,' Rebecca said.

I bent to help Petrella to a sitting position, but she writhed away from me, shuddering and crying.

'My father may be able to help. I think he has seen babies born,' said Rebecca. 'Shall I rouse him?'

'Yes, but don't wake Maudelyn. I'll get Bessie.'

'Bessie went over to see her cousin. You gave her two days' leave.'

'Lord, I'd forgotten! Get your father then.' I tried desperately to remember what little I'd learned about childbirth. My mother had told me what herbs would relieve the pain and speed the emerging baby, but I had never actually helped at a birth. All my instincts, however, told me that everything was not going according to plan. The pains were so fierce and they came so quickly that the child ought to be born very soon, but Petrella had not begun to bear down and her face was swollen so much that her last vestige of prettiness was gone.

Joseph Benacre, nightcap on his head, hurried in, tying the sash of his gown.

'I know little of these women's matters,' he said briefly.

'We know less,' I told him. 'Do you think she ought to be bled?'

'She's narrow-hipped,' Rebecca said.

'Give her some of your rosemary tisane,' he advised. 'Have you tincture of poppy?'

'In the store room.'

'Put a pinch in. The mixture will help her to sleep.'

'But she needs to bear down,' Rebecca objected.

'Later. When she has rested.' He patted the girl's shoulder and motioned me into the storeroom.

'Is it bad?' I asked in a low voice.

'As bad as it can be,' he answered, equally low. 'The babe is lying in the wrong position but even if we manage to turn it I doubt if she could give birth normally. Her pelvis is too small, too narrow. The head will be crushed.

'I'll send Gideon for a physician.'

'It would do no good, but send by all means,' he began, when there came a sudden anguished cry from the other chamber.

Petrella, her back arched like a bow, was straining, pushing, her teeth clenched and her lips drawn back in what looked like a snarl. She had bitten her tongue and blood dripped from the corners of her mouth.

'Get the poppy tincture down her,' Joseph ordered. 'The child will be born dead and she will be badly torn, but we can save her if we stop this convulsion.'

'Hold her head, Rebecca. I'll try to open her mouth.' My own voice shook almost as much as the goblet of rosemary tisane in my hand.

'Drop by drop. We cannot go about to choke her,' Joseph cautioned.

'She isn't swallowing,' I said desperately.

'Wet cloths bound about the temples!' Joseph ordered.

On the bed Petrella gave one long, convulsive shudder and relaxed, her eyes rolled back, foam on her snarling lips.

'She's gone,' Rebecca said blankly. 'She's not breathing.'

Joseph seized a candle and held it near to the mouth and eyes of that contorted face.

'Her heart could not stand the strain,' he said at last.

'The poor wench is dead.'

'But the babe still lives.' Rebecca pulled back the covers to reveal the distended flesh revealed under the rumpled, sweat soaked shift.

'It has a right to be born,' I cried, 'otherwise Petrella died for nothing.'

'It might be possible — to cut,' Joseph said. 'I read once that the great Roman Julius Ceasar, was torn from his mother after her death.'

'If we try and fail it will be murder.' Rebecca licked her lips nervously.

'If we don't try the child will die anyway,' I flung back.

'Have you a sharp dagger?' Joseph spoke with grave dignity, but his face was drawn.

'I'll get it.'

'There's one on the wall. I hung it out of harm's way because Maudelyn is forever playing about with it when he should be asleep,' Rebecca pointed.

It was the dagger that Godwin had given to my son. Such a fierce, dark anger rushed through me when I reached for it that I saw the others step back a pace. 'I'll do it, then the blame is mine,' I said, and my voice held a calm authority.

I had never cut into human flesh before, had never realised how difficult it is. I think I said a prayer. I know I closed my eyes. And then the shock of the slicing travelled up my arm from the quivering nerve ends and black blood oozed up, and there was something red and slippery and hideous in my hands.

'Don't faint now!' I heard Joseph order sharply. 'The cord must be cut and tied. Rebecca, get the thread.'

The babe was crying. I heard it draw its first breath and then it cried, and its tiny frame was pink where it was not bloodied.

'A girl. It's a girl,' Rebecca said. She was wiping the babe clean and snatching up a cover to wrap it in. It's eyes were screwed tight against the candlelight and it turned its head from side to side as if it were seeking nourishment.

'We'll need a wet nurse,' I said shakily. 'Bessie will likely find one.'

'I'll cover the poor wench's face,' Joseph said. 'The priest will have to come.'

'And the babe will need a name. Have you a name?' Rebecca asked.

I stared down at the child and saw myself in the water garden of Barnard's Castle, and the Lady Joan, her voice whispering, 'Pass on your secret knowledge to a female of your blood born after her mother had died.'

And this was my niece, a little scrap of hope born out of betrayal and death.

'I will call her Diana,' I said slowly.

'A pagan goddess?' Joseph commented. 'The Abbot won't like that!'

'The Abbot won't have the rearing of her,' I said shortly. 'As Diana she will have a choice, don't you see? She may choose to be virgin, hunting where she pleases and tearing those who love her to pieces with her hounds. Or she may choose to be warm and fertile like the many breasted Artemis. But it will be her choice. No man will force her or betray her.'

'Diana then,' said Rebecca softly.

It was dawn and I took that also to be a symbol. We looked at one another in its pale light and smiled through the reek of blood and the sickly sweet odour of corruption that filled the chamber.

The Abbot, as Joseph had prophesied, thought the choice of name an odd one, but I said, gravely that it had been Petrella's wish, so he agreed to it, and she was baptised in the monastery on the same day that her mother was buried there. She lies there still near to my grandmother, Eadgyth, with my own mother, Alfreda, and Ralph's parents not far away.

I wrote to Dorothy, giving the letter to a pedlar who came by. I told her that Petrella had come with me but had fallen sick and died, and that I would write to her again when I was at Kenilworth. It was not the whole truth, but it would suffice.

At the autumnal Equinox we had a second baptism, but this time it was a secret one.

Joseph, Rebecca and I rode over to the monastery, leaving our mounts among the trees at the edge of the river, crossing the bridge and climbing the serpent path on foot. For the first time in over ten years I used the key and we filed down the rocky passage into the high, vaulted chamber.

We had brought lamps and candles and these, as we kindled them, revealed, as they had done to me before, the painted Archangels who welcomed us from the walls. We had wrapped the baby in the new shawl and she slept peacefully, sated with the rich milk of a young bondswoman we had managed to hire.

Joseph's appearance had changed subtly since their arrival in the Temple. He looked taller and he moved with authority, his features a carven mask in the lamplight. In his hands he held the dagger that had given life to Diana and the hazel wand he had cut and polished himself. I took my place in the west and Rebecca, having laid the babe on the central altar, went to the north.

Now Joseph circled the great chamber, inscribing in the air the banishing pentagrams that held evil at bay, and, returning to the eastern quarter, ignited the incense we had brought in the small charcoal brazier. Three times he censed the child, three times sprinkled her with salt water. Then Rebecca and I lifted her between us and presented her to the Elemental kings, to Peralda, Djinn, Necsa and Ghob, invoking for her swiftness of air, loving heat of fire, mobility of water and stability of enduring earth.

We laid her, still sleeping, on the altar and Joseph dedicated her to the Great Mother, that hidden Female side of the Creator out of whom the goddesses evolved in an age long forgotten. One by one the names were recited — Artemis, Athena, Selene, Bast, Levanah, Diana, Ge, Rhea and Mother Isis who is in all women as maid, wife or hag according to the changing faces of the moon.

And when the ceremony was ended we snuffed the lights and, locking the door upon the Mystery, came out into the starlight again.

13

'You will have to tell the boy about his father,' Joseph had said. 'He needs the security of knowing his beginnings.'

'He doesn't ask any questions,' I said defensively.

'And that in itself is not natural,' Joseph said. 'He does not ask because he fears the answer. But he needs the influence of a father, Mistress Gida, for he is becoming difficult. He is sullen and uncooperative.'

'He has a will of his own,' I said, flushing.

'And that will ought to be controlled and disciplined. He is almost nine years old now and he is becoming spoiled. It might be well if you gave him into the care of the monks.'

'The Abbot is too harsh with him,' I said, 'I cannot believe that thrashing a boy ever put lessons into his head.'

'It is not learning that is Maudelyn's problem,' the old man said. 'He is intelligent, but he has a liking for mischief — not childish high spirits but something sly and — I am fond of the boy, my dear, but I must be honest with you. He is doing no good here.'

It was true, although I was reluctant to admit it. Maudelyn was bored at Marie Regina and he was puzzled. I guessed that Diana's birth had brought his own situation to mind and his sullen manner was simply a way of making himself noticed.

It was Bessie, who collected most of the gossip by some means known only to herself, who told me that the Duke of Lancaster had ridden to Kenilworth to see his latest child.

'A daughter this time, mistress. Now Katharine Swynford has borne him four children and they do say he is more in love with her than ever.'

Looking back, I think that was the phrase which decided me. It was not that I wanted to hurt or embarrass Katharine or the duke, but it seemed so unfair to me that my son should be unknown and myself forgotten. I made arrangements therefore to travel to Warwickshire. Gideon, one of our two retainers, was to accompany me, and when I had settled Maudelyn I intended to return. Exactly what I would say to the duke I wasn't sure, but first I must tell Maudelyn something of the purpose of our journey.

He stood before me, fidgeting a little because it was a fine afternoon, his fair hair straggling into his greenish eyes. In his belt was the dagger that Godwin had given to him, and on his face was the blank, slightly insolent expression he had begun to affect.

'If it's about winging Brother Sixtus,' he said, 'I was only having a little practise and the arrow was blunt anyway.'

'It wasn't about Brother Sixtus,' I said a trifle wearily, for I knew I would hear of the offence sooner or later from the Abbot. 'It's about your future.'

'I want to be a knight,' he said swiftly. 'I'll not go to any monks' school.'

'To be a knight you must start as a page in some noble household,' I said. 'You must learn the arts of chivalry, my son.'

'Where?' His sullen expression lifted slightly and he looked at me eagerly.

'To the Duke of Lancaster's household. The duke is a fine man and you can rise high in his service.'

'Can we go now?' he asked.

'Soon. Very soon.' I was pleased that he had asked no further questions but ran off to inspect his small stock of weapons.

We left Marie Regina a few days later. It was high summer and the young king had been two years on the throne, but I saw no improvement in conditions as we passed along the roads. Serfs with leather collars around their necks toiled in the fields and large-eyed children with matchstick legs huddled at the doors of their hovels, with grubby palms outstretched for alms some charitable traveller might bestow.

My heart jumped a little when we came to Kenilworth. I was tired, for we had stayed the previous night at an inn where the pallets were thin and the lice thick, but I could not help feeling a tingle of anticipation as we passed into the courtyard and I saw the sunshine gleaming and sparkling on the panes of the many windowed hall.

By a stroke of fortune I could scarcely believe the duke stood on the steps. He must have just returned from hunting because the carcass of a roebuck was slung between two poles and he was talking to the servant who carried the lead pole. There was a lad with him too, a pugnacious looking boy with spiky red hair who was squat rather than handsome. I recognised Prince Henry and thought inanely that he had grown in the years since I had cared for him in the Death.

The duke frowned slighty as I dismounted and walked towards him. It was clear that he had forgotten me completely and a sick disappointment stifled my joy.

'My Lord Duke, you look well,' I said boldly. 'Thank you, Mistress — ?' He paused, looking at me.

'It's Gida, my father. Gida Falcon who used to look after me!' Henry said.

I had not expected the child to remember me at all but he came forward, clasping my hand with evident pleasure, staring past me to where Maudelyn stood.

'Gida! My wits must be addled with age!' The duke embraced me with a heartiness that betrayed his acute chagrin: 'You look splendid, absolutely splendid! Where have you been hiding all these years?'

'You did give me permission to go visiting,' I said dryly.

'And is this a visit or are you come to stay? Cullen Beaumont died, you know. Yes, died of a kidney stone some years since.'

So that was why he had never followed me to London.

'He never married,' the duke said cheerfully.

'Neither did I, my lord,' I told him.

'Ah, well, not all are cut out for the wedded state,' he said.

'But I do have a son,' I nodded towards Maudelyn who stood very straight, slight apprehension in his face.

Henry, his eyes darting between us, said, 'He must be one of yours, my father. He has the same nose and holds his head as you and I and my Beaufort brothers do.'

I had never noticed it before but the prince

was right. The duke saw the resemblance too and flushed deeply, his eyes meeting mine in silent question. At that instant he looked irresistibly like Maudelyn about to be scolded for winging Brother Sixtus.

'He is nearly nine years old,' I said steadily. 'I reared him as a good Christian, but he cannot stay with a woman for ever. He wants to become a knight.'

'What do you call him?' the duke asked.

'Maudelyn Falcon. I want the name Falcon to remain.'

'And he is my son?'

'I will go away again if it displeases you,' I said swiftly. 'I never bore you a grudge, my lord, for I was as much to blame as you.'

'You ought to have told me before,' he said. 'I have had much on my mind, I know, but I would have found time. I was — at fault a little, I fear.'

'The boy wishes to become a knight I wish him to have a noble education.'

'Here?' He gave me a long look and then strode to where Maudelyn waited.

'So you are my son!' he said genially. 'Will you like to live with me, do you think?'

'Yes, my Lord Duke,' Maudelyn said promptly.

'I must tell Katharine,' he announced, turning to me.

'Will she be angry?' I asked.

'Because of a lapse I made nine years ago? Katharine is the most tolerant woman in the world,' he said. 'Henry, escort Mistress Gida to the women's quarters and then bring her to the solar. You, lad, come with me and I will introduce you to the sweetest woman in England!'

So Katharine Swynford was the sweetest woman in England and I was a lapse of nine years since. A mixture of wry laughter and humiliated weeping strove within me for mastery as I went into the great hall.

'I am glad you are come back, mistress,' Henry said. 'I have often wondered how you did.'

'And I have thought of you,' I said. 'How are your sisters?'

'Pippa and Bet are both wedded, with households of their own.'

'And you are — twelve now?'

'Ready to go campaigning with my father,' he said proudly. 'My half-brothers are too young. Will you be visiting us for long?'

'Only for a day or two. I am going to seek permission to return to Marie Regina.'

'My father is your guardian, isn't he?' The boy regarded me solemnly for a few minutes, then said, 'He is not hurtful or neglectful out of malice, but he has much on his mind. He has to govern England, you know, because my cousin is only a youngling.'

He was sensible for his age and I liked him, hoping that he would be friendly to Maudelyn and influence him for the better.

'You know where the solar is? Shall I wait?'

'No, I'll come down when I'm ready.' I lingered a little, patting my hair into place, smoothing my dress, feeling absurdly shy. It was foolish because I was a grown woman and it was time I realised that the duke's brief passion for me had long since died into ashes.

I paused at the threshold of the solar and took in the scene, and I knew I was right not to hope.

Katharine had gained a little weight but it suited her and there was the unmistakable glow in her face of a woman who is completely happy because she knows that she is loved. A small boy was perched on her knee, but she set him down and came to greet me with outstretched hands.

'Gida! After so many years! And you have brought your son to us. John has told me about the matter. I am sorry for it, my dear, but the boy is a fine boy. We will make him happy here.'

I was certain that she would. Katharine

Swynford was one of those women who blossom as their families increase. She led me across to the gilded rocker and showed me the newest addition, and her eyes shone as if nobody had produced such a wonder child before.

'We named her Joan, after the king's lady mother. She has been so very kind to us. This little one is Tamkin and the two wrestling down there are Johnny and Harry. They are being bearcubs at the moment. And you remember my children by my late husband? Tom and Blanchette?'

'Maudelyn will settle among us well,' the duke said. 'This is my haven, Gida, where I can forget the affairs of state.'

'The duke does not get the support of his brothers as he should,' Katharine said, frowning slightly.

'Edmund's nose is stuck in a book most of the time,' he said, 'and Thomas cannot hold a conversation without losing his temper.'

'And Parliament must vote more money if the war is to be brought to a successful conclusion. The Isle of Wight is actually overrun with Frenchmen! And there is great danger for the herring fleet.'

'My darling, when you try to talk politics, you are extremely comical,' the duke said. 'Boys! Boys, why don't you go down to the butts and take Maudelyn with you? Gida, you will be visiting us for a while, Katharine will miss your company when I am gone again.'

'I wish you would not speak of your going away again,' she objected. 'Let us enjoy the time we have together.'

'This time I will take Henry with me. Tom and Maudelyn too.'

'And me?' The biggest of the Beaufort boys swung round as they tumbled out of the door.

'In a year or two, Johnny. You must stay here now to protect your lady mother in case the French invade.'

'Is that possible?' I asked in fear.

'They are poised for invasion,' he said, 'but we will beat them back. I am persuading the Commons to levy a small tax. Every man, woman and child will pay according to circumstances.'

'The peasants too?' I enquired in surprise.

'According to circumstance,' he said. 'If the war is lost, then the peasants will be the first to scream against their betters for not guarding the realm. So let them help to pay for that defence if they will not risk their necks in the field! But do let us talk of other matters. A man has no wish to bring his troubles home and chew upon them.'

'We will have supper,' said Katharine smilingly, 'and then we will gossip. My sister Philippa was enquiring after you when she wrote to me at Yuletide. She and Geoffrey are still very happy together though she has no children.'

'Geoffrey is becoming quite a considerable poet,' the duke said. 'I am having his latest volume bound in silk as a gift for Katharine. You must see the additions I have made to the library, Gida. You were always fond of books, were you not?'

It was so strange to look at him and see only kindness in his eyes, to talk to Katharine whose friendly manner showed no hint of shock or hurt at the revelation that had just been made to her. Only a completely happy woman could be so free from jealousy.

I was pleased, at supper, to see that Maudelyn was apparently accepted by the other children. He would develop in this atmosphere into the fine man I wanted him to become, but I felt a pang at the thought of leaving him.

After supper Katharine walked with me in the rose bower that the duke had planted for her the previous year. There was fragrance all about us. If I close my eyes I can smell it still and catch the echo of her voice.

'John has behaved badly to you, Gida. I

wish you had confided to us sooner, then we might have done something more for the boy.'

'The duke has much on his mind,' I reminded her.

'The weight of the realm,' she agreed. 'The king is a fine lad, but he is only twelve years old and he is headstrong. Fortunately he trusts John and dislikes his other uncles, and the Lady Joan guides him wisely, but the time will come when he refuses to be controlled and then I cannot think what will happen.'

'The duke will surmount it.'

'Of course he will, but the people hate him. I cannot understand why for he is the kindest, most tolerant of men, the loyalest subject any monarch could hope to have.'

'He is a proud man.'

'And has cause to be. Is he not the son of King Edward and brother to the Black Prince?' Her voice was warm with indignation. 'No man has driven himself harder to extend the king's domains! He has never spared himself, even to marriage for political reasons that we might gain a foothold in Spain.'

'He has his best ally in you,' I said smiling.

'It is all I am fitted to do,' she said.

'I bear him children, and I make this a refuge, a haven, where he comes to spend a little time as a private man. For that I am called leman and whore, and he is accused of plotting and scheming to increase his power. His brothers hate him. Edmund of York whispers slanders and Thomas of Gloucester bullies and blusters. And they would pull the realm to pieces between them if John were not stronger than either of them.'

She broke off, laughing at her own vehemence, and put her hand on my arm saying. 'You must not mind what I say. John tells me I talk treason fifty times a day, but I am indignant on his behalf. He does not trouble to defend himself against his accusers and it makes me furious.'

I left Kenilworth the next morning, hiding my hurt when Maudelyn wriggled out of my embrace declaring he had no time to linger because he was due at the butts. The duke gave me a purse of gold, telling me it was what remained of my dowry, and ordered that four of his own retainers must accompany Gideon and me back to Marie Regina. He spoke kindly, kissing me farewell, but I sensed that he was glad to see me leave. I reminded him of his earlier indiscretion too clearly. Maudelyn was a boy among his other sons. I was the woman he had neglected.

'You will come back to see us?' Katharine asked, and I promised that I would, but I had no intention of keeping that promise. That part of my life was over and I would spend my next years at Marie Regina.

As I rode away I reflected sadly that the duke had accepted Maudelyn's existence easily because he had never really loved me at all. And I wished I had some magic potion that would stop me from loving him, but it seemed that I was one of those women fated to love only one man and fated also not to be loved in return.

The duke's retainers left me at the castle gates in Marie Regina, for they were to go further south and I went in to be welcomed by Rebecca and Joseph with as much pleasure as if I had been away for a month! It was if they had become my family now, and Diana was the child entrusted to me in place of the child I had given up.

We settled into the rhythm of the seasons, summer giving place to the harvests of autumn, winter bleakness greening into spring. I was happy — no, that isn't true! I was busy. The household was small but even a small household must be controlled, servants paid, animals fed and slaughtered, horses exercised, fish caught, supplies ordered in advance, herbs planted, plucked and dried, tapestries mended. We were working the land with fair success, but the poll tax bore heavily on us all. At Yuletide there was a letter from Katharine, telling me that the duke was on campaign again and he had taken both Prince Henry and Maudelyn and her own son, Tom Swynford, with him. She enclosed a letter in Dorothy's hand which had been sent to Kenilworth and I broke the seal eagerly.

'Dear Gida,

I send this letter to the duke's estate in the hope that it will reach you. There was great trouble when you left because the Greys were so angry with Petrella that they suspected you of having helped her to escape.

When your letter came they repented their unkindness, for indeed it is a sad matter to lose a daughter. I do not believe they would have put her into a convent when their tempers had cooled, but there! it is done and no sense in blaming anyone now. I pray that the poor maid rests in peace, and I pray that Godwin will not come back to cause more trouble.

Now, let me come to the burden of my letter which is joyful. Ralph wed a month after we heard of Petrella's death. Ann

Todmore is a widow, or was, I ought to say, near thirty but comely and respectable with a decent dowry. They have two babes already, Giles and Enid, and are happier than one might have expected. But he does not talk of Petrella and we seldom see the Greys.

I am well in health though my rheum troubles me in damp weather. I think often of you and Maudelyn, and I think too of Marie Regina. When I am old, really old, I think I may return to Kent, for I lived many years in the castle, as you know, and have many happy memories of the place.

We are full of war news here, with great chains slung across the port mouths lest the French arrive. I have seen the little king in procession and he is a beautiful lad. But the Duke of Lancaster is hated, for people say he uses the war to add to his own profits, I don't believe that, but there is much misery in the city, and fear, with many beggars and robbers and rogue apprentices. I pray there will be no riots while the duke is away but I am not easy in mind.

I send you my best and most obedient regards,

Dorothy.'

So Ralph had taken a widow to wife and already had two babes. He had done what I could have done when Cullen Beaumont offered me marriage, but I could never have accepted second best. I wished Ralph well and put him out of my mind in that part of my life that was over and done.

Diana was growing out of babyhood into an exquisite child. She suited her name for her hair was the colour of pale ash and her eyes were of a pale, spring sky blue. She was going to be tall for her years and there was already a grace in her movements that enchanted the eye.

She was a sweet natured child who had a smile for everybody and a particular affection for old Joseph. She trotted round after him, holding his hand and chattering. She was bright for her years and we promised ourselves that as soon as she was old enough to understand the importance of keeping a secret we would take her with us to the Temple. Already she knew the names of the herbs I plucked to cure ailments and the powers of sigil and colour. Her memory was good, but she seemed to know many things by instinct.

I looked forward at the time to the long years of teaching her, to the joy of watching her grow up. I ought to have known that one cannot count on anything.

It began with a herald riding through the hamlet of Marie Regina and calling upon all within earshot to pay attention. The king was gravely displeased because though a shilling poll had been levied on every head the returns had been so meagre that cheating was suspected and so an enquiry was to be held and the tax levied again.

'But we have paid,' Joseph said when I told him. 'Surely we don't need to pay twice over.'

'I will go to the Abbot,' I said, frowning. 'He will have more reliable information. After all, I have been given a receipt for the tax already paid.'

'The Government cannot expect to collect the tax twice over,' Rebecca said confidently.

The Abbot when I went to see him was less sanguine.

'Half of those who collect the taxes cannot read anyway,' he said, 'and a receipt is no guarantee in these times. I am informed that riots have broken out in Brentford and are spreading. A friar named John Ball is preaching sedition, travelling from parish to parish telling the poor folk to rise and seize by force what cannot be got by persuasion. Dangerous nonsense, fomenting discontent and anarchy.'

'Cannot the king do something to heal the wrongs?'

'The king has no power. 'Tis the Duke of Lancaster who rules, and he is in Scotland.'

'There is surely some Court of Appeal?'

'You could go to Maidstone and lay your case there,' Brother Simon said, 'but you would be better to wait quietly and hope the tax is not demanded again.'

It's odd when I look back, but I was concerned about the tax collectors who might try to wrest more money from me. I never gave a thought to the peasants whose grumbling discontent was now erupting into violence. We lived so quietly, offending nobody, and I paid fair wages to my labourers. It never entered my head that I was regarded as a member of the ruling class.

It was Rebecca who drew my attention to the glow in the sky when we were taking our evening walk.

'A fine sunset,' I remarked.

'Not in the east. That's a fire, a big bonfire,' she objected.

'You don't think the French could have invaded?' I asked in alarm.

'Perhaps it is a warning.'

'Or a riot over Maidstone way! We'd best get indoors.'

'Nobody is rioting here,' Rebecca said in

her calm fashion. 'Will you set double guard, or shall we go over to the monastery?'

'For sanctuary? I think we ought to keep our heads. If there is riot it's not likely to be here. I'll send Gideon to see what's afoot.'

'He will likely slope off to the tavern and come home in his cups as he did last month,' Rebecca said gloomily.

'Then I'll ride out myself,' I decided. 'I'll go to the monastery and get the Abbot's advice, and if it is bad news I'll come back and we can set guard or go back to the monastery if that's what you'd prefer.'

'You'll be careful?' she begged.

'Lord, but you speak as if the country were ablaze!' I said impatiently. 'I've ridden these fields since I was a child and no harm ever came to me.'

And I gave her a friendly wave and ran round to the stables to get Silver. It occurred to me as I rode towards the monastery that there might be trouble, but I still had no real fear. I still lacked the prickle that raised the hair at the back of the neck and the instinct of danger.

The Great Silence had begun in the monastery, but Brother Sixtus opened the side door and admitted me, finger to his lips.

'Mistress Gida, we expected you, but

where is the rest of your household?' the Abbot asked, rising as I entered the parlour.

'I came alone to seek the cause of the fire,' I said.

'Riot,' he said briefly. 'Have you not heard that the town of Maidstone is overrun? The whole place is crowded with peasants, who murder, burn and loot as they come. They are declaring they will go to the king and lay their grievances before him. They have found themselves a leader — Wat Tyler is his name and the good God alone knows from what dunghill he is sprung. My laybrothers brought me the news not an hour since.'

'I have been in a riot before,' I began nervously.

'This is no local disturbance,' he said impatiently. 'They are animals these serfs. If they were not the Lord would have sought to place them in a better position, but they go against His Will by seeking wealth and privilege that is not theirs by right of birth.'

'I will ride back and tell the others,' I said. 'We will ride here if you permit it. Surely they will not attack a monastery!'

'They will attack anything that is not wattle and daub,' he returned.

His words echoed in my head as I rode back to the castle. If Joseph and Rebecca could make their way to the old wattle hut where my mother had once lived they could keep Diana safe until the rioters had passed. I had already decided that I would stay at the castle. Yes, it was foolish of me, but I had been born in that castle and it was my home even if it was not my own property. I was nearing the avenue of oaks and the sky was bright, not with stars, but with the light of the fires. There seemed to be fires all about with no limit to them, and I reined in my mount, looking about me in terror. The sky flamed with torches, the road resounded to the tramp of marching feet, and on they still came. They seemed sprung from the ground like dragon's teeth, and what frightened me more than anything was their silence. No private quarrels were being settled here. They moved with flaming torches over the landscape, each man bound to his fellow by common purpose. I turned Silver into the safety of the woods, and I rode her harder than I had ever ridden her before to the castle. Joseph and Rebecca were already mounted with Diana on the saddle in front of Rebecca. Her little face peeped out gravely from the hooded cloak she wore against the night air.

'Go down to the river,' I said. 'Hide among the trees near to that tumbledown hut I showed you, Rebecca. They'll not see you and even if they do you'll be taken for cottagers.'

'What will you do?' Joseph demanded.

'I'll follow you,' I said. 'Don't stay to argue but ride! Wait! Diana, you keep this until I come.'

Some impulse made me draw from my sleeve the seal that the Duchess Blanche had let me choose so many years before. I had grown into the habit of carrying it as if it were some talisman, and now I pressed the claw into the child's small hand, and hit the pony on the rump with no further word of farewell.

And then I rode on into the castle calling to Gideon to bar the doors, and we began the long night's waiting.

Afterword

The peasants never came. We sat there all night, Gideon and I, with Bessie shivering and weeping and taking nips of courage from the ale jug. We heard the measured tramping, saw the glint of torches, but they passed us by. There were ten thousand men, I'm told, who marched out of Kent that night. Oh, they had cause for discontent, for hatred too, but I can feel no pity for them. Not even now when almost twenty years passed and I am near fifty. They had no call to do what they did, no reason save blind passion and a hatred of anything alien to their own pattern of life.

When the next day broke Gideon and I unbarred the doors and rode across the fields to the river. It was a lovely morning with spiders webs lacing dew sparkling grass and the clouds scudding through the blue sky. I could see the river foaming between the trunks of the trees and I raised my voice to call, expecting figures to emerge into the open.

There was no answering call, no sign of anyone, Gideon gave me a troubled look and spurred his horse ahead, calling as he went. I followed him, guiding Silver in and out of the trees. We found Rebecca first, spread eagled on the bank, her eyes still open. Joseph lay at a little distance, blood congealed on his head. They had fought fiercely to defend themselves and for a moment I was puzzled as to why they had been attacked at all. Then I saw the Star of David, the golden symbol that Joseph wore beneath his houppelande, torn off and lying near to his hand.

Perhaps the marching serfs had caught up with them too soon and recognised that people of their own class don't wear warm cloaks or ride well-groomed horses. Perhaps Joseph tried to bribe them with the gold, and they had realised his origins. Jews were universally despised and distrusted.

Of Diana there was no sign, though we searched up and down the river banks for hours. The Abbot, pale after a sleepless night when he had expected an attack, was very kind. He ordered that a full search should be made and that a reward of one hundred pounds should be cried for information leading to her whereabouts.

'For if she has been stolen, my dear, no peasant will be able to resist such a lure,' he assured me.

No peasant, indeed nobody at all came

forward with information of any kind. Perhaps they feared it was a trap of some sort. Or perhaps she had died or been killed. There was so much killing in the weeks that followed.

We heard of it later, from runners and pedlars bringing news from the south. The peasants had marched not only from Kent but from Essex and Sussex, Devon and Cornwall. They had sacked and plundered as they marched, dragging landowners from their beds, freeing prisoners from the gaols. They had camped at Blackheath and the next day they had entered the city, demanding audience with the king, declaring that all men were born equal and free. Free to murder anyone set over them, I suppose! Even Archbishop Sudbury who was noted for his mildness had been beheaded at his own altar.

But the king, boy though he was, had ridden to meet the insurgents and had talked with Wat Tyler, their leader. It was unfortunate that the Mayor of London, seeing the rebel chief reach for his dagger in token of surrender, had assumed the king was in mortal danger and had run Tyler through. The peasant army had bent their bows then for an instant the Government of England had trembled on the edge of anarchy, and then the king had shown himself true son of the Black Prince. He had spurred his horse forward, crying to the rebels, 'Follow me! I am now your leader!'

They had followed him, crying out that he was a brave lad and they trusted him to redress their grievances. And I believe he had been sincere in his promise, but a lad of fourteen, even though he be king, has not the power to change the fabric of society with one gallant gesture. John Ball, the renegade friar, and more than a hundred leaders were arrested and hanged, and the serfs their fellowship disbanded, had slunk back to their villages.

The duke had returned from Scotland and his grip upon the country was firmer than ever. But I believe he was fair minded, and I wish now that he had been more greedy, that he had taken the throne for himself. We've had little joy out of King Richard since he grew out of boyhood.

I've lived far from public affairs these past years. The lease is mine now, for when the Lady Joan died, that would be about four years after the peasants riot, the Abbot offered it to me. I've lived here at the castle ever since. It's been a quiet life, quiet and peaceful, and there are those who would envy me, I suppose. I have no husband to bully me, and I live comfortably, if frugally. There is a new Abbot at the monastery now, a brisk young man with a lively sense of humour. He is forever telling me that I ought to travel more, that the new century is dawning and I must wake up my ideas or be left behind. I say nothing, but I smile inside, because it seems to me that I have lived longer and more intensely than most women.

Dorothy had died twelve years since. I received word of it from Ralph Aston in a curt, formal letter that made it clear that he neither expected nor desired a reply. He sent no word of his own circumstances, but I could picture him as he was now, a trifle weighty and ponderous, but prosperous. An unyielding man, I thought sadly, who might have been happy if my brother had not come back.

A year ago I had a visitor. I didn't recognise her at first, for she wore the garb of a pilgrim, and her face was hidden by the wide brim of the straw hat, but I knew her when she spoke.

'Gida, it is so many years since we met, I am pleased to find you here.'

'Katharine Swynford — I beg your pardon!' I remembered that she was the Duchess of Lancaster now, for he had married her when his Spanish wife died.

'I am making a pilgrimage to Canterbury,' she said, 'and finding myself near thought I would call for an hour.'

'Is Maudelyn well? I had word from him six months since and he visited me at Easter.'

'Maudelyn is well. He is with my Lord Duke.'

'And you are not?' I led her up to the tower room and offered her wine.

'I make the pilgrimage as an offering for peace,' she said. 'You know that Prince Henry seeks to wrest the throne from King Richard?'

I nodded, remembering the falling crown in the vision I had had years before.

'One cannot blame Henry,' she said wearily. 'The king is half-mad, I think, for he listens to no advice. Even John cannot control him now. His follies and extravagances have brought us all to the edge of ruin. Henry would make a far more able monarch, but John sets great store on loyalty and so is torn between them. He is not well either, for he is no longer young.'

'We are none of us young,' I said, and we sat in melancholy for a little while.

Then she roused herself a trifle, saying cheerfully, 'Blanchette wished me to convey her love to you. She says that spinster

347

ladies ought to stick together! Oh, and Tom is taking another wife. Meg Darcy is a considerable heiress.'

'And the rest of your family?'

'Are all well. They support Henry, of course, and have nothing to say to Richard.'

'These quarrels shake the realm,' I said.

'And the haven I provide is no longer sufficient,' she said, and there was a wry twist to her mouth.

'You have been the great love of his life!' I exclaimed.

'And am grateful for it, but we have been together for many years now. The brightness is dying. Forgive me for saying this but I have sometimes thought you had the best of it. One rounded, perfect experience to remember.'

'That's nonsense,' I said. 'Memory doesn't keep a woman warm on cold nights, and a body can get tired of talking to herself.'

'Maudelyn visits you.'

'Every few years, out of duty. His affection lies with his father, as I hoped it would do.'

'He is a fine young man,' she consoled me.

'Aye, and you have had the rearing of him since he was nine, so you must take the credit for it.'

348

'If he would settle down and take a wife,' Katharine said, 'then there might be grandchildren to visit you.'

'When he's a mind to it. I was never one to force people,' I said.

'You were always a good woman,' she observed. 'My sister, Philippa, was fond of you.'

'And I of her.' It was hard to believe that the chattering Philippa had been in her grave for ten years. Sometimes it was hard to believe that I was not fourteen years old still and on my way to Court for the first time.

Katharine took her leave shortly afterwards, kissing me warmly, and riding away with her pilgrim hat crammed firmly on her head, and I could not stop myself from picturing how it might have been if I had not worked the love spell at Philippa's request.

In all these years there has been no word of Diana, and inevitably the sharpness of her loss had blurred. She would be twenty-two years old now, and I believe she would have been beautiful, most beautiful. I blame myself, you know, for having made the wrong decision all those years ago.

This morning a pedlar came by, with his cart full of laces and trinkets, and rolls of silk, and his mouth full of gossip.

'The king won't hang onto his crown for much longer now that Henry of Lancaster has landed in the north. With the duke dead there's none to stand for Richard now.'

'The Duke of Lancaster dead?' My hands, appraising silks, were still.

'Aye, old John of Gaunt is gone! A heart attack a month since. It's a sad thing for the realm in my view, for grumble people may, about his high handedness, but he held the balance between his son and his nephew. And he made an honest woman of the Swynford lass.'

'Yes. Yes, he did.' I spoke automatically, my eyes dry, my heart heavy as lead. At the same moment a voice within me cried. 'Foolish! Foolish! He forgot all about you years ago'.

'They say his widow is to retire into a convent,' the pedlar said.

'Oh.' I forced myself to smile a little as if the news were only a passing interest, and I began to sort through the articles on the tray he had carried through to the hall. 'Your prices are no lower I see.'

'But prices everywhere have risen, mistress!' he protested. 'I shall give you good value for whatever you buy.'

He was still talking but his words meant nothing. I was staring at the seal in my hand, the falcon's claw that I had given to Diana eighteen years before. I turned it over slowly in my fingers and saw my initial scratched on its back. I'd done that myself in an idle moment, and now I looked at it again, unbelieving.

'That's a pretty seal, mistress,' he said, noting my interest. 'I got it in Cheapside from a young man who needed a coin to jingle.'

'What young man?'

'I never asked his name. He wanted money, that's all.'

'I'll buy it,' I said shortly. 'And two rolls of the blue silk. Here's gold. Go into the kitchen and ask my servants if they need anything.'

He would have gone on talking, but I went up into the privacy of the tower room, the seal clenched in my hand.

I've been looking at it on and off for hours. It's possible that it was stolen when the peasants killed Joseph and Rebecca and has passed through many hands since. But I know that Diana is alive. I know it more surely than I have ever known anything before. Somewhere in the land is the child to whom I was bidden to reveal my secret knowledge. And I have lived here too quietly for too long. It's time now to go on my travels, to journey first to Cheapside to begin my search. The falcon's claw is the sign. I *know* it!

We do hope that you have enjoyed reading this large print book.

Did you know that all of our titles are available for purchase?

We publish a wide range of high quality large print books including:
Romances, Mysteries, Classics, General Fiction, Non Fiction and Westerns.

Special interest titles available in large print are:
The Little Oxford Dictionary
Music Book
Song Book
Hymn Book
Service Book

Also available from us courtesy of Oxford University Press:
Young Readers' Dictionary
(large print edition)
Young Readers' Thesaurus
(large print edition)

For further information or a free brochure, please contact us at:
Ulverscroft Large Print Books Ltd.,
The Green, Bradgate Road, Anstey,
Leicester, LE7 7FU, England.
Tel: (00 44) 0116 236 4325
Fax: (00 44) 0116 234 0205

Other books in the
Ulverscroft Large Print Series:

**HIJACK
OUR STORY OF SURVIVAL**

Lizzie Anders and Katie Hayes

Katie and Lizzie, two successful young professionals, abandoned the London rat race and set off to travel the world. They wanted to absorb different cultures, learn different values and reassess their lives. In the end they got more lessons in life than they had bargained for. Plunged into a nightmarish terrorist hold-up on an Ethiopian Airways flight, they were among the few to survive one of history's most tragic hijacks and plane crashes. This is their story — a story of friendship and danger, struggle and death.

म म M M